ARMED AND DANGEROUS
by NENIA CAMPBELL

Armed and Dangerous by Nenia Campbell

Copyright © 2013
All rights reserved.

Armed and Dangerous by Nenia Campbell

DEDICATION

To my awesome fans (i.e. all of them).

Armed and Dangerous by Nenia Campbell

Chapter One

Prelude

Christina:

My psychologists suggested that it might be therapeutic to write about what happened. That it would be beneficial, as they put it, for me to confront my demons head-on. What they failed to take into account was the fact that I might not *want* to confront the horrors of my recent past, let alone document it all in the written word for any and all to see. Whatever you say can and will be held against you, and with the IMA it would be at gunpoint.

The IMA were a terrifying group. Mercenaries trained like soldiers. The moral code of assassins. They took no prisoners if they could help it: the less evidence, the better. Was it so hard to believe that some skeletons might be better kept buried?

One visit to the psychologist was all it took for me to realize that these sessions would be a complete waste of time and money. I would not be able to tell her anything about my problems without fearing more for my life than I already was, and she wasn't equipped to deal with them besides. I had expected that, and I wasn't too disappointed. Since my mother had been the one to select Dr. Linden, my expectations had been low to start. I knew she did not hold my best interests at heart. Mamá, that is, not the therapist — although Dr. Linden probably didn't give a fig about my interests either, beyond what the session bill required.

Considering that I had been the one who was kidnapped and held hostage by hardened criminals, I figured if *anyone* in my family had a right to be traumatized, it ought to be me. But no, at the urging and endorsement of Dr. Linden, whose motives I now questioned, my mother was in the process of writing a memoir about her "three months of terror." Critics were singing her praises in anticipation of the book's success, calling her "brave" and "inspirational."

I had been forced to endure unimaginable cruelties too, at her expense — and what had I gotten out of it? A temporary prescription for sleeping pills and anti-anxiety medication to help with the panic attacks. My mother, who had chosen to save her own life instead of mine, thereby forcing me to pay for the mistakes made by her and my father, had a book deal. In what universe is that fair?

My mother's egocentric one, apparently.

Worse, I was concerned my mother's memoir would put me on another hit list. Despite stealing from large corporations by hacking into their computers as though he thought he were *Neo*, my father hadn't realized what he'd been messing around with until it was too late. My mother was just foolish when it came to the IMA. If she revealed a detail that the IMA did not want revealed, we were both dead. They might kill us to err on the side of caution.

When I brought these points up with my mother, she was dismissive, even hostile, telling me that I had no right to talk to her as if she was a child. "But don't you think you should quit while you're ahead?" I asked. "You have your fashion line. Think about fall — winter ball — *prom*," I concluded, a little desperately. She was horrid while designing clothes, treating me, her size fourteen daughter, as though I were a fat cow for not being able to squeeze into one of her perfect double-zero gowns. She would be worse if her memoir was turned into a Lifetime movie.

"Christina, in today's economy, people do not want to buy fashion. They want to buy sob stories that will make them feel better about their own miserable lives."

I followed her down the hall, into the master bedroom. She had converted her walk-in closet to an "office," and because she never did anything by halves, she had purchased a vintage Royal Arrow typewriter with glass keys. It was incredibly noisy, and since her office shared a wall with my bedroom I heard her pinging away well into the night. Not that I'd have been able to sleep anyway.

The office was hardly big enough for her antique desk and swivel chair, let alone for me. I knew what she was trying to do, shutting me out, pushing me away the way she always did. It made me angry enough to persist with, "Great. I respect that. But why don't you write about your own life? Why do have to drag me into this — again?"

"I cannot work with you standing there pestering me."

That was kind of the point. "But — "

"Go." Dismissive wave. "Be sure to change into something nice for dinner. John is coming over at six."

"But I hate John."

"This is not up for discussion."

I clenched my hands into fists. "You know I can't stand him. You *know*. Why would you invite him over here while I was staying? I don't visit you often. Would it really be so hard to accommodate me? Just once in a while?"

"You are upsetting me, Christina."

I was upsetting her? *She* was upsetting *me*.

Armed and Dangerous by Nenia Campbell

"John is the only reason I have been able to get through these past few months with my sanity."

He's doing a pretty crap job, then. "Does he have time-traveling powers, too? Because Dad told me you'd only been going out for about a month."

She jabbed a finger at the door. "Out."

"Fine," I snapped. "But when I come down, it'll be because *I* want to, *when* I want to, and I'll be wearing an *old, ratty t-shirt.*"

Her office door slammed shut, shaking the walls.

Ever since her and my father's divorce, my mother had gone through a series of boyfriends, each as unlikable as the last. Dr. Linden, on our one and only session, had proposed that I felt "threatened" by these men who I perceived to be "taking my father's place," and that I still felt "angry" about my parents' separation. No. Freud said it best, I think, when he said, "sometimes a cigar is just a cigar." Sometimes your mother's boyfriend is just a loser.

This current model was named John, an irony that went over my mother's head. John was twenty-nine, younger than the typewriter she was using to write her memoir, and an aspiring actor. "Aspiring" in this case meant that he wasn't enrolled at a film college, wasn't actively looking for an agent, and didn't have any work lined up. He seemed to be operating under the belief that if he spent enough time in our bathroom oiling his hair like a 1950's greaser a talent scout would drop out of the sky like the finger of God Himself and say, "You, with the cowlick, I want *you* to be in my next Big Picture."

Maybe that was why my mother liked him; he shared her delusional style of thinking.

Not only was John a loser, he was also a total creep. I found him prowling around in the hallway outside my bathroom door when he knew I was taking a shower, and he'd "accidentally" brushed up against me a couple times. Once, he'd even asked me if my mother and I did threesomes — something he denied when I told my mother about it, which put the blame back in my court, of course, as the girl with the scheming Electra complex. It would have escalated from there, but I'd asked him if he was aware of my ties to the mob, and whether he'd ever had a bullet go through his penis, adding casually that if I spoke to the right people, he could easily find out.

Not that Michael would do that. He was only cruel when he was paid to be, or so I liked to think. He wasn't a sadist, but he also wasn't around, and therefore wasn't worth thinking about. In any case, after that conversation John stopped sniffing around my bedroom door, and that's all I really wanted from the exchange anyway.

Mamá made good on her threat. Six o' clock found the three of us in the conservatory of her newly renovated Victorian, eating limp, green things that could have been weeds salvaged from the roadside. John whined about how he needed meat to build up his muscles for his headshots. Mamá was, by turns, consoling and condescending, saying that maybe he should spend more money on her so they could go out. Just one fucked-up happy family, that was us.

I snorted.

Mamá turned the full-force of that look on me. "Do not make the noises of a barn animal at the table, Christina, or you will be eating your dinner outside like one."

"Sorry." I lowered my head.

Mamá pursed her lips, looking at me closely, then shrugged it off. I could see her making the conscious decision to ignore me. "I finished twenty pages of my memoir today," she informed us, speaking to John as she laid her hand on his bicep.

John looked up from his stare-down with the mystery greens. "That's fantastic, babe."

"I was so inspired," she gushed. "The words just flowed out of me." *So does crap.* "It feels so good to unburden myself from the horrible events I was made to endure by those heartless, *heartless* men. But God works in mysterious ways, no? And now I can share His wisdom with others. To give them solace where I had none."

Provided that they're willing to shell out the $9.99 for your poorly edited ebook. I put down my fork. If I had to listen any more of this, I thought I might scream. "May I be excused?"

"Christina, don't be rude in front of our guest."

"He is not a guest. He practically lives here."

"Christina!" Mamá narrowed her hazel eyes. "You will stay seated, and you will eat your *kale.*"

"The memoir sounds great, babe," John cut in, ever eager to get in my mother's good favor. "Fantastic."

"You said that already," I informed him, prompting Mamá to snap at me in Spanish, telling me not to "ruin her last chance at happiness by being a pettish brat."

"I bet they'll make your memoir into a movie." John shoveled a mouthful of kale into his mouth and she beamed at him. Like he'd just said something exceptionally profound instead of smarming it up with his mouth full. "And if they do," he added, spattering bits of chewed vegetation on the tablecloth, "I can play as myself."

"God help us," I muttered. Quietly.

"Naturally, Penelope Cruz will star as me, though she is a little heavy in the hips."

I glared at my plate and stabbed at one of the green spears. "Don't you think you're being a little overly optimistic? Your book hasn't even been published yet."

"Christina, I find your negative attitude extremely hampering to my creative process."

For God's sake. I drew in a deep breath — *count to three, Christina* — and said, "I'm not being negative. I'm being realistic. There's a difference."

She sniffed. "You are being difficult. You should be more focused on your personal advancements. Dr. Linden informed me that you terminated your sessions with her prematurely. Do you realize she does not give refunds? You wasted hundreds of dollars."

"Dr. Linden is a quack. And just what the *hell* do you think you're doing, talking to her behind my back? Haven't you heard of doctor-patient confidentiality?"

"I am your mother."

In name only.

I hadn't realized I'd said it aloud until my mother said, viciously, "What was that, Christina?"

"Nothing."

"It did not sound like nothing."

"Well, it *was*," I said, just as coldly.

"Are you gonna take that lip, babe?" John butted in.

"You keep out of this," I snapped. "You're not even a part of this family — and you're only ten years older than me." That was a not-so-subtle dig at my mother.

She set down her wineglass. "Go to your room."

"No."

"Excuse me?"

"I said no. I'm not going to my room. I'm more adult than anyone sitting at this table, and I'm not going to be treated like a child. I'm going to Dad's."

"At this hour?" my mother squawked. "I forbid it!"

"You can't forbid it. If you don't let me leave, that

would be unlawful imprisonment."

My mother's shoulders tensed. She had that wariness about law enforcement particular to immigrants, having grown up on such urban myths like, "Don't misbehave, or you'll get deported back to where you came from." I heard her and John conversing worriedly as I stormed up the stairs. Potential criminality aside, we both knew the real reason she did not want me to go to my dad's. Being kidnapped had put things into a new perspective for my father, who had realized belatedly that the fantasy woman he had been married to for all these years had been exactly that — a fantasy.

Dad and I didn't have the perfect relationship, but we had far more in common with each other than either of us did with *her*. My mother knew this and despaired about being left out of the loop, convinced we spent every minute of our time together gossiping about her like schoolgirls.

Or, as she put it, "I do not like it when you and your father conspire against me. It hurts my feelings."

I grabbed a light sweater from my closet and shrugged it on. "We have better things to talk about than you."

"You should talk to a therapist about this hatred you are harboring against your own mother!"

"Why don't you do that for me? Go tattle to your precious Dr. Linden."

"Perhaps I should. While I am at it, perhaps I should also tell her how self-centered my foolish daughter is. How she thinks of no one but herself. That she is, *como se dice, una sociópata.*"

"It's *sociopath,*" I said. "Which, by the way, is heritable. I wonder which side of the family I got that from." I stuffed more clothes in my bag. "Why don't you ask Dr. Linden how she feels about you making diagnoses on her behalf? See what she has to say about that."

"You know nothing about psychology," she scoffed.

"Neither do you. Go on — ask her. Call Dr. Linden right now. Better yet, put her on conference call. John can talk to her too, and tell her all about how he's going to star in the memoir you are writing about me without my permission."

"You are a horrible wretch!"

"And you are a horrible mother," I said quietly.

"See if I help you move into your college apartment, if I am so horrible." With a cry of theatrical anger, Mamá stormed down the stairs while muttering about ingrates and how children who spoke to their parents the way I did would have gotten the attitude beaten out of them back when she was a girl.

I did my best to ignore her, as usual. I was already keyed up, though, and felt the tingling flood warnings in my tear ducts: an emotional dam ready to burst. I threw the last of my things into my ratty old backpack and trudged out to the car, letting the front door slam behind me. Nobody came out to stop me. Nobody came out to say goodbye. I hadn't been expecting anyone to, not really, but still; I couldn't help feeling disappointed.

You will never learn, will you?

I turned on the radio. My Belanova CD was playing. The upbeat pop music was too happy for me to bear, and I switched it back off. Released the parking brake. Glanced back at my mother's house in the rear-view mirror. The warm glow of the lights grew blurry from my tears. No, I hadn't learned my lesson, and I suspected I never would. I thought I might understand how a kicked puppy feels.

Armed and Dangerous by Nenia Campbell

Chapter Two

Breakdown

Michael:

The problem with being on the run? It forces you to hurry. When you hurry, you make mistakes. I made a mistake. I lingered for too long in Seattle. Maybe I was tired of running. Maybe I just didn't care. In any case, I'd led them on a merry chase across the western seaboard. Lots of time and resources wasted. Take that, cocksuckers.

I knew from the start that I couldn't run forever. When I started to get tired and they started to get too close, I bought myself a case of rum which I then proceeded to knock back deliberately and methodically while I waited for Callaghan's men to catch up. The burn felt good, seeping into my brain and body like liquid heat, relaxing me in a way I wasn't capable of sober. By the time they had broken down my door, I'd already finished off the better half of the carton. I had been drinking for about six hours.

There were five of them. They were spinning a little and one of them kept growing another head, but all were present and accounted for. I was surprised Callaghan had only sent five. There'd been a time when it would have taken at least ten. I guess the IMA had its respect for me.

Armed and Dangerous by Nenia Campbell

I squinted. The leader was a man I'd seen around the base a handful of times. He'd never been important enough to bother learning his name, just a grunt, though if he was here now that must have meant he'd been promoted.

Jesus, what is this? The off-brand recovery team?

From the look on their faces, the disappointment was mutual. "Michael Boutilier?" From the look on his face, it looked like he kind of wanted me to say 'no.'

"Who's asking?"

"It's him," the leader said. "Michael Boutilier, you are coming with us."

"That right?" I saluted with the tumbler. "At least tell me your name before we fuck."

He pointed his pistol at me. I heard the safety click off. "Don't make me shoot you, Mr. Boutilier. I'd hate to have to explain to Mr. Callaghan why we brought you in dead."

"*Alohrs pas*. He doesn't like failures." I set down my glass. The liquid sloshed over the edge. "Why don't you *passe* on the hell out of here, before I *passe* you a goddamn ass-kicking?"

"He's drunk," the same grunt from before said.

"You're drunk," the leader said to me.

"You don't say. They teach you to tell that in spy school? *Cho*-fucking-*co*. Sure is nice knowing the American tax dollar is being put to good use, eh?"

The guard set his teeth. "Boutilier, I'm warning you."

"Fuck you, *chure*. Kill me if you want. I don't care."

"We aren't going to kill you."

Something smashed into my head. It took me a moment to realize it was the rum bottle. It took me another moment to realize that one of his men had crept around behind me to brain me with it. Glass shattered. Liquid splattered. *Aw, hell. That was good rum.*

"But by the time this is over," the guard continued, "you might wish we had." His voice was throwing off shimmery echoes. I had time to think, *Oh shit.*

And then everything went dark.

Christina:

My father's house was only about fifty miles away from my mother's. It felt like a different country. *He* lived in one of those cottage homes from the 1920's. Small, cozy, not really room enough for three. The second being his new wife, Emily "just call me Aunt Em" Parker nee Rutherford.

Emily — sorry, Aunt *Em* — had a degree in Library Sciences and had first met my father when he had been returning some overdue programming manuals. He had argued with her about the due date. She couldn't locate him in the computer system when she attempted to double-check the library's records. My dad helped her update the backed-up files and she looked the other way while he quietly wiped his fines in lieu of payment. The two of them then went out to dinner, and the rest, as they say, was history. It was a cute enough story but one I'd heard far too many times. I didn't like the way Aunt Em told it, either, which was in a theatrical, overblown way far too reminiscent of my mother's.

Thankfully their shared penchant for drama was the only attribute they had in common. Apart from that one trait they had in common, Mamá and Em were different in both looks and personality. Mamá, in her cruel and cutting way, had even christened Aunt Em *La Ratona* because of her mousy looks and nervous gestures.

The one instance they had met was when my mother had come by to pick up some of her things from our old house. The meeting had been catastrophic. Obviously. I hadn't been there since I'd been touring college campuses on-site, but from what I'd gleaned from the various sides to the story (and there were many), my mother had called Em a "dried up old hag," and Em had retorted that at least *she* wasn't an "aging cougar who still thought herself a sex-kitten."

I imagined the look on my mother's face was priceless.

It was only eight-thirty when I pulled up in their driveway and their lights were still on. They were probably awake then, but just in case I had brought the key my father had given me. As quietly as I could, I unlocked the front door and met the sound of a gravelly baritone in stereo that I recognized from the evening news. The two of them were sitting in his and hers matching armchairs, drinking tea.

Dad jumped when I closed the door, his bald head gleaming in the blue backdrop of the weather screen. "Sweet Pea?" he said, turning to look over his shoulder while Em fussed with the tea he'd spilled on his shirt. "Is that you?"

"Mm-hmm."

Em tossed her napkin — a cloth one, never paper — on the end table between their two chairs and said, "It's a little late."

"Yes, weren't you staying at your mother's this week?"

"Mamá was being horrid."

"When isn't she?" Em muttered.

"*Especially* horrid, then."

"Girls, please," Dad interjected, looking a bit desperate. For obvious reasons, he tried to avoid talking about my mother as much as possible. Twenty-five years of marriage had left him paranoid.

"She had John over."

"You might have called first," Em said.

"I didn't know! I just thought — I mean, since I have my own key — I figured it would be okay."

"You're always welcome here, Christina," Dad said. "But it would be nice to get some advanced notice next time, if possible."

"I'm sorry. I would have, but I didn't even know I was going to leave until she — oh my *God*, Dad, she was planning the TV adaption of her *memoir* at the dinner table."

"What memoir?"

I helped myself to some tea from the stove without asking because Em was an old fusspot, and because I knew it bothered her, and because I knew she was still too insecure about her relationship with my father to say so. "The memoir about her 'harrowing experiences.'"

Dad looked genuinely ill. "That woman. I swear — " He shook her head. "What is she thinking? No publisher will be able to touch that. Not without heavy censoring."

"She's self-publishing."

Dad swore, violently and explosively. "She's going to get us all killed."

"That's exactly what I said. But no, she thinks she's Penelope Cruz."

"Maybe if Penelope Cruz had no taste," Em said stiffly, taking a sip of tea. Pinky extended. Pointedly so, it seemed. *Does she have a sense of humor after all?*

"I'll have Mr. Rosenzweig call your mother's lawyer about that book. It's good she's keeping busy but she shouldn't be dragging you into this. I'm sure we can work out some kind of arrangement — "

"Fat chance of that. I don't understand why I have to see her at all. It's so blatantly obvious she doesn't want me there."

"You know how your mother is when she gets upset."

"Awful."

Armed and Dangerous by Nenia Campbell

"Her feelings get hurt very easily."

"Because she acts like a *child*." I paused. "And her new boyfriend — John — he does, too. He's *twenty years younger than her*, Dad. People think he's my brother."

Dad sighed. "Christina, please. It's one thing to talk about the book — because I do wish she would stop her fame-mongering, especially because of them —"

Em's lips went white. "Rubens," she said warningly, looking around the room. As if the IMA had bugs in our house and were listening in on us right now.

Actually — that wasn't as paranoid as it sounded. Em had good reason to be afraid of them. They had ears everywhere. "If they did do something, Mamá would be the pretext. Not the reason."

"You're too right. I wish you weren't." Dad sighed, exchanging a long look with Em. "Well, you're certainly welcome to stay with us for as long as you want. I believe the guest room's clean, and since we aren't expecting anyone else that means it's all yours. You lucked out, kiddo."

"I shouldn't be here for too long. School starts soon."

Armed and Dangerous by Nenia Campbell

The undisguised relief on Em's face annoyed me. "You're starting college soon, aren't you?"

"Yes, at Coswell. I'll be a freshman."

Dad almost dropped his teacup. "Coswell? What? Where the hell is that?"

"Arizona — remember? I was telling you about it a couple months ago, on the phone."

Em righted his teacup as he spluttered, "I thought that was your safety school in case you didn't get into Stanford. Which you did. I remember you telling me you did."

"Perhaps this isn't the time," Em posited delicately.

We both chose to ignore her.

"I did get accepted into Stanford. But I don't *want* to go to Stanford. I told you that, too."

"You don't want to — " I rarely saw Dad get angry. When he did, he developed a twitch over his left eye and his entire face turned purple. He looked seconds away from having an aneurysm, a heart-attack, or both. "Do you have any idea how many people would kill to have the opportunity you've so candidly passed up, Christina?"

"Lots. I know."

Armed and Dangerous by Nenia Campbell

"Rubens — " Em valiantly tried to edge her way into the conversation. Again. Dad and I continued ignoring her.

"I don't think you do."

"I do, believe me. I took everything into account. But I'm tired of being front and center all the time. I want to be on the fringe. I'm a lot happier there."

"Christ." Dad mopped at his forehead, turning towards Em but speaking at me. "My daughter just gave up her full scholarship to Stanford."

"It wasn't a full scholarship — and it wasn't a spur-of-the-moment decision, either. I've been thinking about this for a long time."

"Is that supposed to make me feel better?"

"Well. Yes, actually."

Dad shook his head.

He might have looked like he was hamming up his anguish, but he didn't have a dramatic bone in his body. He could never afford to, being married to Mamá. That made his hurt and anger worse, because it was real. But at the end of the day, this was still my life, *my* choice. Going to school with the best, the smartest, the richest, the superlative-est — it didn't really appeal to me. It wasn't what I needed.

What I needed was tranquility, peace. Solace.

Armed and Dangerous by Nenia Campbell

I no longer trusted myself in crowds. Not after learning that the so-called real world is just the white light being emitted through the neutralizing prism of our society's norms. Not after viewing the full-color spectrum of the human capacity for emotion and intent, and being blinded by that dizzying intensity. Not after seeing how much I wanted all that, despite knowing that lifestyle would ride me hard and leave me with a broken soul.

No. What I needed was safe, quiet exile.

"I'm sorry, Dad."

"Christ. Where's the bourbon? I need a drink."

"Rubens, so late? But your heart — "

"That is exactly why I need a drink."

"Dad, no — "

But he had already gotten to the bottle and was knocking back the shot glass as Em and I watched, scandalized. He pinched the bridge of his nose and coughed, then looked at us sheepishly. "Doesn't go down as smoothly as it did when I was younger — "

"Thank heavens for that," said Em.

"But it certainly takes the edge off."

"It's psychosomatic."

"Whatever works."

Armed and Dangerous by Nenia Campbell

"*Really —* "

"I'm sorry," I began again.

"It's okay, Sweet Pea." He coughed again, shrugging off the napkin Em was trying to press on him. "Really. It's your life, and I'll get over that. If Coswell is where you want to go, then, well, Coswell is where you'll go."

"How are you going to move your things?" Em asked.

Trust her to notice the details. "Um, well — " I bit my lip, remembering the argument that drove me to my father's house at night in the first place. "Mamá was going to help."

"That was, er, nice of her," said Dad.

"Was?" said Em.

"Yeah. I think tonight might have changed her mind."

Dad sighed. "She'll change her mind again, don't worry. And if she doesn't, *I'll* have a talk with her. Or her lawyer will. She isn't allowed to blackmail you into choosing sides."

I sure hope not. "Thanks Dad." I yawned. "I think I'm going to go to bed. I'll leave my stuff in the car for now."

"Goodnight, Daddy — Em."

"Goodnight, Sweet Pea."

As I was climbing upstairs I heard Em say, "Well. She's quite a character."

"Liliana, or Christina?"

"Christina."

"She's her own person," Dad agreed. "I don't know where she gets it from. Her grandmother, maybe."

"Certainly not her mother."

"No," Dad sighed, "I thank God every day for that."

Me too, I thought, carefully shutting the door behind me. It was heartening that they didn't think me quite so much like Mamá as I'd feared.

Armed and Dangerous by Nenia Campbell

Chapter Three

Impasse

Michael:

My head was pounding, each pulse of my heart delivering pain as well as blood, only partly due to the alcohol I'd consumed. The back of my neck felt sticky. Sweat — or blood? I couldn't check. I couldn't move my hands. They were cuffed behind my back.

"Hell," I said, closing my eyes to the bright beams of light overhead. And then, feeling this somehow wasn't enough, "*Fucking* hell."

That was more like it.

Forehead throbbing and eyeballs fit to burst, I studied the room through cracked lids. Cold tile floors. The kind that were easy to clean because of what got spilled on them.

This wasn't good.

"I really ought to kill you for defying this organization with such blatant disrespect."

Of course *he* was here. Who else would bother with a manhunt? "You won't," I said tiredly.

"This time," he agreed. His shoes squeaked annoyingly as he paced around the cell. "Your little runaround had the unexpected benefit of being a rather useful screening tool, permitting me to weed out those suspect individuals who have led me to question their value in the past."

"So nice to feel appreciated."

"I wouldn't go that far."

He leaned against the far wall, arms folded over the front of his three-piece suit. Not smiling. *Really not good.* I'd pissed him off. That explained why the guards, who I'd noticed hovering near the door, were also keeping their distance. One or two of them usually tried to get in an extra kick while I was down. I swayed to my feet, because that was better than sitting on my ass. It was a mistake. The disorienting pain made me stumble back against the wall.

"Such a pathetic display," Callaghan said softly. "It isn't like you to be so self-destructive."

"Jealous I beat you to the punch?"

He slammed his fist into my temple. White bursts of pain exploded inside my head. I retched, collapsing in a heap. Over the ringing in my ears he said, "You were never this weak-willed before. Curious. What has possessed you? *Who* has possessed you? I should say."

"You can say whatever you want. I don't have to answer."

He fingered the holster of the gun hidden inside his suit-coat. "Don't make promises you can't keep."

"Can the pleasantries, then." I managed to struggle into a sitting position. The pain was blinding, but it was better than lying there prone. "Let's get right to it — what the fuck do you want from me?"

"You and I had an agreement."

We did? "What was it?"

"You know what I'm talking about."

"No, I fucking don't," I growled, wincing inwardly at the volume of my own rising voice. "I'm hungover as fuck. So unless you have caffeine, aspirin, or some combination of the two, stop playing the fucking mental cryptic and answer the goddamn question."

"You're awfully confident for someone in your position. Remember, *you* work for *me*. Have you forgotten that, perhaps?"

"Right now, I can't remember shit."

"I could assume that the cockiness is the alcohol speaking through your veins, but I somehow think not. After all, insubordination is something that seems to flow in you far more thickly than blood."

That was too much. I wasn't going to put up with that. Not after that dickwad had framed me and nearly gotten me killed after delivering the fucking Judas kiss to our boss. Fuck, no. I hocked up a ball of phlegm and spat it at him. It landed, quivering, on his shoe.

There was a pause.

When he lunged, I was ready. I swept his legs out from under him with a single well-placed kick. He threw out his hands to break his fall, and rolled away before I could deliver the follow-up. The guards rushed forward, jumping to like a pack of well-trained dogs, but Callaghan held them back with a raised hand. "Stupid boy. Did you honestly believe for a second that this front of yours fooled a soul?" He pulled out his gun. "That it fooled me? I *own* you."

"The fuck you do, you psycho mick — "

He pushed himself up to his feet. To the guards, he said, "Hold him, and open his mouth."

What?

Two of them grabbed me. I snapped my head, catching one of the guards under the chin. The one on my left jabbed me in the kidney with the butt of his gun. I leaned to that side, guarding against further damage, and received a debilitating blow to the back of my legs that drove me to my knees. When I opened my mouth to draw a breath Callaghan shoved the barrel of his gun past my lips and teeth, until the muzzle of it was brushing against the back of my throat. Beads of sweat dotted at my temples. I pulled away, and received a sharp jab to the spine for my efforts.

"Your little friend," the bastard said, "how easy it would be, to bring her here—to make her cry, to make her scream." He punctuated this with a shove that made me wince and exhale a ragged snort of air through my nose. "I wonder. Could you stand watching her beg for help you are unable to give? Stronger men have broken for less."

He flicked the safety off.

"Of course, if she were all I wanted, I could simply kill you now and take her—but then you would miss out on all the fun. We don't want that, do we?"

I glared at him over the barrel.

"No," he said, answering for me. "You don't." With that, he yanked the pistol out of my mouth, spraying spit, and I sucked in a breath—which I immediately released again when he kicked me in the stomach hard enough to send me slamming into the wall again. I landed on my pinned arms and let out another curse. "Don't test me, Michael. Don't ever test me. You won't win, not ever, and I'll take you for everything you've got."

He fired the gun up at the ceiling, making everyone jump except for him.

"When the boy is sober enough to tell his arse from his elbows, ship him off to Scotland. He'll be heading the BN mission there." His eyes cut back to me. "He may not be our most qualified agent, but at least we know he'll fit right in with the locals."

Satisfied he had made his point, he left me there to cough up blood and bile and impotent rage.

And fear.

Christina:

Stockholm Syndrome. It's when a hostage comes to feel sympathy or affection for their captor, defending them to the point of obstructing justice and sometimes even falling in love with them. I read up on it a bit after I found myself harboring confusing feelings about the man who had made me prisoner for three months. Over a quarter of kidnapped individuals develop symptoms of Stockholm Syndrome.

Everything is so simple when it has been laid out in black and white facts, and cold, numerical data. It's only when you throw emotions into the mix that everything gets all tied up in knots.

Trying not to think about my captor was a bit like being told to absolutely not think about polar bears and then being asked what was on your mind. In other words, not very well. I had periods of being fine and then I'd catch a glimpse of something — a man with a particular way of walking, a scent, a flash of blond hair in sunlight — that would make me realize I wasn't so fine after all.

Not even close.

I let the book I was attempting to read drop to the floor, unread. I'd been reading the same sentence for the last half hour, without comprehension.

If you listen to the press, they'll tell you that he's ruthless, dangerous: a green blooded mercenary, a cold-hearted killer. He was all of those things. He was everything your mother warned you about when she told you not to walk alone in the dark.

But —

There was another side to him, as well. As cliché and pathetic as it sounds, that was the side that had made me come to some sort of rudimentary understanding of his nature. When he wasn't wearing an assassin's mantle, he was passionate, volatile, intense. Being close to him could make you feel as if you were an island apart from the rest of humanity. He was the realest person I had ever met.

I couldn't tell anyone how I felt because I knew they wouldn't understand. Oh, poor little Christina, they would say. Falling for the bad man who treats her like dirt because she didn't know any better. And isn't it a pity that they don't still teach sex-ed in schools? Or, they would go, oh, Christina, that filthy slut, if she puts out for a man like that, I imagine she puts out for *anyone*. You stay away from *her*.

It wasn't like that at all. Maybe it would have been easier if it was, like ticking a box. Are you the Madonna, or the whore? The victim, or the vixen? The Sabine, or the skank? Nothing in life is ever that simple.

I didn't know where I fit into all of that. Sometimes I would wake up in the middle of the night, covered in sweat and scarcely able to breathe because, like a drug, I hadn't quite managed to flush him out of my system and was suffering the consequences of sudden withdrawal. I'd be all abuzz, with emotions too chaotic and frenzied to put a name to, all of them fueled by an intensity that went beyond mere desire or fear.

I lacked closure.

That, I had decided, was the problem. The root

cause behind all of this. Something lay between Michael and me like a yawning abyss, daunting and unfinished, and I would never get over these anxious feelings until that something was resolved — but that would require seeing him again, which I absolutely did not want to do.

I was afraid of what I might do if I did.

It had to be the Catholic guilt rearing its ugly head. All those years of self-blame and absolution. I shook my head, leaning over to right the book that had fallen, and opened the drawer of my nightstand. Lying coiled on top of my bible like a snake, beside my reading glasses and the bottles that held my pills, was my old rosary. My grandmother's, actually. She'd given it to me as a gift after my first communion.

I ran the beads through my fingers, taking care to avoid the places where the paint had worn clean away to reveal the olive wood beneath. I didn't pray so much anymore but the familiar gesture was soothing. It helped me think.

He's probably found someone else by now.

I hated him, for making me think that. Then I looked down at the beads, guiltily.

Fool. You think he should be pining away for you in an ivory tower somewhere?

Armed and Dangerous by Nenia Campbell

That sounded stupid, even in my head. I wasn't that selfish. I just wanted…meaning. I wanted a sign that what had happened between us had *meant* something. Not romantically. I wanted to know that our battle with the IMA had caused him — and *me* — to change, that we had come out of the experience better off, and wiser about the world.

Most of all, I wanted to talk about my doubts and fears with somebody who understood me. If one more person told me how *lucky* I was to be alive and unharmed, how *lucky* I was to be safe, I thought I might punch them.

I was not safe.

I knew the IMA were having me monitored. It wasn't arrogance on my part, just statement of fact. To assume anything otherwise would be sheer stupidity. The IMA did not like loose ends. I was a loose end. They had chosen to let me live for now because I wasn't worth the resources it would take to kill me. That could easily change.

Michael understood that. Or had, once.

I just wanted to know that God had a plan that didn't involve me being dead, or permanently isolated, for the rest of my life. I didn't think that was too much to ask.

Armed and Dangerous by Nenia Campbell

Now you're questioning God's plan?

I flipped over my pillow and pressed my face against the cool side. Still clutching the rosary, I breathed in the chemical, flowery smell of the fabric softener.

Maybe the rest was all up to me now.

Things would be different at Coswell. I could fade into the liberal-arts-college-woodwork, get my degree in Computer Science, and live a life of mediocrity and relative solitude at some software firm, like the one in *Office Space*.

A boring, ordinary life.

I filled five notebooks that night, front and back. Five notebooks filled with all my thoughts and feelings, all the sights, sounds, and smells of captivity. It took me all night. I knew better than anyone what the smell of old blood soaked in dust and drywall was like, or how it felt to have your innermost thoughts and fears laid bare before the person you hated above all else like so many pearls before swine. I went through ten ballpoint pens of various colors, switching mid-word sometimes when the ink ran out. And with the flagging ink of my final pen, one of the red ones my mother used for her fashion sketches, I wrote these final words. Just to see how it would feel:

Armed and Dangerous by Nenia Campbell

I love Michael Boutilier.

Staring down at that sentence, etched in my handwriting, I felt — nothing. Absolutely nothing.

I sighed in relief. Had I really expected differently? Yes. No. Some explanation of why I couldn't get him out of my head might have been nice. The doctors were all so quick to diagnose PTSD and, yes, maybe that was a part of it, but it didn't explain why I kept seeing him in my dreams, or why my stomach always clenched when I thought of him with someone else. Or, worse still, with me. Or why the words *I don't love Michael Boutilier* sounded more false and unconvincing still.

The next morning, when my father and Aunt Em went to church, I committed my memoirs to their funerary pyre and told myself that the tightness in my chest was relief.

Not regret.

Armed and Dangerous by Nenia Campbell

Chapter Four
Coercion

Michael:

When your boss sends you halfway across the globe on assignment it's fairly obvious that he wants you out of the way — especially if he has made no effort to keep his opinions a secret. International travel is expensive. So is getting rid of a body. Not that I was particularly shocked or surprised. I knew that. And Callaghan knew that I knew that. This was a man whose idea of subtlety involved thumbscrews and sodium pentathol.

The flight was a rough one, spent in coach. Bad enough those seats weren't made with a man of my size in mind but with recent injuries, each jostled limb and bout of turbulence was agony. I had a mean mother of a headache and couldn't find my suitcase on the baggage claim.

I kept one eye peeled for the team I was supposed to be meeting here while I rooted through the endless loop of near-identical bags. Customs had stopped me for a "random search," groping me with an enthusiasm generally reserved for one-night stands while they searched through my shit.

Had they done something with my suitcase?

Had Callaghan given them a tip-off to fuck with me?

I clenched my teeth, letting my hands drop as I straightened. Well, fuck that. I'd just as soon buy new things to replace what I'd lost than deal with his gloating.

I turned to leave, only to run into a squat red-haired man in a monkey suit holding up my suitcase. "Mr. Collins?"

The words were spoken in a gruff brogue. It sounded native, but good accents can be faked and that alias sure as hell hadn't been on that suitcase. It couldn't be; I hadn't used Mr. Collins since Mr. Richardson's regime. "Yes?"

"Please come this way."

So this is how it's going to be, I thought, when he gripped my arm tightly enough to cause discomfort. Despite his short stature he was strong, and clearly trained in something. *Shut up and take the blue pill.*

"What agency did you say you were a part of?"

"I didn't," he replied.

Definitely trained.

I got into the glossy black Mercedes, my suspicions confirmed when I saw one of Callaghan's men inside. I wished I had a gun. I would have liked to shoot him in the foot just for that. He patted me down and finding nothing to confiscate, settled back in his seat. I watched him as the driver started the car.

The Scottish man closed the door behind me and left. On the other side of the one-way glass, I saw him walk away. That made me sit up and take notice. "Just what the fuck is going on here?"

"I have been assigned to retrain you."

"Yeah? Good luck with that."

"I don't need luck, Mr. Boutilier."

Boutilier now, not Collins. That meant the Scotsman might be only peripherally involved. Which would explain his abrupt departure. When I glanced around for a drinks cabinet, I ascertained that all the rear doors were locked. No escape. No alcohol, either. I twisted the cap off a bottle of water. Frowned. It hadn't been sealed.

"So the BN shit was a farce?"

"No." He watched me set the water back down with the others with an odd smile. "Not thirsty, Mr. Boutilier?"

"What do you want with me? Why am I here?"

"It has come to Mr. Callaghan's attention that you have been growing soft. You *will* be leading our operations here, make no mistake, but prior to that we shall be reviewing your instruction. You will receive a refresher course in combat, weapons handling, stealth, agility, and tech."

I hid my annoyance. "If he wants to pay me to fuck off in a course for new recruits, fine."

"Your training will be unpaid."

"What?"

"Furthermore, in the event that you decide to 'fuck off,' as you put it, you will receive an hour of torture for each percentage below average your score falls, should we deem it unsatisfactory.

"If you resist your training, or the disciplinary actions resulting from failure to meet our expectations thereof, a close friend of yours will be abducted. *She* will be tortured, instead of you. I believe you know whom we are referring to, yes?" I nodded tightly. "It will be filmed, Mr. Boutilier, and you would watch it in place of your usual sessions."

"This is bullshit," I said.

"Wrong, Mr. Boutilier. This is an education. I suggest you pay attention."

Christina:

My mother was reading the latest Nora Roberts

book purchased last-minute at the Portland airport. The night before, she had called to inform me that she had changed her mind about helping me move as long as I was willing to admit I'd been wrong. I had been so angry, but Em had been dropping hints all week about an upcoming vacation and the loss of dignity was worth getting on with my life. So I sucked it up, the way I always did.

She was wearing Juicy Couture sweats in size four with a pair of sunglasses perched jauntily on her head. She dressed like a celebrity trying not to be noticed, so naturally she got noticed. At least four different men had hit on Mamá since we left the airport, some of them only a few years older than me. What would John would have to say about that? Whatever. Not my place to get involved.

I was spared from public notice. Nobody paid any attention to me at all. I might as well have been invisible.

The stewardess came by with a rustling plastic bag, wearing a blue polyester uniform that probably hadn't seen an update since the 1950's. "Trash?"

"Yeah." I scooped up my empty cans of orange juice and dropped them in. "Thanks."

We both turned to glance at my mother who was making no move to discard her empty coffee cup and lipstick-stained paper napkins. With a sigh, I did it for her. I believe the term for this is *enabler*. The pitying looks from the stewardess and surrounding passengers only served to further my humiliation.

The fasten-your-seat-belts icon popped up on the LED display above the door leading into the cockpit. Over the intercom, the pilot informed us that we were landing and would arrive in the Phoenix airport in approximately fifteen minutes — oh, and to wait until the plane had stopped before removing baggage from the overhead compartments and to please make sure we disposed of all trash in the proper trash receptacles, and thank you for choosing our airline.

I looked over my mother's shoulder to watch the plane's landing. There were lots of desert shrubs. Tumbleweeds, Joshua trees, and the occasional grove of saguaros scattered over the sand dunes that crested like ocean waves over the burnished landscape. Beautiful, but inhospitable. An endless sea of desert with islands of red rocks reaching up, cathedral-like, towards the sky.

"You're breathing on me, Christina, and your breath stinks. Stop it." Mamá shoved a tin of mints at me with an impatient expression, and I took two to make her shut up before the cute guy down the aisle heard her chastisements. She gave me a final irritated look before replacing the tin in her purse and turning to the window. "*Uy*. What a dump."

"*Mamá* — " I trailed off. There was no point in correcting her. I should have known she wouldn't be able to appreciate it beyond a potential landfill.

"What? It is true, is it not?"

"No."

She spritzed herself with a portable mister, taking care to avoid her carefully coiffed hair so it wouldn't frizz. "What were you thinking, Christina? Clearly you weren't. Remember this moment, when you regret your choice. It will be a lesson for you to curb your impulsive ways and listen to your mother."

"Is this why you came along?" She looked up from the mister. "So you could nag me?" I clarified.

"No." She put the spray back into her purse. "I came along because I had hoped to talk some sense into you, but clearly you have none."

I somehow managed not to laugh in her face.

She caught a glimpse of my expression. "Are you going to be sick? Turn your head, if you are. I am wearing designer."

"I'm not going to vomit," I said dryly. "Thank you for your concern about my health."

She winced at my word choice. "Good."

At least she hadn't commented on my weight.

Only because she hasn't had occasion to do so yet.

Indeed. When we stopped for a quick lunch at a pretzel stand, she managed to squeeze in four snide remarks about my weight, her weight, carbohydrates, and diabetes.

"Don't glare like that," she said. "You'll get wrinkles."

Sometimes, I really hated being right.

We took a cab to Coswell from Phoenix. I hadn't brought much with me. With a little creative rearrangement the driver managed to fit all my suitcases in the back seat and trunk. My mother sat up front with the driver, who looked down her tank top at every right-hand turn. "Planning a trip?" he asked the reflection of her boobs.

"My oldest is starting her first year at college."

He tilted the rear-view mirror and met my accusing glare. After that, he stopped trying to stare down her cleavage. He even helped remove the luggage from the car without either of us asking. My mother gave him a tip she couldn't really afford. "You did not bring much," she said.

Armed and Dangerous by Nenia Campbell

You didn't carry much. I thought you were supposed to be helping? I shrugged. "I brought what I needed."

"This is hardly enough. How many coats did you bring? One? What if it gets dirty?"

"I'll wash it."

"And go coatless in the meantime?"

"For all of *two hours*, yes. It's Arizona, Mamá. It isn't like Oregon. They don't have cold winters here. They don't even really get rain, let alone snow."

"What a nightmare."

I wasn't sure, exactly, what she was referring to. Better not to know. "Please, Mamá. People are staring —"

That was a mistake. Her gestures got more dramatic, the idea of a live audience proving too tempting to resist. "Why are you being so self-destructive?"

Was she talking about me? "Excuse me?"

"Is this to punish me? Was I not a good enough mother?"

She had been referring to herself. What a surprise. "Maybe this isn't about you," I said. She stared at me as if she couldn't possibly fathom a world that dared exist without her edifying presence, and I added, carefully, "Maybe I want to escape. To get away."

"From them?"

"Partly," I conceded. "And partly not."

She fairly wailed. "I don't understand."

"It's quiet here," I said. "Peaceful. I know you don't understand that, that Coswell isn't glamorous like some big city on the coast, but I like that simplicity. It suits me."

"Yes," she said after a moment. "Yes, I suppose it does." She tossed her head. "Just so long as you are not throwing your life away because of *him*. It is foolish, Christina, to destroy your future for a man. Especially one like him. Men like that, they do not like to be reminded of personal obligations."

"Yeah, well, he's not the only one."

There was a heavy silence. I hadn't even realized that I had spoken my thoughts aloud until I saw her flinch. I opened my mouth instinctively to apologize, then shut it. What was she going to do — demand that I pack up my things and return with her to Oregon?

Fat chance.

"I am trying to give you advice," she said.

"It isn't wanted."

"You need to stop blaming me. Us. Your father and I, we are not responsible for what happened. You need to take account for your own actions. Dr. Linden says — "

"I don't give a *toss* what Dr. Linden says. I am your child. You're the adult — or at least, you're supposed to be. Take some responsibility for once, Mamá, instead of looking for someone to absolve you of it."

"You never used to speak to me this way."

"I didn't used to have a choice. But now I do. And I'm choosing to leave, just as you did when you abandoned me. No," I corrected myself before she could speak, "what you did was worse. At least abandonment is passive. You — you took a more active role. You sold me out. You knowingly put a price on my innocence, my well-being, and my *life*."

Mamá released a string of barbed Spanish curses that had passerby turning heads. I hoped none of them spoke Spanish. I would die if a single one of them understood what she was saying.

"At least he rescued me," I said, when she had finished her offensive slurs.

"Christina."

"Ask yourself what kind of person does those

things," I said. "What kind of a woman willingly condemns her own daughter to death? What kind of woman refuses to help her daughter move into college because she doesn't want to hear how much of a scuzz-bucket her new boyfriend is? What kind of woman sets out to ruin her daughter's new life before it's even started? Ask yourself those questions — I think you'll find it's you. It's always been a competition between you and me…and I would have gladly let you win, if it had only meant that you would love me."

She made a small sound, like a choked-back sob.

"I'm sure I can take care of the rest." I scooped up my luggage. I didn't want her to see the tears forming in my eyes. "See you at Christmas, maybe."

I heard her step forward and tensed, afraid that she was going to hug me. But she couldn't bring herself to do it and I was relieved because I thought I might have slapped her if she had.

Armed and Dangerous by Nenia Campbell

Chapter Five

Transparency

Michael:

I'd grown up on the streets, been disemboweled, even spent a week on death row, but my retraining had been vicious enough to earn a place in the running of the rat-race my life had become. They hadn't been joking about the torture. Sleep-deprivation, starvation, sharpened blades. Resistance was not just futile, it was fatal. The plane ride back to the United States had been the first time I had been able to relax in almost three months. I spent the entire ten hour flight asleep.

When I arrived in my cheap motel room I received a text message with an address from a number I didn't recognize but I knew who it was from. It looked like my suffering was going to be an ongoing event. I popped some caffeine pills and called a cab. It dropped me off in front of an old Victorian for what I was sure was going to be some prime time shits and giggles.

A flickering screen wavered before the men and women assembled in this stuffy room as the office grunt fiddled with a remote I was pretty sure he had no idea how to work. This had once been the library of a large manor home. Over the years it had been modified and rewired to serve as a base of operations for the IMA.

Forcing an old house to service the grade of technology we use is a bit like hiring a seventy-year-old hooker for trying out new sex positions.

"This is the Night Bureau." Office Grunt had figured out how to work the remote. "Also known as the *Bureau du Nuit.*" He clicked one of the buttons. A corrupted image of the French flag appeared. The image was in gray-scale. "The BN are a semi-terrorist organization sited primarily in France, though they presently have bases of operation running in Cambodia, parts of Eastern Europe, and the Sudan. This is their flag."

He pressed another button and the screen faded to black. He set the remote down on the table and mopped at his forehead with a handkerchief. "Until now, the BN have not been a major source of conflict for us—beyond the occasional inconvenience." He attempted to shove his handkerchief into his suit pocket and missed.

"We have no bases in those parts of the world, with the exception of Romania, and bar a few extremists the BN have left us alone. A favor we have always perfunctorily returned. However, the BN are encroaching upon our territories in England, to the point where our clients are beginning to perceive them as a threat.

"Likewise, the BN is interested in obtaining political recognition. Should they succeed in establishing themselves, the potential threat they pose to us will be great. They are left-wing radicals and notoriously anti-military. They see our clients, and therefore us by proxy, as a threat to political and global security, and have already killed two of our operatives in cold blood. I know what you are thinking: if they are anti-military, why are they using violence to prove their point? The BN operate under traditional utilitarian principles—that pain can be a necessary expenditure for the well-being of the majority."

Office Grunt paused for dramatic effect and except for the rustle of papers and the subtle creaking of chairs, it was silent. Pleased, he continued, "Our mission objective is simple. Target the individual leaders of the BN and bring them to heel. Should we be unable to reach some form of agreement, a rougher form of justice will be necessary."

The kind of justice accompanied by mental implements and clamps.

I rubbed at the back of my neck, which had gone clammy. I could feel my pulse; it was rapid, far above what was acceptable for a normal, resting heart rate. My heart was doing some very interesting things in my chest. I wondered if I was having a heart-attack, if I'd overdone it with the caffeine pills. My palms were sweating.

Callaghan got to his feet, clapping slowly. "That will be all. Dismissed, Mr. Rivers."

Rivers rushed to comply, coming close to knocking over the projection screen in his haste. Callaghan watched the flustered man leave the way a cat tracks a wounded bird. Then he turned to face the remaining operatives. "Ladies — "

His eyes locked with mine. I lifted my left arm, fist clenched, and hit my elbow. *Fuck you.*

"Gentlemen. The attacks by the BN have been strictly hit-and-run. Their numbers are great, though not as great as they would have the world believe and certainly not as great as ours. They are trying to engage us in a game of cat and mouse. To eliminate our operatives one by one. It is the strategy of one who has everything to lose, which means that they are already afraid. As they well should be." He glanced around the room. "It is also why we shall not be playing by their rules."

Spoken like a true psychopath.

"What are your orders, sir?"

"As Mr. Rivers so eloquently put it, our goal is to hunt down the individual leaders. So far they have managed to elude us, thereby permitting them to remain silent. Remedy that. Find them. Catch them. Make them feel talkative."

The woman who had asked the question nodded and said nothing more. There was no need to elaborate. Not for her, anyway. One aspiring sociopath sitting up front leaned forward, wanting more juicy details. The eagerness on his face was repulsive. "What methods will we be using?"

"Effective ones. If you have any further doubts, I suggest you speak with Mr. Boutilier sitting in the back there. He is well-acquainted with the precise nature of my methods — isn't that so, Michael?"

I glared at the man who'd asked until he looked away. I knew the type. Eager for blood until he saw it on his hands. That changed a man, seeing it up close. It made him harden, crazy, or sadistic. We all made our choice.

I said nothing.

Callaghan cleared his throat. "I will be assembling teams to investigate the suspected locations of their various bases. These teams will be announced at eighteen hundred hours, on SecNet, where they will remain for an hour. Synchronize your watches, and don't be late."

He paused a heartbeat.

"The rest of you are dismissed."

Thank God. The caffeine pills were losing their potency.

"Boutilier — a word."

I lowered my arms mid-stretch. *Just one?* I schooled my expression and turned around. "What is it?"

"I hadn't realized you'd returned to the States already."

Bullshit. "I returned hours ago. You summoned me."

"You didn't think to check in with me first?"

That was why he was pissed. I wouldn't let him track me like a hound. "Aww, did you miss me? So sorry. Next time I'll send you a postcard."

"If you can't curb your tongue, I'll have one of my men cut it out. The same goes for your obscene hand gestures. You are a soldier. You will act with the discipline of one. Because if you do not, I can think of several men offhand who would only be too happy to take you to task."

I reached for my gun. The throbbing in my ears grew to a deafening level. "I don't think so."

"You know what happens to worthless curs who can't be trained, don't you? They get put *down*. So put the bloody gun away, Michael, and if you don't tell me why the fuck you put one of my best riflemen into the hospital for doing his duty, I'll be having you put away as well."

"My finger must have slipped," I said coldly.

"And the bullet just happened to miss all his vital organs?"

"Maybe it's the luck of the Irish."

"Aye. That's lucky all right. That's very lucky indeed." His eyes narrowed. "Don't bullshit me. You shot a bullet into his stomach, causing an excruciating but nonlethal amount of pain."

"I didn't fire any guns. You won't find fingerprints."

"So you hired someone else to do your dirty work. Back less than a day and already causing trouble."

"Pretentious little shit got what he deserved."

"Your Christina Parker has also been in a spot of

trouble as of late, it seems. But perhaps you know already."

"I've been stationed in Scotland."

"That isn't an answer, Michael."

"And that wasn't a question, *sir*."

He resumed pacing. "Post traumatic stress syndrome is very difficult to treat. Scientists understand the mechanism, to be true, but they still aren't quite clear on why some stimuli trigger the symptoms and others...don't. I hear the girl has been seeing a psychiatrist. It would be a pity if her condition were to suddenly take a turn for the worse."

It would be a pity if I shot you in the dick.

"I can see you're wondering what it is I want. Let's cut to the chase. You have completed your training satisfactorily. Now I want you to lead the team I'm sending to England."

"More retraining?" I spat.

"No, no, no. You've been stationed in Scotland, as you've said. That particular training is done. This is more for convenience's sake. You're already acquainted with the exchange rates and all those other mettlesome cultural details — unless you feel further tutelage is necessary."

I set my teeth. "Perhaps you have forgotten that the Scots don't like the English. They are still embittered about the Battle of Culloden and the Jacobite uprisings."

"It's a small island. You'll learn your way around it."

Maybe the BN conflict was really a set-up to take out some of his old enemies. Rumors were circulating afresh about his mysterious origins. Supposedly both his parents had been involved with the IRA, and the IRA was notorious for harboring anti-British sentiments. Membership with that group would explain why Callaghan was unwilling to make the trip to England himself. If he had been expatriated from the United Kingdom for acts of treason, he couldn't.

Keeping this information in mind as something to look into when I got back, I said, "Your men don't listen to me. They still regard me as a traitor. Due to rumors that you have done nothing to discourage, I might add."

"If I tell them to listen to you, they will."

"I had no idea you were so popular."

"Their loyalty is to their paycheck. What about yours?" Upon seeing my expression, he added, "By the by, I've started having the girl watched. You wouldn't know yourself, not being a graduate, but university can be very taxing upon its students' readily available cognitive resources. Some students find that they just can't cope."

"Lay a finger on her and I blow you straight to hell."

"Are you threatening me?" he asked, amused. "Perhaps Watson didn't train you as well as I thought."

"I'm not threatening you," I said. "I'm making you a promise. Touch her and die."

"You're a powerful man, Michael Boutilier, but even you couldn't take on fifty men without kevlar. Try, and I'd have you gunned down where you stood. Oh, but that would be a blessing for you, wouldn't it, dying a hero's death? I couldn't have that, no. I'd be sure you saw her killed first, knowing your death would be in vain."

It took me a moment to speak. "I see," I said.

"Blackmail for a blackguard. Rather fitting, wouldn't you say?" He paused. "I assume this is a hypothetical case. An exercise in power — a war game, if you will. Yes, that must be it. Because I'm sure even you, with your brute intelligence, wouldn't do something so utterly stupid."

"No." I turned on my heel to leave before I could do or say anything that would leave me in a state of further disgrace. My pulse throbbed in my temples, sending white bursts flashing up like sparklers in my periphery.

"One more thing."

I didn't turn around this time. "What?"

"From now on, keep your safety on when you're dealing with my men. You aren't the only one who can cause accidents, Michael Boutilier."

With that threat hanging in the air like a bullet suspended in time, I left to sleep the sleep of the dead. When I woke up, I would find myself covered in sweat.

Christina:

Dad wired me some money before he left for Napa with Em. "Just make sure you keep a budget," he told me. "Record all your transactions in an excel spreadsheet, and break them down into food, utilities, school, and personal use. I want to be able to see where your money is going." I agreed — it was a good deal — and when I checked my account online I had a shock. Dad must have felt guilty about not helping me move. That was the only explanation. That, or he'd added an extra zero somewhere.

With my funds in place I set up accounts with PG&E, AT&T, and all the other acronyms responsible for basic utilities. The apartment came with free wi-fi, or so it said on the board outside, but I didn't trust it. Not after eyeballing the ethernet jack and concluding that I'd be sharing the same channel with everyone in the complex. What a bandwith nightmare. I shelled out for my own modem instead, and a just-in-case ethernet cable.

When I finished setting up my internet, I went online and found a mattress company that didn't charge extra for delivery. The mattress came within an hour. I dragged it into my room, off in the far corner where it wouldn't be in the way. I unpacked my sheets and dressed the bed. Then I took a quick nap. My dreams were hazy and muddled, but unpleasant enough to keep me from feeling refreshed. I cracked open an energy drink that tasted like warm pee and went dumpster diving. I found some beat-up but serviceable furniture outside the sorority buildings. I didn't bother with the frat houses. I figured anything I found *there* would be too gross worth salvaging.

Getting the furniture home was a problem, but

when I rang the doorbell of the alpha-kappa-sigma house, the girl I spoke to was really friendly. She owned the shiny red minivan parked in front, and agreed to drop the furniture off at my apartment for ten bucks. On the ride over, she chattered about rush week and I ended up back at my place with a nightstand, a battered dresser, a funky-looking floor lamp, and a pamphlet detailing all the reasons I should join a sorority.

Time for another nap, I thought. But no, I still didn't have any food. Simple tasks. Basic tasks. Things I had taken for granted while living with my parents. They became Herculean labors in an apartment that didn't have air-conditioning. It was even worse outside. I had opened up all the windows in the hopes of catching a breeze. Nothing but dead air. It was one-hundred-and-five degrees outside and it seemed like the air might just catch on fire.

Eventually the power turned on but then the AC didn't work. I called management to complain. Turned out the water wasn't on yet. I called and complained some more, only to be informed that the water should be working. Obviously, it wasn't. Someone in blue overalls came down to fix it. The air-conditioning switched on, as if by magic. After that, I vowed to run the AC nonstop, regardless of whether I was in the house or not. The welcoming rush of cold air would make up for the guilt.

I took another nap in my cooling apartment, and then a cold shower. I no longer had the energy to go grocery shopping even though it was finally starting to cool down outside. My muscles were on fire and I was starving. Plus, I wanted to get the lay of the land before I went out wandering. I didn't want to get lost. Nothing would scream "new" like getting marooned in the desert. I decided to phone in for pizza and kicked back on my bed to wait.

Forty minutes later, my doorbell rang. I dragged myself up to answer it. "Medium pizza, Hawaiian, and a two liter soda?" The guy on my porch spoke quickly, as if reciting from a cue card, not looking at my face. He seemed a little too interested in the writing on my tank-top.

I looked down, and realized with horror that my sweat had all but rendered the white fabric transparent. *Oh my God.* I cleared my throat, crossing my arms as casually as I could, and said, "What do I owe you?"

"Eleven seventy-five."

I paid him the flat rate, pretending I had to scratch an itch on my elbow. "What about my tip?" he complained.

Armed and Dangerous by Nenia Campbell

"Here's a tip," I said, struggling to balance both soda and pizza box. "Don't talk down to women, even if it's just to their boobs." I slammed the door on his startled face with my butt, set the pop down, and locked it. God, he had looked about seventeen, too. I'd just robbed some high school delivery kid of his tip. I felt bad about that, but not bad enough to chase him down and give him the five bucks.

The little pervert.

I bit into a slice, scattering chunks of pineapple into the box. With my right hand, I opened my laptop and visited the college website. Classes started in just two weeks and my registration day was dead-last. That concerned me. Everything worth taking would surely be gone. Why was I stuck with such a crappy priority number? I was a scholarship student. I turned down Stanford to go to this dump. I…was beginning to sound an awful lot like Mamá.

I uncapped the bottle of soda and took a long swig. Maybe I should have stuck with something non-caffeinated. When I'd eaten my fill, I stuck the leftovers in the fridge for tomorrow. Then I located my toothbrush and toothpaste, changed into pajamas, and slept like a stone.

Armed and Dangerous by Nenia Campbell

Chapter Six
Regret

Christina:

I woke up around noon the next day, all my muscles screaming. Breakfast was cold leftover pizza washed down with flat soda. After cleaning the inside of the dresser, I began folding up my clothes in the drawers.

At three o' clock sharp I logged into my account, Cmparker. I opened up several tabs in the browser window to make registration as easy for myself as possible. Course catalog. Undergrad requirements. RateMyProfessor. But the moment I saw the available courses, I knew I was in trouble. Medieval Literature. Ancient Peruvian Art. The Philosophy of Biology. *Macrame*. Were these even real classes? I could feel my eyes crossing as I read the syllabi.

To think I had poured my heart out to the admissions people in that stupid personal statement. All that garbage about "healing journeys" and "finding myself." I kind of wanted to march down there and redact everything I'd said.

"Crap," I muttered, "Crap, crap, crap." I couldn't just take *nothing*. I wouldn't be insured if I wasn't a full-time student with at least twelve units. Feeling increasingly frantic, I quickly skimmed through the general ed. requirements for undergraduates and selected a handful of courses that fulfilled some of my prerequisites for graduation. On a memo pad, I mapped out a sample schedule. Two of the courses had time conflicts and one of them was taught by an asshole, so those got scratched out.

All of the classes left on my sheet sounded equally bland and unappealing. Which made sense; if they were interesting, they'd be full, too. Supposedly if I kept my grades up and stayed in good academic standing my priority number would get ratcheted up next semester. Until then, I was essentially paying them to teach me nothing in the good faith that they would later teach me something.

For now, there was nothing I could do except pay for the classes I had and hope I'd get some better ones later. That didn't mean I was happy about this decision. I wasn't, not at all. I didn't like feeling helpless. Coming to Coswell was supposed to help me *forget*. So why did I keep getting forced to remember?

I closed the registration window and finished off the last of the pizza. The pineapple and ham did hula hoops of unease in the pit of my stomach. I took an anti-anxiety pill to settle my stomach and went grocery shopping.

I also bought a knife.

A nice one, with a retractable blade.

If I got caught with it on campus having the knife in my possession would not be as likely to protect me from trouble as put me right into the middle of it, but seeing it in my purse made me feel better.

Were the IMA watching me right now? Laughing at my pitiful attempt to arm myself against them? I was living on borrowed time. Every waking moment, I wondered, "Is today the day that they will come for me?"

I knew I would never see it coming. Not unless they wanted me to. Not until it was already too late.

Michael:

The black corset could barely contain her breasts. They wobbled attractively as she straddled my lap, hands cupping my jaw as she leaned in for a kiss. She was wearing stockings. Garters. A whisper of a thong.

Few things in life are as satisfying as the knowledge that sex is imminent — except, of course, for the actual sex.

I rolled my head back, giving her access to my

neck. Her nails scratched down my torso, rasping against my chest hair. I sucked in a breath as she teased the skin just beneath my waistband. So close — and so fucking far — from where I needed her to touch me.

"Tease."

I bucked my hips. Growled when she removed her hand. It seemed like my entire nervous system had been reduced to a two-way transmission between brain stem and cock. She brushed her lips against mine, draping her arms around my neck with such casual possession that said cock strained against my jeans. "So impatient."

"I'm so fucking hard, I could take you right now. Tear your clothes right off, and fuck you through that mattress until neither of us done know what time it is."

"Not yet."

"You're going to be the death of me."

Her lips curved.

"I swear."

"Yes, you do." Her tongue flicked against my ear as her breasts weighed down on my chest. "And your favorite one…is fuck."

With what breath I could salvage, I said, "You

better lose that top real soon."

"You don't like it?"

"I'll like it just fine on the floor."

She smiled again. A shy, sweet smile, self-conscious and all the more seductive because of it. I watched, my breaths coming shorter and closer together, as she began to work the laces. Her patience annoyed the hell out of me. If my hands weren't tied, I'd have ripped out the cords.

"Better?" The garment fell into her lap.

I stared at her firm, small breasts, with the dark nipples already hardening into little exclamation points of arousal. Begging for my touch, for me to take them into my mouth. God. She was beautiful — and fucking sadistic. I wet my lips and managed to say, "Not even slightly."

She gave me a shove that had me pressed flush against the mattress. She tossed the corset aside and leaned over me. Her garters were chafing my abs, sending tight spikes of pleasure shooting through my dick. I wanted to dig my hands into her soft, fleshy thighs and grind her into me. I wanted to be inside her so badly that it hurt.

"You're hard to please," she said.

"You want to please me? My pants. Take them

off."

She ran her thumb along my lower lip. "Ask me nicely."

I bit at her fingers.

"No biting." She smacked my cheek.

"When I get out of this, I'm going to bite every inch of you, and you're not going to be able to do a damn thing about it," I warned her.

"But until then, what do you say?"

"Fucking *please*."

She climbed off me, then, giving me a pleasant view of her ass. I watched her drop to the floor, kneeling up and over the mattress until she was right between my knees. I could feel her warm breath through the damp crotch of my jeans and it was driving me crazy.

"Yes," I sighed, leaning back, immediately bolting upright when I felt the fleeting pressure of her tongue against my shaft as she jerked the button of my fly with her mouth. She looked up at me, her blue eyes deceptively innocent, took the zipper delicately between her white, even teeth, and pulled — hard.

Jesus fucking Christ. I nearly came right then.

"Do you want me?" she whispered.

I drew in a shuddering breath. "Yeah, I want you. I want you to strip buck naked for me, and ride me to the finish line like I'm a goddamn racehorse."

She cocked her head. "Do you love me?" She looked sad, suddenly, as if she might burst into tears.

I stared at her without comprehension as lust tangled up with other puzzling sensations that didn't quite fit in with the raging feelings of want boiling in my blood.

"*Do* you?" she persisted, leaning forward. Dark tendrils of hair tickled my thigh. I could feel the burn of her breath on the head of my cock like a brand.

"*Yes*," I said, and I wasn't sure what I was affirming.

But it seemed good enough for her, despite the tears now falling from her eyes and spattering my skin. She parted her lips and I sucked in a breath, bracing myself — and promptly woke up with a choking gasp in my hotel room. Alone. With a raging hard-on.

Goddammit. Not again.

I stumbled into the bathroom, hissing a little when the light flicked on. I leaned against the wall and waited for my vision to adjust. Fucking dreams. I sat down on the toilet lid and finished myself off with a little help from *Victoria's Secret*. One of the merry-widows looked suspiciously similar to the one which had hugged Christina Parker's lithe, curvy body in that fucking dream. Or lack thereof. She had been so close. So close to fucking me with her gorgeous, full-lipped mouth.

I quickened my pace. My orgasm was as quick and as savage as a punch to the gut. Leaning back against the toilet tank, depleted, I felt like a fucking thirteen-year-old. I threw the magazine aside in disgust. It hit the wall and landed, open, on the bathmat. Taunting me.

I needed to get laid.

No — no, I had tried that. It hadn't been satisfying in the least. I could have done a better job with my hand, and for free, too. There was only one thing that worked all the time, every time, satisfaction guaranteed.

Stop thinking with your dick.

Not just my dick. My life would be much simpler if all I wanted from that girl was a quick tumble between the sheets. It was far more complicated than that.

Most women, they have an idea about me, a fantasy, and act disappointed when I don't play the part. I'm nothing but a role for them. Christina saw me for who I was. She looked behind the curtains, saw the horrors behind them — and still saved my worthless hide at her own expense.

I liked that. And I didn't want to see her get hurt, not because of me. I'd done my share of that hurting, and so there was no fucking way this was ever going to work. Not unless I somehow managed to get a fucking time machine.

She probably hated me now, anyway. How could she not after that note I had left her, thanking her on the sly as if she were a drunken one-night stand? I'd burned that bridge between us. For her own good — and for mine.

The IMA were sending me to England tomorrow. I needed to pack. Plan. Draw up some maps and phone up old contacts. I relaxed as the blood swirled back into the slightly less stupid head. Cold, dependable logic. A familiar world. A sterile one.

There was no room for Christina Parker here.

Armed and Dangerous by Nenia Campbell

Chapter Seven

Danger

Christina:

Even though classes hadn't started yet I thought I'd get a heads-up on where they were so I could plan out my modes of transportation accordingly. I needed to purchase my textbooks, too.

I had thought that with a week to spare the campus would be deserted — pun intended — but it wasn't. Clumps of upperclassmen checked out the girls rushing the sororities. Lost freshmen huddled with their parents, wielding rolling backpacks and oversized maps and looking comically lost. People were trying to locate their classrooms, to buy new books. They desperately wanted to see and be seen. To establish ties. To make new friends.

It was like something out of a back-to-school special.

I walked past a sign advertising student ID pictures. They were taking them on the second floor of the Student Union. Right now mine had a blank square that said NO PIC. Did I look good enough to have my picture taken? I hadn't signed up for that when I got dressed this morning. I was wearing the lightest, summeriest dress I owned and still the heat weighed down upon me from all sides, crushing me into a glowing cube of hyperthermia. I figured I looked as good as I was going to get. With this heat, it wasn't as if I could curl my hair and makeup was completely out of the question.

I studied the discreet map in my planner and decided I'd work my way over to the SU gradually, since it was all the way across campus. I liked looking around. The school grounds had a quiet beauty. Rock gardens, adobe, tasteful arrangements of cacti. Here and there were verdant patches where someone had managed to coax some wilting grass. If not for the suffocating heat, it would be very peaceful.

That — and also the fact that my schedule was *awful*.

I had a 7am freshman seminar on Mondays, Wednesdays, *and* Fridays. It was a writing workshop, a unit-filler, and would not fulfill any of my graduation requirements. More useful than the bonsai-growing class, or the class on macrame, though probably not as fun.

At 3:30 p.m., I had Communist Theory. It fulfilled my Sociology prerequisite, but sounded so boring. *"A critical analysis of the Communist Manifesto"*—really? When I looked up the professor's ratings, the comments made him out to be a neurotic weirdo with a fear of authority figures.

Tuesdays and Thursdays at 2 p.m., I had Medieval Literature. That one I was actually looking forward to because one of the books in the curriculum was *Don Quixote*, one of my favorites. Unfortunately, they were using a translation different from mine, which meant I had to buy this one, too, and there were eight required books for this class, in addition to four optional, supplementary readings. In total this class was costing me about $500.

At 6 p.m., I had Introductory Psychology. Boom — Social Sciences requirements complete.

I was a declared Computer Sciences major, and yet absolutely none of the classes in my schedule were pertinent to my studies. This was completely ridiculous. Classes hadn't even started yet and already I was a jaded college student who desperately wanted to graduate.

College had once been my greatest aspiration; it stood for everything my mother did not — intellectualism, feminism, freedom. But being kidnapped had given me plenty of time to think, and somewhere between all that fear and dread, I'd realized that was the wrong reason to go to college. That the potential for those things had been inside me all along, only I'd never realized because I hadn't believed myself strong enough to break free without an intermediary.

While in Seattle, I'd seen entire constellations of possibility I'd never previously been aware of, I'd been so blinded by the bright, glaring stars of expectation. Freedom, I was beginning to think, had less to do with *where* you were, and more about *who* you were trying to be.

A mission-style bell chimed, disconcertingly similar to the one at Holy Trinity, and when I looked up I saw a large, two-story building painted in the peaches-and-cream color of adobe looming before me. The Student Union, I presumed. What other building would be worthy of a clock tower? I went inside, marveling. It was like a mini-mall in here. There was a bakery, a coffee shop, a gift shop, even a post-office. Best of all, it was *air-conditioned*.

I walked upstairs, entertaining the thought of treating myself to some sushi from the cafe for making it this far in the heat. Signs pointed me to the place where they were taking photos. Outside the room there were a cluster of freshmen comparing their student ID pictures. Even I could tell they were freshmen — it was such a high school thing to do. I remembered, we used to collect class photos like trading cards. Bonus points awarded for boys.

Armed and Dangerous by Nenia Campbell

The girls ignored me, didn't even see me. A few of the guys reflexively glanced in my direction and then looked just as quickly away. One of them was even a little cute. Eurasian features, built like a soccer player, chipped-tooth smile. He was the type I might have gone for before —

"Your dress is unzipped."

I stared at him in disbelief. He made the circling gesture with his finger. *Behind you.* "Shit," I yelped, and fled into the bathroom. The sound of their laughter made my face and neck burn. There was a full-length mirror across from the sink. When I looked over my shoulder I could see that the zipper had, indeed, come loose.

"Shit," I said again. I made an underhanded reach for it, but couldn't quite reach —

"Need some help?"

"Thanks, but I think I — "

I froze. The voice had been male, and very familiar.

I felt the zipper being pulled up. I jerked away and felt a hand close around the back of my neck. "No — " I hit the mirror, my face squashed against the glass. "Don't you dare touch me, you — "

"Do not scream," he said. "Do not say a single

word."

And he pressed a gun to my temple.

The Sniper was a man of indeterminate origin who spoke at least four languages. He was also one of the IMA's best riflemen, though in such close proximity that distinction hardly mattered. A whimper escaped my mouth as I leaned closer to the mirror, trying to escape the press of the rifle. The glass resisted my body, a few pounds of pressure from cracking.

He nodded his approval when I relaxed in his hold, the weight of my backpack dragging me slightly off-balance. "That is better. Much better."

I said nothing, but watched his reflection like a hawk. In the mirror, his eyes met mine.

"This is just a routine check-in. It can even be a painless one. That is entirely up to you."

"What if someone else comes in?"

The Sniper cracked a polite smile. "Still thinking about screaming, perhaps?" The smile disappeared. "I would not do that, if I were you. I think you will find that this restroom has been closed for maintenance. It would be a pity if an innocent life were to be sacrificed for your foolishness — don't you think so?"

"Yes," I whispered.

He pulled my hair back from my face. Whispered, "Have you been a good girl?"

I brought my head down in a swift jerk, simultaneously pulling away from him.

He tightened his grip again. "Not talking to anyone you should not be?"

"No."

"Good answer." He smiled, though this time there was nothing courteous in it. It was the same condescending smile a smarmy teacher gives a pupil he perceives as slow. I was okay with him thinking me slow-witted, though, if it meant him letting his guard down. The Sniper wasn't as familiar with me as Michael and Adrian were, and had only seen me at my most reckless.

I fingered the lump of the pepper-spray canister through the pocket of my dress. *Three seconds. That's all I need. Three seconds. Four at the most.*

"What are you doing here?" My throat still hurt where he had grabbed me.

"Exactly what I said before. Just checking in." But he didn't put away the gun and the coldness hadn't left his eyes and I began to wonder if I was going to die.

The prospect wasn't as terrifying as it might have

been only a year ago. I now knew that there was much worse.

"I don't believe you." My voice shook a little, betraying my attempt at sangfroid. "It's been a year. You've only just now started watching me?"

"No, no, I have been watching you since you arrived back in Oregon. Or at least, I did until Michael decided to use me for target practice for one of his men." He ran his fingers along the barrel of the gun, stroking it the way one might pet a dog. "Then I was temporarily replaced."

I wondered what the Sniper had done to provoke Michael — not that he needed much of an excuse. The Sniper was far too eager to get into Adrian's good graces. He deserved what he got. "Sucks to be you."

"No, Christina. I am afraid it sucks, as you say, to be *you*. You see, while we may require the services of Michael Boutilier at the moment — infrequent and objectionable though they may be — we have no such necessity for you."

The room dipped and spun like the prow of a ship at sea. *He's just trying to scare you. They have no reason to hurt you.*

Yes, they did. Because sometimes just knowing something could be reason enough to pose a threat.

Reason enough to want someone dead. 'A' had died for that reason, and I had proved myself to be a greater nuisance than she had ever been. For starters, I was still alive.

But thinking about 'A' was painful. Not just because it triggered a whole set of memories that would do me no good at the moment, but also because I had caused her death. The only person in the complex who had shown me kindness without expecting anything in return.

She had died because of me.

Incorrectly interpreting the thoughts swirling through my brain, the Sniper said, "No need to worry. At the moment I am but a passive observer."

"Passive," I repeated. I couldn't keep the sarcasm from my voice. He, like all operatives of the IMA, was anything but. I edged towards the opening beneath his arm and he slammed me back against the mirror, causing cracks to rift through the cheap glass, brittle pieces flaking to the tile at our feet like confetti. "Stop it," I said. "Please. Just stop it. Go away. Leave me alone. You can't — "

"Begging already? My, how the mighty have fallen. I seem to recall you once saying that you were not afraid of me. But that has all changed now, has it not? Whatever is the matter Christina? Not quite so brave now that you are no longer Michael's whore?"

"Shut up," I snarled.

"I see I have hit upon a raw nerve."

"It's called self-respect, you bastard."

"Hmm. Well. I can think of several men at the IMA who would only be too happy to take you up on your, mm, *self-respect*, as you call it."

"I would *never* — "

"Yes, that is what they all say at first. Until they hear the alternative."

"Don't tell me you're offering."

I didn't have to see my reflection to know I looked completely repulsed. And terrified out of my mind.

"I am afraid you are not my type. I prefer my women with a little less…kick."

At my sides, my hands clenched into fists. He glanced down, shook his head.

"Mr. Callaghan, on the other hand, has always been appreciative of a good fight. But I believe you are already aware of this, yes?"

I closed my fingers around the pepper-spray. *Give me a window*, I thought. *Just one.*

I said nothing.

The Sniper continued his diatribe. "Michael is a difficult man. Recalcitrant. Insubordinate. Retraining, threats—they all do nothing. At the moment he is working for us solely because he believes it has so far kept you from harm, despite dragging his heels and fighting us every step of the way."

It's that bad? Something in my chest wrenched. Hard.

"Why are you telling me this?" I tried to sound defiant, to mask the pain in my voice with self-righteous anger. It was none of my affair how Michael was assimilating into the IMA. "Why should I care? I don't."

"Michael is growing arrogant, my dear, and Mr. Callaghan feels that it might be opportune to give him a sense of urgency." His fingers closed lightly around the place where my throat met my collarbone. "It would be helpful to us, and far less painful for you, if you cooperate."

A spike of anger riveted through me. Even after all this time, after all I had been through, I was still the easily-cowed little girl. *I don't think so.*

I brought up my empty hand. He had been expecting an attack, clearly. With the way he was provoking me, I might even say he had been looking for one outright. He was going to get one.

Armed and Dangerous by Nenia Campbell

The Sniper moved to parry me, digging two fingers into my wrist, twisting it. The pain was excruciating; he intended to break it. But he had left his face open. Gasping, I reached into my pocket. I aimed the little can at him and thumbed the button. There was pause. Then the yellowish cloud sprayed out, attacking the mucus membranes of his eyes, nose, throat, and mouth.

He let go. It was all he could do to breathe. *Take that, you son of a bitch,* I thought but did not say. It was all I could do to keep from inhaling the caustic fumes.

I ran from the restroom with watering eyes and a drippy nose. I kept coughing. That crowd of students was still standing outside, though a few of them had peeled off. They gave me a collectively searching look with undertones of judgment. Probably thinking I sneaked in there to smoke pot. I didn't care. Being subject to their scrutiny was worth being safe. The Sniper was too professional to make a public scene. He hadn't even cried out when I sprayed him. He had too much to lose to bother chasing me, but that didn't mean there weren't others waiting in the wings.

Michael, what have you gotten us into?

What have you done?

And why was I being made to suffer for it?

Armed and Dangerous by Nenia Campbell

Michael:

I tugged at the stiff, starched collar. It was like wearing a neck-brace made out of cotton. This was exactly why I didn't care to wear suits. They were un-fucking-comfortable, and difficult to fight in.

Maybe that was the point.

Thomas Agnew, the Princeton graduate from Fairbanks, Louisiana, did wear suits, however, and it wasn't like Michael Boutilier had a say in the matter. So here I was, wearing the monkey suit like a fucking patsy. I stretched out my legs. At least they had put me in first class this time. I wouldn't even need to clown around with a fake accent provided that I tempered the Cajun lilt and avoided any French curses. Praise the Lord for small favors.

How long would they go on for?

I leaned back in the seat, trying to enjoy the legroom, forgoing the struggle with my shirt-collar for now. View was nice, too. To get to England from America, most planes pass through the Arctic Circle. It's faster that way, though it means passing over Alaska, Greenland, Iceland. Outside was a blanket of white, snow indistinguishable from cloud.

The steward came by with the rolling cart,

delivering the obligatory bundles of crap "courtesy of our airline." "Can I get you anything, sir?"

"Scotch. Make it a double."

He gave me a disapproving look. Thinking I was nothing but a corn-pone hick, probably, about to get drunk off his ass and cause a major ruckus. I did him the favor of pretending I didn't see it, though he took his sweet-ass time coming back with the scotch. When he did, I ignored the tumbler he offered. "Won't be needing the glass."

I wanted to laugh right in his face when I heard him mutter under his breath. He'd drink too, if he were in my place. Once you've been in my line of work for a while, it gets to the point where alcohol is the only thing that shuts up the body chatter. The doll-sized bottles put some fire in my belly but did nothing to melt the coldness in my chest.

Infiltrate the BN. Gather information. Reconnaissance. As if it were all as simple as ordering fucking take-out. I lifted the bottle to my lips, frowning when nothing but air poured into my mouth. *Time to move on to door number two.* I cracked the cap off with my teeth and took a swig.

Anything synonymous with the phrase "turncoat" had me concerned, even if it was the enemies of the IMA I was turning traitor to. It's a hard label to shake off, regardless of which side you actually work for, and I suspected that I was being set up for some kind of fall.

Wouldn't be the first time if I was.

On the other hand, would Callaghan have wasted all that time and money 'retraining' me if he only planned to kill me afterward? *Only if the payoff was even bigger.* The BN was a pain in the ass, but they sure weren't the mother lode of figurative hemorrhoids.

"The fuck are those assholes planning?" I muttered, scratching the stubble on my chin. It was starting to itch.

A woman down the row kept turning around to stare. I glared back at her until she returned to her book. When I saw what she was reading, I snorted. Fucking mommy porn. She heard the snort and turned red, squirming in her seat, trying to hide the book in her too-small purse.

I rolled my eyes and turned away. I knew I was being cruel. But I had just graduated from the Ivy Leagues. I was on my way to a high-paying job. Why shouldn't I laugh at some frazzled housewife reading the literary equivalent of garbage? Doing so was in character, and if it gave me some small amount of pleasure, who the hell cared?

Armed and Dangerous by Nenia Campbell

That's right. You're a college graduate. Life's a party. So smile and eat shit and pretend it's fucking caviar.

When the steward came by again, I tugged his sleeve and said, "Another scotch, if you please. There isn't enough alcohol in here to get a mayfly buzzed."

Armed and Dangerous by Nenia Campbell

Chapter Eight

Frustration

Christina:

I felt hunted, trapped.

Not quite so brave now that you are no longer Michael's whore?

I shivered, forgetting the smothering heat for a few chilling seconds. How did they do that? How did they always manage to strike right where it hurt most? How did they *know*?

Stupid question. They knew because they had been trained to—and it wasn't exactly like I had the world's best poker face. Far from it.

I ended up going straight back to my apartment without getting my photo ID taken. My encounter with the Sniper had left me too rattled. I didn't believe for a second that he hadn't meant me any harm. While he wasn't a complete sadist, unlike his boss, he hated Michael and he didn't like me. He had now proven that he was not above vengeance. Spraying him in the face with pepper-spray probably hadn't helped my situation.

Why was he here? Had he been going to kidnap me?

Worse?

Armed and Dangerous by Nenia Campbell

I can think of several men at the IMA who would only be too happy to take you up on your, mm, self-respect, as you call it.

Worse.

I tried to swallow the lump that had formed in my chest starting circa thirty minutes ago and my eyes blurred with unshed tears. I yanked the stop cord on the bus and hurried off before anyone on it could see me cry. As my skin heated up from the mid-afternoon sun, my tears began to feel like ice as they evaporated. This was bad. This was really, *really* bad.

Keep it together.

Where was my key? Had I left it there, back in the restroom? Did the *Sniper* have the key to my apartment? *If he does, you are officially too stupid to live.* My breathing hitched as I dug around in my pocket. Please, no. Please, for the love of God, no, no, no, *no*. My fingers closed around warm metal. I let out a breath. Oh, thank God.

The key stuck in the door's lock. I had to jimmy it around a little and as I did so, I heard a strange click. Was it jammed? Did I just break my door? Maintenance was so going to hate me.

But then the hinges yielded to the push of my arm and with a shriek of rusted metal I was in. The cold air hit me like a tidal wave and I leaned back against the door, slamming it closed. I did up all three locks and collapsed where I stood. The cold hadn't penetrated as far as my bedroom yet, which faced directly into the sun and got ridiculously hot. So hot that I could never sleep past ten or the heat of my own blankets would wake me.

I'd survived this long. I wasn't about to let myself get knocked off by mere heatstroke. Or stupidity.

But in the meantime, what was I going to do?

Don't think about that. I swiped my hand over my forehead. Droplets of sweat spattered the carpet. The movement made me feel a little dizzy, as if my brain was a buoy bobbing in the vast sea of my head. When did I last have a drink? Had I even eaten? I couldn't remember. I couldn't even tell if I was suffering from dehydration or paralyzing terror. *Maybe it's both.*

That was more in keeping with my luck.

When I no longer saw the heat shimmering in front of my eyes I got up and went to the fridge. I grabbed the orange juice and drank it straight from the carton. It had been propped up against the back, close to the freezer, and was partially frozen. I closed my eyes and drank the slush until my throat ached from the sweet, chilly tartness of it. I crossed myself, belatedly blessing the food, set the carton aside, and wiped my mouth with the back of a shaking hand. My stomach hurt a little but I no longer felt faint.

I had let my sympathetic nervous system take over again, going on autopilot. Abandoning myself to terror. That was bad. Not just because it made me do stupid things like forgetting to eat and drink and sleep, but also because it meant that I had elevated cortisol levels. Enough to kick-start me into unnecessary spurts of fight-or-flight.

Not so unnecessary in this case.

The IMA were back in my life, and I wanted to know why. I hadn't done anything circumspect. Perhaps Michael had, and because Michael was inaccessible they were taking their wrath out on me. The Sniper had implied as much and Michael himself had warned me this might happen. Kent, too, before he took me back home.

I have been watching you since you arrived in Oregon.

Did that mean he knew where I lived? My lock — had it been jammed because of its cheap component parts, or a trick of the heat warping the metal, or because the IMA had broken into my apartment? A few days before I might have brushed that off as simple paranoia and popped one of the anti-anxiety pills my psychiatrist had prescribed for just these types of situations. "Panic attacks," they were called.

Except when they were warranted. Then they were called "common sense."

I closed the fridge. The IMA used the Sniper for visual surveillance, in addition to marksmanship. His renown as a "good shot" carried multiple meanings; he could snap a photo as easily, and with as much finesse, as he could snap a neck. That made him a valuable commodity.

If they had sent him to me, specifically, there was a reason, and that reason was that the IMA was interested in keeping an eye on me. That they suspected something.

But what?

Back in Washington, the Sniper had bugged Michael's apartment. He had spied on us while we were on the run. It looked like he was doing the same thing now, which meant that somewhere in my apartment were various bugs.

I chewed on my lower lip, trying to remember if I had done anything incriminating recently. They would put the camera somewhere they could see me come and go, I guessed. They would want to establish patterns in my schedule, see who I was in contact with. In the Seattle apartment, Michael found the dime-sized camera squirreled away in one of the knotholes over the front door.

Armed and Dangerous by Nenia Campbell

He hadn't showed it to me, though. He had destroyed it first. I had no idea what real bugs actually looked like, what I was looking for. I doubted they looked like they did on TV — big, futuristic looking devices that blinked out "I am a bug!" in Morse code.

At least try.

I backtracked through the hallway, dragging one of the cheap IKEA chairs with me. I ran my hand over the wooden frame to check for signs of tampering. Uneven spots, lumps, peeling paint. Nothing. A big, fat *nada*.

I stomped into my bedroom, which was a mess, relatively speaking. I began cleaning, working my way from the door to my bed, keeping one eye peeled. Nothing *looked* moved, and I would notice, Mamá being the snoop she was. If the IMA had been here, they had been careful. My computer looked fine, at a glance, and I could run some software scans that would tell me if they had installed a keylogger. My phone had been on me at the time so I wasn't concerned with that, either — for now. I checked the framing on all my windows and doors. That was a bust. So was the bathroom.

I went into the kitchen. The appliances worried me because they had come with the apartment, so I wasn't entirely sure what they were supposed to look like normally. I didn't want to tinker around with them, either, and risk losing a hefty chunk of my security deposit to sustain damage costs. Better to leave it all alone and just avoid hanging out in the kitchen if I could.

I did find something strange fitted into the thermostat in the living room, which faced the front door. A strange ring with a tiny blinking light and what looked like an optics device. I crushed it under my shoe and felt a little better. Not much, though. There were probably more.

This cloak-and-dagger warfare was a message, a warning. It said: *We know where you are. We are watching you. And if we want to, we can hurt you.*

College was supposed to include the best years of my life. Instead — this, all this. I was beginning to suspect that God might not want me to get on my life. That, or my faith was being tested somehow, like Job, But if this was a test, what was I supposed to do? I wasn't capable of fighting against the IMA. Not on my own. I'd tried.

Michael could, I thought, surprising myself. He had been fighting against the IMA in his own way since he was first recruited. Michael knew what bugs looked like and where to look for them. Michael would know what to do, where to go, and when to run.

In the face of my survival I had taken his abilities for granted, but really, when it came down to it, he was the main reason I was still alive. Yes, he had gotten me into this mess in the first place, if not personally then by proxy, but he had also been the one to defy the odds to get me back out. That had to count for something.

I could talk big, stall, even run and hide — but Michael knew how to fight. And it was starting to look like the IMA was demanding one.

Michael:

When the plane landed my armrests bore divots in the leather from my fingers. I'd half-expected the plane to blow up. Rookie fear, I know, but that would be just like the bastard — to take a bunch of innocents down along with his target and then blame the act on terrorists.

Callaghan liked that, lulling people into a sense of false security and then catching them with their pants down. I knew I had a limited shelf life — I'd come to terms with that a long time ago — but for now, I was alive. I hadn't yet outlived my usefulness. I just needed to keep it that way for a little while longer.

My luggage had disappeared again, not unlike the Scotland trip, so I wasn't surprised, either, when I got pulled aside for another "random" security check. By the time I got out of the London airport I was an hour and a half behind schedule.

Those assholes had no respect for me or my time.

I had been set up in an over-priced, under-furnished hotel. Crystal chandeliers, red carpet, rococo wallpaper. Suitable for a hot-shot who judged things by cost and not quality. This kind of place was a trap for bourgeois tourists. It was even called *La Chançard* — 'the lucky fellow.'

Someone appreciated their own sense of irony.

I strolled up to the concierge's desk. I could see him around the corner, talking into the phone, but I was getting into the swing of my role and found I was developing a taste for being a dick. I slammed the bell, gratified to see him jump. The annoyance left when he saw my suit.

"Yes? What can I do for you?"

Fake posh accent and everything. Now that was class.

"Mr. Agnew," I said. "I believe I called earlier on about a room."

The concierge studied my ID for a long time. I watched him glance from me to my driver's license as though memorizing my features. I suspected he was trying to get the measure of me, so I stared right on back. I was better at this game and he knew it. We both did. When he handed back my license, he didn't meet my eyes. "It's two-hundred pounds a night. That includes a continental breakfast."

"Great."

"How long will you be staying with us?"

I eyed him. "I'm roughing it."

He seemed to accept that. Of course he did. "Form of payment?"

"Credit."

"Very good." He slid the card through the scanner and then handed it back with a key. The key was dull brass and hung from a tooled leather fob. "Three thirty-seven is your room, sir. Please enjoy your stay at our hotel."

I waved my hand in thanks.

The room turned out to be on the third floor. Not my preference. I preferred lower floors. Easier to escape that way in a pinch. Something I'm sure Callaghan took into consideration when making the arrangements. He probably put me as far from the fire escape as he was able, as well. At least it had a view. I could see the London skyline, occluded by a shroud of misty vapor and air pollution. Sulfur-colored skyscrapers. I closed the blinds, tossed the keys and luggage on my bed, shrugged off the suit-coat.

Better already.

I unpacked the gun from my suitcase, removing it from the special holster. The holster was made of lead and special computer cloaking technology that scrambled the readings of the x-ray and scanner software. The gun went beneath my pillow in the space between headboard and mattress. To my left, where it would be in easy reach. My knife went into the nightstand drawer, right on top of the fabric-bound bible.

When I bent to shut the drawer my shirt-collar cinched tight around my neck like a noose. I untied my tie and unfastened the collar, letting out the first unconstrained breath I'd had since I'd put the suit on this morning. I undid the buttons and tossed the shirt on an upholstered chair. The slacks followed.

Just like that, exhaustion slammed into me like a battering ram. I kicked the suitcase to the floor and leaned back against the slippery coverlet. As soon as my eyes closed I found myself recalling that dream. Still so vivid, I could almost feel her skin against my naked chest.

My breathing changed, my body's willingness to sleep disappearing as it was jolted into ready awareness, and I cursed. I had a fucking standing ovation going on in my goddamn pants, and it was demanding an encore.

But the leading lady, she was nowhere in sight.

Chapter Nine
Messenger

Christina:

I awoke with the dulled sense of malaise that comes from a night of sleep plagued by nightmares. For the last couple days, it had been like this. Sleep had taken some of the edge off my fears, but none of the logistics behind them. I was right to feel frightened; I no longer felt safe. It was hard to argue with that. So I didn't.

Fear could be a useful emotion. It could keep you alert, and ready to deal with whatever problem happened your way. Panic was detrimental. I would not panic.

I yanked on a pair of denim shorts and a billowy peasant top that hid some of my butt. Right before tromping down the steps I gulped down some of the orange juice I'd opened yesterday, while cramming my books into my backpack with my other hand. The bus was coming in fifteen minutes. It took five to walk down to the stop and my watch told me I was running the wrong side of late.

Today was my first day of college.

"Shoot." I grabbed my lanyard and my photoless ID.

Armed and Dangerous by Nenia Campbell

Sunlight speared into my eyes when I opened the door. I squinted into the dazzling brightness of it, everything gilded, golden, sparkling, lit up like desert sand. It was warm but still a few degrees shy from hot. Across the street, an older man was getting into his car.

The five minute walk felt closer to ten minutes than five. I only just made it to the bus on time. All the seats were full, except for one at the back behind an intimidating-looking goth guy with headphones.

Outside the window was the black car I'd seen the old guy get into. It was trailing slowly after the bus. There was plenty of room for him to pass, but he wasn't taking it.

Following the bus? Following me?

No. I couldn't let fear get the better of me. But I wondered; oh, I wondered. The timing was too great to be mere coincidence, and I'd long suspected that there was no such thing. Everything was connected, just like the circuits in a motherboard. You only had to look closely enough.

I tried to put the incident out of mind as I headed for Medieval Literature. It wasn't difficult. The air-conditioner in Howard Hall was broken, and with its large, spacious skylights, the building was as hot and humid as a sauna. I parted with some of my pocket-change for two over-priced but ice-chilled drinks for the vending machines. One of them was already empty.

Our "professor" for the class was a graduate student in the process of obtaining his doctorate in Chivalric Romance. Despite the heat he was wearing a tweed suit about ten years out of date that looked as if it had been purchased at a thrift store. I couldn't tell if it was meant to be ironic or not. He had to be boiling in it because there were damp circles under both his armpits. I hoped mine didn't look like that.

"Medieval Literature may seem like an oxymoron," said Professor Ross-Ross-being-my-first-name-not-my-last-name. "The Dark Age was notorious for its backpedaling in arts and sciences alike. However, there were still creative works being published at this time, though many of them focused on religion, and especially the crusades."

He went on to talk about courtly love and the idealization of purity and honor; the overpowering presence of God looking down on everyone, all the time; the importance of avoiding sin and temptation; the crusades and their glittering triad of gold, God, and glory.

Sounds like Mamá when she gets worked up.

I thought about the Sniper and the man I saw

Armed and Dangerous by Nenia Campbell

outside my apartment early that morning. Had I seen that car before? I might have, but that also might be the paranoia talking. If the man was following me, he had to be under the employ of the IMA: somebody posted to keep an eye on me until the Big Guns arrived.

Professor Ross's lecture was interesting, but I floated through the whole lesson. I kept thinking a van was going to pull up behind me as I walked away from the bus station. That I would feel a gloved hand clamp over my mouth, taste the biting leather and the chemical sting of chloroform, when I went to the SU to get a coffee—

But nothing happened.

Nothing happened *yet*.

I was worried about my 6 p.m. Psychology class. That got out at 8, and by that time it was plenty dark enough for someone to creep about, unseen. After about 5 o' clock p.m., the college pretty much looked like a ghost town.

Luckily, I had remembered to bring my key-ring pepper-spray. I was considering bringing the knife, too, even though the campus had a zero-tolerance weapons policy. It all came down to one simple question: which would be worse? Possible expulsion, or getting abducted by people who didn't care one way or the other?

Exactly.

Michael:

There's an old quote that soldiering is 99% boredom and 1% sheer terror. That old axiom holds true in my line of work as well.

When I finished napping I did a brief work-out. Push-ups. Crunches. A round of jujitsu. Then I did some reading. I didn't relax. I never relaxed. I was perpetually on, whether I wanted to be or not.

The room's telephone rang. I snatched it up. "Hello?"

"Mr. Agnew?"

"Yes?"

"There is a message for you at the front desk."

I changed into business casual and shoved the gun into its holster beneath my coat.

The chandeliers in the lobby were turned up high. Their aggressive glare made my eyes water. I flashed my ID at the concierge. He handed me an envelope. How very old-fashioned. It was like something out of an old black and white spy movie. I shouldn't have been surprised. The BN were romantic dreamers; the saw themselves as heroes setting out to change the world. Most people do, just as most people lie to themselves about who they really are.

I wondered who the messenger had been, whether the concierge would tell me if I asked. Probably not. His silence had, in all likelihood, been bought for a generous price. I could outbid them, easily, but it wouldn't be worth the vague description I would undoubtedly receive from him.

I flexed the envelope, testing the quality of the paper. Firm, unyielding. Expensive. Risky, making the drop-off at a big place like this. These people liked their teatime chatter.

Perhaps that was why Callaghan wanted them out of the way. He didn't play well with others, didn't like to share his toys. If the BN were strutting around his playground, it made perfect sense why he'd want them gone.

I tipped the concierge, then turned away to open the envelope. Instead of a letter it contained a small card. A business card. The word *Annie's* was written on it in large block letters, along with the phone number and store hours. On the back, scrawled in a messy hand, was some additional information:

6:30 a.m. Ask for Charles.

Armed and Dangerous by Nenia Campbell

Christina:

That evening's psychology lecture consisted of a brief overview of the course and an in-depth analysis of the syllabus that had several people in the back snoring. Bored as I was there was no danger of *that* happening. I had not been able to let my guard down in public since my kidnapping.

I was happy the walk between the psychology building and the bus stop was a short one. Not only had I been lucky enough to find an apartment for rent on the busline, but I'd also somehow managed to pick classes that did, as well. I couldn't have done it better if I had planned it.

I *was* concerned about how dark it was tonight, though. That hadn't factored into my plans. The labyrinthine sprawl of classrooms was shadowy and foreboding beneath the moonless Arizona sky.

I took notes without paying attention, jotting down keywords that were overtaken by a sea of doodles and random scribbles. My notebook looked like a wall of graffiti. It was an accurate portrayal of my own frenetic thoughts. If only there were someone I could contact, somebody I could go to for help and talk to without being judged. But I was pretty sure they didn't have "Help!-I-Was-Kidnapped-and-Can't-

Get-Over-It" support groups. My God, it sounded like the punchline to a bad joke.

Besides, that wasn't the kind of thing you could "get over." I was beginning to understand that victims have three choices: they can try to make themselves forget, they can let the past haunt them, or they can make the experience a part of themselves and try to grow over it, like scar tissue on a wound.

Life doesn't come with an eraser. Experiences leave their mark, for better or for worse. Anyone who tells you otherwise has never been hurt.

The professor dismissed the class early. I yanked the sweatshirt that I had brought over my head to hide my bust and long hair. One of the girls at Holy Trinity had taught me that trick; she worked at a restaurant and occasionally got some creeps who would try to follow her home on the way back from the late-shift.

I was tall and had been taking self-defense, but some men didn't need an excuse to bother women. Because, in all honesty, there *are* no excuses. Not for people like that. Even so, I wasn't about to give them one. Hence the pepper-spray—and the knife.

The talk of my departing classmates seemed to get sucked straight into the void of darkness, like an aural black hole. I could hear the nervous chattering of crickets coming from the scrub. Their high-pitched warbling mirrored my own sense of unease perfectly.

Calm down, Christina.

I tried to stay my breathing and unclench my muscles. I remembered reading somewhere, probably in one of those pamphlets from the YWCA, that attackers can read fear in body posture. That's what they look for in a victim.

I am nobody's victim, I thought to myself. *Nobody is going to fuck with me tonight.*

If only I could believe it.

I passed the doughnut-shaped science building, keeping my head high and my shoulders back. A few lights were still on in some of the labs. Coswell wasn't a research university so the equipment they had was pretty low-tech. Strictly high school-level stuff, though the hollowed-out center housed our acclaimed botanical garden. Accredited research universities had a lot of interest in our botany department and its large collection of desert flowers. I caught a whiff of pollen as I circled around, which meant somebody had left the door to the inner-garden open.

Sand and grit crunched under my sneakers as I stumbled down the steps and into the courtyard separating the drama and computer departments. Here was a small grove of jade plants, artfully surrounded by jagged, saw-like blades of cacti that looked like shadowy teeth in the night. A sweet, tangy scent suggested jasmine. The crickets hiding in the plants halted their chirruping as I passed, startled into silence. In that heartbeat of stillness I heard a crunch. It was the sound of rock and sand beneath a heavy-soled shoe that wasn't mine.

I went cold, just like that, straining to listen to the silence that now seemed as taut as a cord ready to snap—and when it did, what would happen? The sound did not happen again. This only served to reinforce my conviction that I was being followed.

Shit.

My first instinct was to run, but running would only alert whoever was following that I suspected something. They would drop all pretenses of subtlety and chase me, regardless of the well-lit walkway and its security cameras overhead. I made myself continue at a steady pace. I jumped over one of the cactus plants: a jovial, carefree gesture meant to disguise my quickening pace as I ducked around the corner of the drama building and temporarily out of sight.

Whoever was following me was keeping well behind. If it hadn't been so silent, I wouldn't have heard that telltale crack. I had bought several seconds to make a decision. To my right was a crosswalk, too far for me to reach in time. To the left was the student theater. I ducked behind one of the freshly painted sceneries I'd watched the art students working on early. It was for our school's rendition of *Midsummer Night's Dream*. The plywood backdrops had been left to dry overnight, painted sides facing inward so students wouldn't try to touch. From the side facing the street, in the dark, I suspected they would look like a solid fence or wall. It was my only shot.

I hoped it worked.

Half-stumbling in my haste, I crouched in front of the primeval forest. The sour smells of particleboard and damp paint stung my eyes and nose. I heard footsteps again. Faintly but there, and growing louder all the while. I peeked around the edge of the board and saw a man—tall, muscular, dangerous.

Not anybody I wanted to tangle with.

I didn't know him, had never seen him before in my life, but he fit the profile of someone the IMA might hire. Except for his impressive physique, he looked perfectly ordinary. He could have been a jock at the school, maybe in his early twenties. Unaware of my frightened watch, he looked around and cursed. He spent several seconds muttering to himself, then raked his fingers through his dark hair and drew out a mobile phone from his coat pocket.

I didn't dare breathe.

A brief but intense conversation followed. I could make out the words "girl," "easy," and "escaped," punctuated by bursts of sarcasm, and discussions of money, both in an affronted tone that made me wince. The gist of it was, he'd been assuming that a female college student would be easy to find and overpower, and he was pissed off that I had managed to get away. His supervisor was chewing him out for being a chauvinistic moron, and seemed to be ordering a return of the down payment my stalker had received for his services. The man was refusing, demanding a second chance.

It was getting ugly. I backed farther into the shadows, more determined than ever not to get caught. He hung up the phone, pacing the deserted sidewalk with ill-concealed frustration. About five minutes later by my watch, a jet-colored car with tinted windows pulled up to the curb. I tried to read the license plate in the dim glow of the taillights but couldn't quite make it out — not without moving from my hiding spot and exposing myself. *S9J* was as far as I got before the car roared off.

I stayed put for a few minutes longer just in case

they decided to double-back for a final sweep. I was shaking, and not from cold. When it looked as if they really had gone, I stepped out from the wall of paintings and started back for home. I kept to the shadows, taking care to avoid bushes, cars, and other objects someone could potentially use to lie in wait.

By the time I made it to the bus stop, I was ready to fall apart. Only about three other students were waiting. A boyfriend and a girlfriend couple, and that same goth guy who'd been sitting in front of me during the ride over. No mysterious, sinister strangers. I collapsed on the bench and willed myself to hold it together. At least until home.

Fate was working against me that night.

That same black car—the one I had seen this afternoon, and then again this evening when it picked up my pursuer—was parked across the street from my apartment complex. The plate matched. There was no question. They know who I was, and where I lived, and they knew I had given them the slip.

I was in trouble.

Big trouble.

What should I do? I lowered my hand from the stop cord. That's what they would be expecting. I got off at the next stop instead. From there, I looped around to the back of the complex, near the laundry room. I had the advantage; I knew the area better than they did. There was usually someone in the laundry room, even at night, and it was always well-lit. Plus, the doors locked automatically, and only someone with a key could open them up again. Smashing through the glass would trigger an alarm.

I went inside the laundry room, took out my phone, and dialed the number for the city police department. The operator answered, "Coswell Police Department. What is your emergency?"

"There's a man following me."

"Excuse me? Speak up, ma'am."

I was gasping. I drew in a breath and said, too shrilly this time, "There's a man following me—well, two of them now. One of them was outside my apartment earlier, the other was outside my classroom, and now both of them are in a car in front of my apartment. W-waiting for me, I think."

"Can you give a description of the vehicle?"

I could do better than that. I gave her the plate number, in addition to a brief description of the car and the two men inside it.

"Can you get to someplace safe?"

"I'm hiding in the laundry room of my apartment

complex. It locks."

"Good. Stay there. Someone will be out shortly."

"Please hurry." I injected a whimper into my voice that wasn't entirely fake. "I'm scared."

She assured me again that the officers were on their way. "Would you like me to stay on the line with you until they arrive?"

"N-no. That's okay."

The operator hung up. I tucked the phone into my pocket, and peered through the window. I could just barely make out the street from here, and through the trees, the black car. My breath fogged the glass. One of the dryers rattled, the pungent smell of the fabric softener filling my nose like a perfumed smog.

Another car drove by on the street. Unmarked. It stopped behind the black car. An officer got out of the vehicle and began walking up to the black Sedan. Before the cop could reach them, they gassed it and roared off. The cop raced back into his car to pursue, phoning for backup, but I knew it was fruitless. Either the car had been stolen or the plates had. They would find the vehicle abandoned on a roadside somewhere, all traces of both passengers long gone.

That was because the IMA were professionals. They were the people you went to when you wanted to be above or below the law. They made the FBI look like amateurs. The police wouldn't be able to help me.

I ran up the stairs to my apartment and locked the door behind me, tightening my grip on the pepper-spray as I did a quick search of the rooms. It was empty; I was alone. If I had been wearing my iPod, the way I sometimes did, I wouldn't have heard that guy following me. Not until it was too late.

I slid down the wall until my butt hit the floor. My fingers were still curled around the reassuring curve of the pepper-spray canister. I looked at it and felt stupid. Pepper-spray? A freaking butter knife? Who was I kidding? They had guns.

I couldn't stay vigilant forever. I wasn't a robot. When I let my guard down, as I eventually would have to, the IMA would kidnap me. Or worse.

I'd barely survived their internment base the first time, and that had been with Michael's help. If they put me there again, alone, with the Sniper or Adrian as my guard, I wouldn't stand a chance. I didn't like pain. I wouldn't be able to stand up to torture. I'd be a goner. And even that was assuming that they didn't just save themselves the time and resources by putting a bullet in my head.

So what are you going to do, Christina? Hide with your head buried in the sand like an ostrich and wait for them to kill you?

If I kept my phone on me at all times as I had done so far, the IMA wouldn't be able to bug it. A phone was a handy lifeline. In the meantime, I'd only eat sealed foods. I'd find a buddy, preferably a man, to walk around with me at night, and I'd use the campus escort service.

Actually, no, I wouldn't, because that followed a schedule. The IMA could run circles around regular police officers. I didn't want to think about what they might do to our underpaid, hourly salary rent-a-cops.

God help me.

Armed and Dangerous by Nenia Campbell

Chapter Ten

Enemies

Michael:

Annie's turned out to be a downtown greasy-spoon. The sort of dive that could double as a cafe or a coffeehouse depending on the hour and the special of the day. Tired-looking businessmen hunched over their eggs and cracked mugs of coffee, oblivious to everything but the ticking of time. I looked around. Nobody seemed like they were waiting. I sat down at the counter and ordered an espresso and watched the Premier League soccer match they were showing on the TV hung crookedly on the back wall.

A tall shadow crawled over my steaming cup. "Mr. Agnew, I presume?"

"Presume all you want." I gave the man a quick once-over. My suspicion wasn't feigned.

"You aren't one of the regulars."

"Are you Charles?"

"Close enough." He made an attempt at an enigmatic smile. It made him look constipated.

"We talking here?" I asked, picking up my espresso and taking a sip. Tasted like shit, but it gave me an excuse to stall without being obvious.

Armed and Dangerous by Nenia Campbell

"No, Mr. Agnew. This way, please."

I followed 'Charles' down the darkened hallway. My fingertips brushed against my hip for the weight of the gun that I'd decided would be a bad idea to bring. Rightly so, it seemed. I hoped 'Charles' hadn't seen—or read—too much into the gesture.

Be more careful, you fool. Remember your training.

That was a laugh. How could I possibly forget?

Most IMA agents, it's easy to tell that they're into something physical. We have to be in top shape, ready for any situation that gets handed to us. Most of the men and women working the field are under thirty years of age, in the prime of their lives.

Studying those assembled in the back of this small room made me realize that the BN were a very different kettle of fish. Political ideologies and techniques aside, some of the men were strikingly slender, and several were older than Kent. I slipped my hands into my coat pockets before they could betray me any more than they already had. If these people read nervousness out of the gesture, so much the better. It could make them underestimate me.

"Mr. Agnew," said one of the men. "You came highly recommended to us."

I inclined my head.

Armed and Dangerous by Nenia Campbell

One of the women said, "Perhaps you don't realize what an honor it is to be here, standing before us."

"Not really." I gave them a lazy grin. "But I'm sure you folks are just rearing to tell me."

I saw a few of them exchange dubious glances.

"Yes," the same first man said. "We are."

Another spoke. This one was in a suit ten years out of date. "The *Bureau du Nuit* is a very prestigious organization, and not for everyone."

He had an accent I couldn't place. Eastern-European. An ex-Soviet Satellite.

"No, not for everyone," another woman agreed.

"Like a secret society?" They'd expect a question like that from a college boy. "Like the Skull and Bones?"

"Apropos of nothing, yes," the first man agreed. "We expect only the best."

The first woman laughed. It was not a nice laugh.

I let my head loll to one side. "Something funny? I don't see anything here worth laughing about."

"Such an interesting accent. Whereabouts are you from?"

"The U.S. Of A, of course."

"From the South?"

"Well, I sure as shit ain't no Yankee."

I'd be lying if I said I wasn't enjoying myself. Their scandalized expressions were such that any real inquiring student would have been completely offended. For me, it was a real fucking hoot, the most fun I'd had in a while.

"I've never heard anything like it."

"My grandmother was Cajun." I folded my arms and leaned back on my heels. "Some of that patois made it on down to me. Like as not, that's what you're hearing right now."

"Indeed," the first man said. Politely. He didn't seem like he was going to be hard to win over, so I'd have to watch out for him. He could be manipulative—the superficially nice ones usually were.

I cleared my throat. "So what am I supposed to call you people?" That earned me a few more suspicious looks, but again, they'd expect that buddy-buddy shit.

"You can call me Perry."

"I'm Robin." That was the old woman.

Because I had already decided I didn't like her, I sneered and said, "What, no Batman?"

The wrinkles in her face sharpened.

"Sparrow," said the younger woman. Also British.

"Hawk," the second man said. He was the one giving me the majority of those distrustful glares. I hadn't made any friends over in that quarter.

They went around introducing themselves from there, giving me time to take a headcount. There were about twenty people, all told. The handles they gave me were clearly aliases. Birds of a fucking feather. "Nice to meet y'all. Can I be Eagle?"

"Mr. Agnew," Robin said. "Might I remind you, we haven't accepted your application yet."

"How can you not? I'm the best there is."

"Look you little upstart—"

"Now, Robin," Perry cut in. Was that short for Peregrine? Cute. Real cute. "There's no need to beat around the bush—we've already got our bird."

"Mixing metaphors?" I said dryly.

"Oh no. Not at all. We're very interested in your history. Ex-military, aren't you?"

"I served some time, yes." Military documents were difficult to fake, but not impossible. Not if you had the right connections and the proper funds.

"Good," said Perry. "We can use that. You see, we have a vision, Mr. Agnew. We believe that the world's governments are growing corrupted by their own power and greed. That religion is being eclipsed by the ultimate golden calf, so to speak."

"The golden dollar sign," Sparrow said. "Capitalism. Brutality. Oppression. Green-blooded totalitarianism."

"Sounds like a real utopia you've got there." Jesus, they were even more whacked that I'd thought.

"Yes," another man—Jay I think he'd said his name was, as in "blue"—agreed. "That is our vision. A utopia."

"You and Karl Marx both." I snorted. "I think we all remember what happened to him in the history books. You want to wipe out oppressive capitalism, you can't do it by brute force. You have to offer a better system."

"An unfortunate moment in history to be sure," Robin murmured. "But not entirely unforeseen."

"Our goal is on a much smaller scale, Mr. Agnew. We want recognition as an emerging party, the ability to introduce social policies, the ability to vote as a recognized group. We are willing to fight for that right, and if that means going head-to-head with those who oppose us directly then we will do so. There is already one group out there which stands for everything that we are against. Unlike us, they have what we want. Recognition. Reputation."

Boo fucking hoo, I thought.

"Nothing would prove our cause quite so powerfully or dramatically as their strategic elimination," Hawk continued. "On an international level. We do not believe in civilian casualties, Mr. Agnew. I think you will find that is but one of the differences between us. We believe in attacking the problem at the root, cutting off those who may be caught in its parasitic branches against their will."

How poetic—and yet, it did have an advantage over the more traditional "deadheading" approach. Cut off what you can see and hope the rest will go away. That technique hadn't worked so well for Mr. Richardson.

"Who?" I asked. "You better not tell me it's the fucking President or any shit like that. I'm not interested in participating in high-profile assassinations. I don't care to spend the rest of my life in Guantanamo."

"Good God!" Hawk looked appalled — the first emotion he'd shown during this speech. "Are you insane, Mr. Agnew? Have you not listened to a word we said?"

"We are not terrorists," Perry said, in a poor attempt at pacification. "Radical groups receive bad press in the news media, but that is because they share an agenda with those who would oppose us. Such as this group. You probably haven't heard of them, Mr. Agnew. They make a point to stay out of print. However all the right people—"

"Or the wrong people, rather," Hawk cut in.

"Yes," Perry said, shooting him a silencing look. "—*people* are aware of their existence. They are the most open secret in the western world. They monitor millions of conversations a day, screening for mentions of their acronym and its members. Occasionally this does happen, and more often than one might think. Generally on conspiracy sites, or online periodicals."

"We have a collection of screen-shots," Sparrow interjected. "Archived by date, publisher, and subject."

"Interestingly, the websites have the strange tendency to go offline—permanently—after mentioning this group by name."

"So do the authors." Hawk met my eyes. There was a sense of knowing behind that flat, dark stare. I decided he was the one in this group to be wariest of—him, and the two women. "Most of them never turn up again."

"And when they do," Perry said, "it's always dead."

"Scary," I remarked. "But come on, don't keep me in suspense. Who are we really talking about here? It isn't as if we're dealing with the Russian mob." I added an eye-roll for effect, knowing that they would expect this, as well.

"Actually, that is more pertinent than you might believe." Perry wrested the conversation away from Hawk like a driver grabbing at the wheel, and in doing so he ended up swerving right into my trap. "They call themselves the IMA. It stands for Integrated Military Affairs. They're a pseudo-military organization. That means that while they are not government affiliated, they do have government-level technology and training. A very dangerous combination. They hold no specific jurisdiction. Once they were considered a fairly respectable group with modest sociopolitical aspirations. Now, they are little better than a mob. A mob with the power and influence of the CIA or MI6."

"Their leader is an Irishman named Adrian Callaghan," said Robin. "A very powerful man. In addition to all the usual training, he has studied psychology and has the equivalent knowledge base of one who has a PhD."

"At some time unknown he was administered the Hare Psychology Checklist. The maximum score on the test is forty, and many consider the cut-off line to lie around a score of thirty. Here, in the UK, a score of twenty-five is enough to merit serious concern. Adrian Callaghan scored a thirty-eight."

"We want him dead, Mr. Agnew," said Robin. "The things he has done to our men and women are unspeakable."

I believed her—because I'd seen what he was capable of firsthand.

"Him, and his toy soldier, Michael Boutilier," Hawk said, cutting into my thoughts. It had taken a lot of training not to react to the sound of my own name. I met his probing stare calmly and thought, *This could be interesting*.

"How about it, Mr. Agnew? Are you still interested?"

I wondered what Callaghan would make of this information. Speculatively, since I wouldn't be giving it to him. If he didn't already know that the BN was baying for my blood as well as his, he didn't need to.

Armed and Dangerous by Nenia Campbell

With enough double-dealing on both sides I might be able to manipulate them both into shooting one another in the back. Save myself the trouble.

My hands formed fists in the pockets of my coat. "Yeah," I said. "Yeah, I think I'm real interested in this proposition of yours."

Christina:

I woke up several times that night. Sounds that were perfectly innocuous during the daytime, like the creak of the apartment settling or the thwack of a tree branch against the window, took on a new and sinister context in the dark scape of my fear.

Being followed home by that monolith of a man hadn't helped. I kept thinking, *what if …?* and torturing myself with hypotheticals until my brain went blank as a sheet of paper on which my nightmares could scrawl themselves down for my own viewing pleasure.

I was tempted to take one of the Ambien tablets the psychiatrist had prescribed me, but they made me feel woozy. For obvious reasons I didn't want to be in a mental fog.

No, it's just going to be me, the nightmares, and the insomnia.

Armed and Dangerous by Nenia Campbell

My eyes felt stiff and swollen, as if they'd been scrubbed with sand. I picked sleep dust out of my eyelashes and glanced at my cellphone. The glowing numbers read 3:49. My vision blurred. I fell back against the pillow, digging the heels of my hands into my temples. I had that stupid freshman seminar in less than four hours.

The best thing to do—the wise thing—would be to close my eyes and go back to sleep. Depriving myself of a full night's rest was a bad idea; it was in my interests to stay alert. My brain just wasn't getting the memo.

I hoisted myself out of bed and trudged to the kitchen. I filled the pitcher with cold water and switched on the coffee machine. Extra-strong. Black. Eight cups of Ethiopian brew.

When the coffee was ready and I had it prepared the way I liked in my favorite mug, I went back to bed and propped myself against the wall, fingering the Saint Anthony medallion I'd taken to wearing around my neck. He was the patron saint of lost things. I'd found it at one of the thrift stores and it seemed like it would be bad luck to leave it there, especially since I'd been feeling lost myself.

I wondered if the medallion could help me find hope, or if that was too abstract, even for a saint.

Armed and Dangerous by Nenia Campbell

Maybe I would sit out on freshman seminar. They didn't even bother to take roll. Better to stay at home than risk being jumped on my way to and from a unit-filler that didn't even matter when I was so exhausted.

If Michael were here, he would know what to do.

Michael was gone, though, and he wasn't coming back, as per his agreement with the IMA. He had gone to work for them again for my sake, because he loved me—or so he claimed. He'd had ample time to rue that decision. I certainly was.

He had done terrible things, and a good deal of them were nigh unforgivable. Rape. Abuse. Threats. Violence. Murder. His employer had been a part of it, but some of those things, like the sexual assault, had been a judgment call. They had been fueled by malice and aggression, not blackmail. If that was what being in love caused people to do, to treat people like crap because you had no self-control and then validate all of it by saying three dumb words, I wasn't sure I wanted any part in it.

Love certainly hadn't made Michael happy. His ill-fated choice had condemned him to a life he professed to hate. A life that he would continue to hate until it likely killed him. He knew it, too: that final kiss was the physical manifestation of a broken heart, bitter and hopeful and sad, all at once.

Did he deserve to experience a life of the grief and pain he had put countless others through for the better part of a decade? In the beginning, back when my wounds and resentment were still fresh and cutting, I would have said, "Yes, absolutely." I would have volunteered to put him into that position personally, and he would have deserved it.

Now, I wasn't so sure. That was a lot to wish on a fellow human-being.

I ended up falling asleep with the medallion clutched in one hand. I woke up with a start when cold liquid soaked into my clothing. For one horrifying instant I thought I had wet the bed. Then I noticed the brown tint to the stain, and the cocoa smell, and realized, to my great relief, that it was only coffee. That was one indignity I was to be spared.

It was my sole consolation that day.

Armed and Dangerous by Nenia Campbell

Chapter Eleven
Turning Point

Michael:

If you have to make a private call, the best place isn't somewhere quiet and secretive. You need busy and loud. That's why I was making my way down a narrow alleyway that smelled like piss. I wasn't about to use my cellphone. Not after meeting up with the B-fucking-N. I wasn't going to dick around to find out, either. I threw the phone in the trash.

I doubted they'd think to ask what had happened to my cell, or whether they'd even notice it was gone, but if they did I could say it had been stolen. That kind of shit happened, especially to well-dressed foreign men who looked lost and seemed careless. It helped that the area I was wandering through was in a bad part of town. That would corroborate my story.

The Halfpenny Gambit was the type of pub that looked like it should be condemned, and was probably a cockroach away from a visit from the FDA, or whatever the hell their Brit counterpart was. In other words, it was a dive lost in time and would almost certainly have a payphone.

I selected the one closest to the men's room. The constant white noise of echoed coughs, running faucets, and flushing toilets would blur out the finer points of the conversation.

I dialed, twisting the steel cable around my hand in a choke-hold as the piece of shit let it ring. I knew he was there. He was reminding me who was in charge. Fucking power plays. I hated that shit.

"Yes?" he said at last.

"It's Michael." I didn't bother to hide my irritation.

"You're late, then. Have some trouble with customs?" So that had been his doing. Fucking *dick*. "Of course, you always did have problems with authority, didn't you?"

"Fuck you."

"You're lucky I didn't give them cause for a cavity search. Believe me, it was tempting."

"I'm sure it was, you twisted fuck."

"Yes, well. Time is money, lucky for you." His tone sobered. "I take it the meeting went as planned."

"Apart from your delay, you mean? And the fact that you booked me into the shittiest five-star hotel in London? Yeah, everything's fucking peachy. I've got a question for you, Callaghan. How come you don't tell everyone about your acing the Hare Test? Too sore you didn't score a perfect mark?"

"Did you actually discover anything worth my time, Michael?"

His time wasn't worth what came out my ass. "I found something. Turns out the BN and I have something in common. We both want you dead. I'm bringing the friendship bracelets to the next meeting."

"I want names. Locations. *Facts*."

"It was the first meeting. They used aliases."

"That means you're just going to have to figure out who's who then, doesn't it?"

"That could take fucking years."

"I don't have fucking years, Michael. And to be frank, neither do you."

The threats were out in the open now. That was never a good sign. "You told me you needed a leader, not a goddamn miracle worker."

"Considering what I'm paying you, it would seem that whatever I expect would be well within my rights."

"Because you hold me in such high regard. Admit it, you want me to fail, you son of a bitch."

"I want you occupied and out of my way. Insubordination requires manipulation, and seeing as how you've got the latter in spades, I'm sure you can figure out a way to speed up the whole procedure."

"I was never insubordinate," I spat. "That was you."

"Not according to the official reports."

"Which *you* fucking wrote."

"Michael, Michael, Michael — let's not be difficult."

Oh, he'd enjoy that. "Are you threatening me now?"

"Not you personally."

Fils de putain.

"I met with the Sniper today."

"He get out of the hospital already?"

"Funny you should mention that. It just so happens Christina Parker put him back there fairly recently. Sprayed him in the eyes with a can of mace, let's see, not two days ago if memory serves."

"Good for her." I meant it.

"But bad for you."

"I fail to see how her actions concern me."

"I think you do. First you take out my shooter, then she disables him further by temporarily blinding him. If that's not grounds for a conspiracy, then I'm the bloody Union Jack. Whose responsibility is she, Michael? Or did you forget why you're working for me in the first place?"

He had me by the short-hairs and we both knew it. I hit the side of the payphone. "I'm not responsible for her behavior. We're not even in contact, for fuck's sake—"

"The Sniper is very eager to see her come to harm. He wants revenge. The hatred he harbors for you and the girl really is quite remarkable. In fact, he offered, unasked, to bring her in to me this very evening."

What?

"I declined as a matter of principle, of course. I have no place for her here at the moment, bonnie though she may be, and she isn't worth the time or the money that I'd lose breaking her in. Still, a very generous offer on his part, wouldn't you say?"

"I didn't mace him," I said. "And I didn't tell her to."

"Yes, but didn't you say so yourself that you wanted to kill me earlier? I can't have that. Not when your allegiance is still so dubious. You might say that I'm merely taking out a life-insurance policy, and Christina Parker is the collateral."

Armed and Dangerous by Nenia Campbell

"What did you do to her?"

"Nothing yet."

"I don't believe you."

"I'm the leader of what is fast becoming a global empire, boy. I have more important things to concern myself with than you and your little girlfriend — though that could change. I warn you, don't flatter yourself into thinking that you're indispensable. Difficult to replace perhaps, I'll grant you that, but not irreparably so. You're not nearly as smart as you fancy you are, and you're nowhere near half as strong.

"As for the girl herself, she is worth nothing to me beyond her ability to keep you in line. Her value equals far less than yours and if she continues to make trouble for me, or if you persist in these petty displays of reckless defiance, that value will hit rock-bottom and I will be forced to dispose of her in any way I see fit."

"That wasn't part of the agreement," I growled. "You don't get to touch her. Not as long as I'm doing what you want—"

"Exactly, Michael. What I want. So I suggest you find a way to charm the BN as effectively as you did that girl. If you could talk your way into her bed, I'm sure you can figure out a way to get *them* into your address book. Didn't you say that you were halfway to becoming the best of mates already? All actors need their motivation, Michael. I believe I just gave you yours."

The phone went dead.

Fuck. I hit the receiver against the side of the box, over and over, until the metal began to dent. "*Mon Christ, c'est completemente* fucked up." Slam. Slam. Slam. "God-fucking-damn it." Slam. "*Merde.*"

"You about done with the phone, Frenchie?"

I shoved the phone at the asshole behind me. He fell into the other booth, full of jeering drunks, as I shouldered my way out of the crowded bar. The man's drunken curses bellowed after me. I only half-heard him. Callaghan had given me my motivation, all right. Just not the kind he'd been bargaining for.

I would see it destroy him.

Back at my hotel room, I grabbed the memo pad and one of the cheap ballpoint pens that had the name of the hotel written on the side in unreadable cursive. I began to compose a list of names of people I had dirt on. Lower-tier members of the IMA. People Callaghan would be annoyed to lose, but not to such an extent that he would lift a finger to help them. I'd be doing him a fucking favor, pruning the drooping, wilting branches of his mob.

Callaghan had never been sympathetic to weakness. I'd learned that the hard way, and it had almost killed me. That was the problem. I needed to prove I wasn't weak. I was still capable of ruthlessness. I, too, could afford to gamble with human lives and win. Callaghan was sick enough to be impressed by that. It would make him take me seriously.

I couldn't afford him to see me any other way.

An added benefit of my sordid plan was that the BN could potentially use the information I was planning on leaking to them to gather more damning information. Information that could advance their own purposes. Information that I could plead innocent on if interrogated.

Kent wouldn't approve. He would tell me I was mixing fire and gasoline, and urge me to remember that my life was not the only one on the line here. Christina's was in danger, too, and so was his. So were those of all my contacts. I suffered no delusions over my own mortality. I was fully aware of the domino effect my demise would have on those who depended on me.

Trouble was, I was already living on borrowed

time. The moment Callaghan decided I wasn't pulling my weight, I'd be dead. But not before he wrung out every single drop of blood and sweat and left me hanging high and dry.

My tolerance for pain is relatively high, but if the IMA really decided to go to town on the torture, I'd eventually collapse like any other human would. It might take a little while longer, but the inevitable would happen. I couldn't wait around for that.

Knowing I was likely being followed — the BN would be doing background checks of their own, it was only to be expected — sharpened my sense of urgency. Over the next couple weeks I'd make a point of installing myself in the public eye, speaking on the phone, visiting people, sending encrypted emails. None of these transactions would hold any real informational value and it would drive the BN batshit crazy trying to figure out what kind of scattering software I was using to encrypt my *communiques*.

That's the trick to misdirection. A search for something that's actually there goes a helluva lot faster than a search for something that isn't; it requires a lot of thoroughness to say "no." These people were paid to be thorough. It was their strength and now, it would also be their weakness.

Meanwhile, the BN's buzz of activity would keep

Callaghan's hands full enough that he wouldn't be able to keep tabs on me quite as relentlessly. Or so I hoped.

Kent tried to dissuade me when I told him of my plan, just as I'd known he would. I could hear his smoker's hack in the background, the rustle of clothing as he shook his head. "You are playing a dangerous game with dangerous men, Michael."

"Yes, but unlike them I have nothing to lose."

"You have one thing," he was quick to point out.

"I also know how it feels to be desperate. *Que c'est q'ca?*"

His response was to sigh. "Your funeral, old boy."

"No," I said. "Not mine. His. Theirs."

My reports to Callaghan continued to be as regular as clockwork. I made sure he had no cause to complain. I'm sure that made him suspicious, but since I was giving him information straight from the horse's mouth he couldn't do a thing about it. As I'd predicted, he was distracted, far too focused on the BN. Everything I told him was useless but it sounded enticing on the surface. I made up facts from what I'd read between the lines from my conversations with the BN operatives during our meetings. This latter, I knew, sounded more convincing still—chiefly because it was.

The BN were even easier to play because they, too, were desperate. Or thought they were. It amounted to pretty much the same thing. They had been having trouble with leaks long before I arrived at the scene, so while I was suspect, I was no more so than any other new recruit. I had taken great pains not to use anything told to me exclusively, assuming correctly that this was a test to gauge my loyalty.

To them, I fed information about Callaghan which I had obtained through contacts not affiliated with the IMA. The BN would never be able to trace that information back to Michael Boutilier. I also let slip a few secrets about the internment bases in both Mexico and Russia, and some of the brutalities that had taken place there. This would carry the most; it was here that they had lost some of their most valued agents.

I knew how to punch their buttons and I was resorting to old tricks. Paranoia, vindication, seductive whispers of justice and revenge; they wanted it all, and I wanted them to want it. I wanted them to do something reckless.

I won't lie. I was enjoying fucking around with the two of them. I'd been feeling close to useless for months—a lethal mindset in my line of work, as it has the tendency to become self-prophetic—and now I was back, playing hardball with the pros and winning.

It was a headrush.

But I could only keep them hanging for so long. After several weeks, Callaghan grew impatient. He hadn't said so in as many words but I did notice that he had started dropping an increased amount of veiled threats.

The BN were also reaching their patience threshold. The heavily guarded internment bases were out of their reach and posed far too much risk to their limited manpower and resources for them to attack. They wanted an easier, more accessible target. It was starting to look as if I had no choice but to deliver.

"Let me see what I can dig up," I told Perry.

"This is very impressive all the same, Mr. Agnew. You have done some fine work here—though we will have to look over it, of course," he added, looking up from the printouts I'd spent all night slaving over.

And try to figure out my sources, thereby eliminating the middleman. I smiled and nodded. "Of course."

That night, it rained. It sounded an awful lot like

the static which now served as a backdrop to my thoughts.

Christina:

The first two weeks of school were tortuous, mortal purgatory. At Holy Trinity I had been able to coast by with a B-average. Actual effort generally got me an easy A. College, on the other hand, did not make allowances for coasters. I found this out the hard way when I received the first D grade I had gotten since middle school.

A D.

I closed my laptop, hiding my online grades from sight. It didn't help much. I knew they were still there, mocking me from cyberspace. What I needed to do was leave the apartment. I was becoming agoraphobic; I was letting my fear make me a prisoner. Even Dad noticed my decline in health when we had last Skyped, asking me if I was eating enough. His go-to question for "are you okay?"

I wasn't okay. Not even close. To be honest, most days I wouldn't have been able to say what I had eaten for breakfast, not even if somebody held up a gun to my head and demanded it. On at least some of those days I ate nothing at all. My jeans had gotten a lot looser and sometimes I caught myself feeling dangerously faint, at which point I'd usually dash to the SU and buy a coffee, or one of their overpriced pastries.

It wasn't that I was intentionally starving myself, because I wasn't. But getting food required going out, and after that terrifying incident on my way home from psychology I tried to do that during daytime hours only.

There were only so many hours in a day, though, and my class schedule was becoming increasingly unforgiving.

My dreams of college parties and sophisticated talk in independent coffee shops were crumbling the dirt in the empty gullies and ravines. I hadn't made any friends. I was too suspicious of everyone around me. No man had looked at me twice. I couldn't sleep, couldn't think. My grades were bad. I hadn't been to Coswell's library once since the semester began. I had no excuse for that. I loved to read. The bus on my route went to the library, as well.

So why not study there?

The idea lifted me. It was so simple, so obvious, that I wondered why it hadn't occurred to me before.

I loved the smell of old books and papery dust.

Armed and Dangerous by Nenia Campbell

The coughs and the squeaks of shoes on polished stone tiles, like punctuation in a sentence of silence. Going to the library would break up my normal routine, too. Staying at home was probably the stupidest thing I could do.

That cinched it; I was going to the library.

I was even smiling a little as I shoved my books in my backpack and headed out to the stop. I was still crushed about the D but now I had a solution. The programmer in me was happy. The Catholic in me was also happy; the smell of the souring milk in the kitchen had been making me feel guilty about my slovenly housekeeping and marked failure as a domestic. I had something to feel positive and hopeful about.

In less than twenty-four hours, that would all change.

Chapter Twelve

Return

Michael:

When I opened my eyes it was as if I'd been bludgeoned by a sledgehammer. I tried to reach up to my temples and found that my wrists were stuck behind my back. There was a familiar coldness against the skin. Shit. Handcuffs.

The day had started off as usual. I did my workout regimen until the hotel kitchens opened, and then I went downstairs for breakfast. I spent the rest of the morning after doing reconnaissance, the fruits of which I would have to deliver to Perry at the end of the day.

But...Perry hadn't greeted me that day. Hawk had. Which had been strange enough on its own, but he had also *said* something that made me falter, something I could no longer remember. I hadn't expected the chloroform rag—by the time I realized what was going on, it was already too late.

And now, I was here—wherever here was.

A man in a suit strolled over, looking me up and down. I figured it was one of the BN operatives, and I was right. When my vision cleared I realized it was Hawk. The arrogance when he spoke would have given him away. "Well, well, well. It appears that our little bird has turned out to be an IMA rat."

His superiority was hardly appropriate considering I was half-conscious, immobile, and tired as fuck. Get him in a ring with me, and he'd be singing a different tune. "How long did it take you to come up with that gem? Did you practice your stage routine while I was out?"

Hawk's face darkened. "Search him."

Figures stepped out of the shadows. They removed my coat, unbuttoned my shirt, even rummaged through my trousers. Good old public humiliation. Some things never change. "I'm pretty sure those are my balls you've found," I said to the man wrist-deep in my pants. "You going to count 'em out for me now? Because I'll save you the trouble. There's two."

"He's clean, sir," the man said coldly, wiping his hands on his pants. "Except for his mouth."

"Pity we don't have any soap," said Hawk.

These two were a regular fucking vaudeville routine.

"So, Mr. Agnew, do you plan on talking?"

"My contact will be hearing about this. I don't tolerate such treatment, not even from my superiors. I don't take kindly to being felt up by some closet-case, either."

"Very convincing." Hawk rocked back on his heels. "I will say this: you were impeccably trained. What was he carrying?" he asked, directing this last to his men. They had divested me of anything even remotely sharp or hard. My keys, one of the hotel's pens, my watch, my shoelaces, and, of course, my phone and knife. "No gun?"

I lifted an eyebrow. "Those are illegal in England."

Hawk shook his head. "It's pointless to pretend at this point. We already know who you are."

I glanced at my car keys. "A man who drives a Lotus?"

"Very amusing. Unfortunately, your reputation and your legendary wit precede you, Mr. Boutilier." He hadn't been bluffing. "Perhaps your organization should have chosen someone less conspicuous."

"I don't know what you're talking about."

"Enough." Hawk was losing patience. That was good. People did stupid things when they got caught up in the moment. "Your stubbornness is an insult to us, and a discredit to your own intelligence."

I said nothing, figuring if I didn't he'd keep

talking. He seemed to enjoy the sound of his own voice. My instincts paid off; Hawk was working himself into a monologue.

"You were a well-respected agent, a rags-to-riches fairytale ending. Until you became disgraced. Now it appears your own organization wishes to be rid of you. Why is this?"

"My gun turned back into a pumpkin."

"I think we know why," one of the other guards murmured in an aside. Hawk sent them a look befitting his moniker before continuing.

"There are no records of the incident and yet…rumors abound. Your demotion appears to be an open secret. The elephant in the room as it were." He paused. "You are a most interesting man, Mr. Boutilier."

I closed my eyes. "What did you do to the other members of my team?"

"Ah, so you are playing along now. Good. Denial is a most dull and tedious game. They are dead, Mr. Boutilier. It takes but one man to answer a question. With your credentials, you seemed the most qualified." He paused. "That isn't saying much, though, I'm afraid."

Now the generic insults to my intelligence. These

guys were going by the book.

"You do yourself no favors keeping silent. Why protect your organization, Michael? Your loyalty is admirable, but they have done you no favors. Quite the opposite—they have let you fall right into our own hands."

Because it wasn't my organization I was protecting.

"Unless it isn't your organization you're protecting," Hawk mused. "Perhaps the IMA has some sort of hold on you. We've speculated as much. A woman, maybe — a girl. There's another open secret in your organization. It seems you had a rather torrid affair with one of the hostages assigned to your charge, isn't that right?"

"No."

How could they possibly know that?

Adrian.

That son of a bitch. Looked like my expiration date was sooner than I'd thought. The bastard had fucked me up the ass at my own game.

"I thought we were past being difficult, Mr. Boutilier."

One of the agents — it felt like a woman's hand — shoved a pill into my mouth from behind. Cyanide? I spat it out with a curse. A gun pressed against my temple. The click of the safety as loud as a gunshot as the barrel dug into that hollow right in front of my ear.

They forced another pill past my lips. Maybe it was the same one that had fallen on the floor. Without looking away from Hawk's cold stare I swallowed it dry. If they wanted me dead they'd have shot me already, and I wasn't about to beg. My chances of surviving their poison were a lot better than pushing my odds with the gun aimed at my left temporal lobe.

"Do you know what PCP is, Mr. Boutilier?"

"Phencyclidine. Anesthetic. Hallucinogen. Neurotoxin. Sometimes used a recreational drug. What is this? A pop quiz? I don't remember signing up for Pharmapsychology one-oh-one."

"Phencyclidine cases aggression — something that clearly comes naturally to you, Mr. Boutilier — and, as you were so good to point out, partial immunity to pain."

What a shame it didn't also grant partial immunity to condescending assholes.

"In extreme cases, there have been reports of people pulling apart handcuffs with their bare hands, often resulting in injury once the drug wears off." He nodded at me. "You may be interested to know that this requires almost ten thousand pounds of force."

Something sharp punched through my shirtsleeve like the stinger of a wasp. I inhaled sharply, jerking my shoulders back. Too late. One of the younger, smaller men withdrew. He had a hypodermic needle. It was empty.

"What the *fuck* did you just inject me with?"

He deposited the syringe into a biohazard canister someone had quietly procured and didn't respond.

"Answer me," I snarled.

"You are no position to fight us, Mr. Boutilier, and struggling will only make the drug rush through your veins all the faster."

I twisted around to glare at him. "Fuck you."

"I suggest you remember your manners before your lack thereof lands you in a far more precarious position."

"Don't fuck with me," I said. "This sure as shit isn't a tea party, so you fucking tell me right now — what was in that fucking needle? Sodium pentathol? Poison?"

"Nothing so barbaric."

Yeah, right.

"You will be happy to know it was a garden-variety sedative, such as that which one might receive at any hospital. It should take effect in a few minutes, depending on your body's metabolism."

"And the pill?"

"The pill in phencyclidine, coated in a slow-dissolving but digestible agent. The sedative will slow the digestive process still further." He paused. "If the drug can cause one to exert such horrific force on a pair of steel handcuffs, imagine what it might cause one to do to the comparatively frail human body."

I stilled. "You're bluffing."

"Did we receive the girl's address from our scout?" Hawk asked one of his cohorts.

"I believe so, yes."

"Good. Make sure she receives our gift. Perhaps we should tie a ribbon around your neck, Mr. Boutilier."

"I'll kill you." My words were turning to mush in my mouth. "You come near me and I'll tear your throat out. You watch. I'll make the *misere* out of you."

Hawk made a dismissive sound. Just before I lost consciousness I thought I heard him say, "Make sure you give Villanueva our generous thanks."

Villanueva? The name sounded vaguely familiar. Where had I heard it before? Where — ?

Then everything went dark and I wondered no more.

Christina:

A heavy thud came from outside. It was loud enough to make me jump. I lowered my textbook.

The sound didn't repeat. *That could be a bad thing.* I looked at the door again. Got to my feet as quietly as I was able. For once, the floors didn't squeak. I went into my bedroom and got my knife, sliding the blade loose as I tiptoed towards the door.

More silence.

An ambush? I looked through the peephole. The stairs were empty from what I could see. That didn't mean it was safe out there, but I was a little reassured.

Keeping the safety chain in place, I undid the main lock and peered through the gap. Drew in a sharp breath. I couldn't believe what I was seeing.

Not the strange men from the black car —

Not the Sniper —

Michael.

Armed and Dangerous by Nenia Campbell

Michael was lying on my doorstep.

Unconscious.

…Dead?

A startled sound made me whip my head around and tighten my grip on the knife. It took a moment for the panicked animal my brain had become to realize the sound had come from me.

I looked back down at the porch steps. I'd half-expected the image of him to dissipate like smoke.

Nope. He was still there.

"Oh shit," I said. "Shit." He was still *there*.

It was beginning to sink in. This was really happening. Michael was here. On my doorstep. I fumbled with the chain.

Oh, bad idea, Christina.

All my senses were telling me that this was a bad idea. Were screaming it, in fact. I told my senses to go to hell. I couldn't very well leave him out there.

What if it's a trap?

What if it wasn't? If someone found him on my porch steps, I would be so screwed.

The metal chain links rattled against the door frame as I pushed the door aside. I jumped and lost my grip on his arm. *Well, this isn't going to work.*

Armed and Dangerous by Nenia Campbell

I set my teeth. The longer I stayed out here the more likely it was that someone would see him.

I squatted down to reach under his armpits for better leverage. His shirt was unbuttoned and damp with something that could have been blood, sweat, or a mixture of the two. Whatever it was, he smelled bad enough to be distracting and his body was *heavy*.

Little alarm bells were going off in the back of my head. That he was dead or dying — and that I was going to be held accountable for it. That this was a trap. That I had finally cracked and was suffering mass hallucinations on a psychiatric scale.

None of those possibilities were comforting.

By the time I got him over the threshold I was covered in a light sweat that wasn't entirely due to exertion. I was a hair away from freaking out.

I paused to catch my breath, steeled myself, then dragged him into the bathroom.

He grunted. Okay. He wasn't dead. That was good. Maybe.

I plopped down on the toilet seat and stared at him. The obvious next step was to dial 911. Had he been any other man, I would have. But Michael was a wanted criminal. They'd have him imprisoned as soon as he recovered. He'd die a traitor's death.

Armed and Dangerous by Nenia Campbell

Regardless of what he had done in the past, I didn't want him killed because of me. I couldn't have his torture or his death on my conscience. I couldn't.

Just the thought of betraying him in such a callous manner, like Judas kissing Jesus before condemning him to his death inspired a guilt so devastating it bordered on actual physical discomfort. I had taken him in. He was my responsibility.

I stripped off his shirt with shaking hands. *Too much responsibility.*

There were no wounds I could see, no open sores, but he had some fresh scars I hadn't seen before. He needed a bath, and badly, but I didn't want to put him into the tub; I wasn't sure I'd have the strength to haul him back out.

I took some washcloths out of the drawer beneath the sink and soaked them in hot water and soap. The hot water stung my hands, ridding me of any lingering hopes that this was an exhaustion-induced nightmare. I wrung out the extra moisture with sharp jerks that made my fingers ache. If only it were that simple. But nothing ever is.

He turned his head away when I began to scrub off the worst of the grit. His face was so filthy that his skin grew lighter in hue with each rinse. There was a bruise on his temple, a knot on the back of his head, dark shadows ringing both eyes. His shoulder was swollen — from a needle, I suspected. Drugs. Maybe a narcotic.

Something in my chest tightened. I hadn't expected looking at him to make me feel so sad. I was still furious at him for all the horrible things he had done because he'd made his choice — and knew what he had been doing when he made it.

Yet, he looked so helpless. So broken.

He isn't.

I blinked. I couldn't let myself forget he was a killer. Not if I wanted to escape this with my heart intact. Not if I wanted to stay alive. He was a professional assassin, and to romanticize that would not only be stupid but also potentially fatal as well.

But what if it's the truth?

His eyelashes fluttered. I'd forgotten how green his irises were. The color of olives, or summer leaves. His most arresting feature, capable of so much sadness. Even ice can be melted into warm water.

"Michael?" I hated the quiver that crept into my voice. I gave him a gentle prod with the washcloth. "Are you all right? Can you hear me?"

His eyes snapped fully open. They didn't look sad now. No, he looked…. I sucked in my breath. He looked angry. Furious. *Murderous.* Something was horribly wrong. His pupils were huge, dilated, *wild.*

I watched, frozen in horror, as he sat up. That sharp, terrifying gaze locked onto me, with all the deadly precision of a sniper rifle. "You."

He had been invalid moments before. I had no way of knowing I was mere seconds away from being tackled like a football at the Super Bowl. But I was. My head hit the linoleum tile with a hard crack. The air escaped from my lungs with a *whumph.*

In a low, terrifying voice, he said, "I'm going to tear you apart, you fucking bitch."

Armed and Dangerous by Nenia Campbell

Chapter Thirteen
Altered State

Christina:

He gave off the scent of sweaty clothing twice dampened and twice dried, marinating all the while beneath the hot, Arizona sun. His sour breath made my eyes water. That was the first thing I noticed.

He smelled like alcohol and a bad dream.

I struggled to get out from under him and he tightened his grip hard enough to hurt. "Ow," I gasped. "Ow! What are you doing?"

"You think you can fucking fool me?"

"What? No. No, I just — "

"Then drop the innocent act."

I didn't understand why he was acting this way. The last time I saw him, he had given no impression of being so unhinged. But then I remembered the empty wine bottle on the rug that last morning, and his propensity towards violence. How he had almost raped me on the floor of that basement in Oregon.

This was bringing it all back in sharp focus. I made myself look into those wild, blood-shot eyes that couldn't quite focus on my face; I saw too much in them. "Are you on drugs?"

Armed and Dangerous by Nenia Campbell

His heavy breathing stirred my hair and stung my eyes. He didn't say anything.

I tried again, anything to pierce this horrible silence pregnant with so many horrific outcomes. "What have they done to you?" I whispered.

His eyes latched on to mine. "What? Who're they? Shut up," he snapped, before I'd even said a word. I closed my mouth. "That's right. Don't think you can scare me with your threats about *them*."

Reddish splotches around his cheeks and nose hinted at burst blood vessels. *Is he drunk?* The thought returned, buzzing as angrily as a wasp in my ears. He was acting a little too crazy to *just* be drunk. Paranoid, delusional, possibly hallucinating — you needed harder stuff for that.

"I know what you are."

My mind reeled, oscillating between mindless panic and desperate cogency. The more I stalled for it, the more I sensed that I was running out of time.

There hadn't been many drug-related incidents at Holy Trinity. We *were* a Catholic school, after all. A couple girls smoked in the bathrooms and the wildest did pot, but neither of those made people *violent*.

I couldn't remember what to do in situations like this. Could I talk him down, or was that unadvised?

God, why couldn't those anti-drug groups teach us anything useful in school? *Okay. Freaking out isn't doing you any good.*

I drew in a breath. I had to focus here and play it carefully. One wrong move could get me hurt or killed. The big question here was: could I get him before he got me?

Michael was still leaning over me, breathing hard. Waiting for an answer. Seconds could have passed. Minutes. All sense of time was being sucked into the terrible void of his madness. "W-what am I?" I ventured.

"A traitor."

"A *what*?"

"I fucking told you to cut that out," he snarled. One of his fists slammed into the tile beside my face. I flinched as the linoleum cracked and blood exploded from his shattered knuckles. I felt some of it spatter my cheek. This time I couldn't hold back my scream. He had *punched* a hole in the linoleum.

That could have been me. "Oh my God," I whimpered. *He could have punched me.* "Oh my God, your *hand*. Oh my God—"

"Shut the fuck up, you little cunt." His uninjured hand closed around my throat. I froze, thinking he was going to snap my neck. His unfocused eyes scraped over my face and the visible parts of my body. I redoubled my efforts to get away and he squeezed. "You're a hot little ride, aren't you?" he said, while I struggled to breathe. "Built to last."

This was disgusting, even for him.

"You look like her," he continued, and his eyes rolled back for a moment. "Just a bit. She's better looking. Big blue eyes. A body that a man could really hang on to. I loved her. Her, she wouldn't touch me if you paid her. *Ha*."

I shook my head slowly. Even if I'd had words to speak, I wouldn't dare voice them aloud.

The movement caught his attention. "What's the matter, *bebe*? Decide I'm not good enough for you? Fucking think you're better than me? Maybe you have more in common with her than I thought. Or maybe you're too busy spreading your legs for them, know what I find? Wouldn't surprise me in the least."

Unexpectedly, I felt the sting of tears. "*Please*."

"What's the matter? You want I should whisper sweet nothings into your ear? *Je veux t'enculer? Tout le* fucking *toi*. That what you like to hear? Is that what gets off the bastards you're wearing the wire for?"

"I'm not wearing a wire." Something hard dug

into my side. My keys, I realized. The mace. I'd left the knife in the other room but I still had the mace.

"We'll see about that." He leaned in, nose brushing mine, as he squeezed one of my breasts hard. "I'm up for whatever you can dish out, *petit*."

With a growl, I sprayed him in the face.

He was off me with a roar, cursing up a storm in French and English. His head banged against the edge of the toilet lid with a loud crack that I half-hoped would knock him out, but all it seemed to do was enrage him further. I shouted at him to stop, terrified that the neighbors would hear his mad raving and call the cops because that would undoubtedly bring the IMA here, too.

Michael was beyond listening. It had never been his forte to start, but now he was in a world of his own and no amount of logic or reasoning could bring him back.

He started for where I'd retreated — following the sound of my voice, I realized.

I shut my mouth, backing up several paces. I held the can of mace out at arm's length, ready to use it again if I had to. Ready to dash into the kitchen and grab one of the knives. I wiped away the sweat that was dripping into my eyes and waited.

Armed and Dangerous by Nenia Campbell

Please, oh please, God, let me get through this without shedding blood.

God must have been feeling merciful. Before violence became necessary, Michael dropped to his knees and vomited all over the bathroom floor he'd just destroyed. I turned away, but I could still hear him retch — thick, clotted sounds that made my own throat tighten and hitch in sympathy.

Don't you dare throw up.

Michael moved again in my periphery. I brandished the mace just in time to see him do an ungraceful faceplant into a puddle of his own puke. That almost did me in. I swallowed hard, forcing the bile back down my throat.

Don't you dare.

I waited several more seconds before approaching him. The smell was terrible, but he appeared to be out cold. With a groan of disgust, I grabbed the soap dispenser from the counter and prodded him with it once, hard, in the side. He didn't move. *Is he dead?*

No — he was still breathing. His hand was still bleeding a lot. Fresh blood. He had a heartbeat. I tossed the soap aside with a clatter.

He deserves to die.

Armed and Dangerous by Nenia Campbell

It was an uncharitable thought. Not very christian. Appropriate in a way because kneeling in puke, with bruises on my throat and wrists, and particles of mace burning my eyes, I wasn't *feeling* very christian.

Maybe he had a good explanation. I'd find out soon enough when he regained consciousness. If he hadn't — if he had become a recreational drug user or turned to petty crime — then I wasn't interested in his story. He could tell it to the cops, for all I cared.

I ripped a swatch of fabric from the bottom of my wife-beater in lieu of gauze and began binding up his hand. I fastened it with a bobby pin I'd grabbed from the counter, piercing the fabric with the little prongs to keep it in place.

Once I'd dressed his wounds, I searched for the soap dispenser, locating it where it had rolled behind the toilet. I squirted the fruity solution onto one of the washcloths. This time I made no effort to be gentle. He didn't deserve it.

It wasn't fair. I'd been trying to come to terms with the evils that had happened to me, and God had brought the most troubling reminder of all back into my life. I scrubbed at said reminder until his skin was an angry pink. *Bastard*.

Finished with his upper body, I consigned myself

to the inevitable and yanked off his pants. Naturally, being a bastard, he wasn't wearing anything beneath them.

I studiously avoided his crotch as I swiped the increasingly scummy washcloth over his legs and feet, trying to ignore his erection. I'd only seen his naked body that one time in the dark and I hadn't seen much. Seeing everything now, laid out under the glare of fluorescent light, was quite a different matter. Frightening and clinical.

I rinsed the cloth in another cascade of steaming hot water and wiped it over the hard muscles of his thighs. I swallowed hard, then ran the washcloth, quickly, over and around the length of him. The skin was tissue-thin and soft, but at the same time solid and corded with veins. He grunted, low in his throat and labored, and it *moved*, and I yanked my hand back as if I'd been stung by a scorpion. My heart was going like a jackhammer. Beside me was the washcloth, like evidence left at the scene of a crime.

I threw the washcloth in the trash—it was beyond salvaging — and washed my hands with soap and hot water. The bathroom was a nauseating blend of piña colada, stomach acid, and sweat. I wasn't looking forward to cleaning it all up.

Maybe I'd make him do it.

Armed and Dangerous by Nenia Campbell

Make Michael do it? I mocked myself. What are you going to do? Threaten him with your pepper-spray?

I dragged him into my bedroom, ignoring my turbulent thoughts. I liked that anger; it gave me something to hang on to, like a lifeboat.

I tore my sheets off the bed and replaced them with some older ones from the hall closet. The mattress now dressed, I heaved Michael onto it, with pushes and tugs, arranging his body under the sheet so he was at least somewhat decent.

"You are a bastard." I rubbed antiseptic into his scraped and bloodied knuckles, nightmares of them turning septic from my unwashed bathroom floor dancing in my head like a horrid nightmare. "You stink. I should leave you outside with the trash, let you get intimate with the flies."

Of course, he said nothing to this. Probably for the best. I highly doubt there was anything constructive he could have added to the conversation.

He had lost some of his fierceness. His eyelashes were short, thick, golden, with the texture of a fine-tipped paintbrush. I took some tissues and wiped the traces of mace carefully from the corners of his eyes. As I did, the stubble around his mouth scraped against the inside of my wrist and my stomach twisted as memories of those lips against mine hit me like a speeding freight train.

I rubbed at my wrist.

This is not good.

Michael:

I woke up with one of the worst headaches of my life. Considering some of the hangovers I've suffered through that said something. The stabbing pain behind my eyeballs grew as I sat up. I reached for the drawer of the hotel's nightstand and my fingers closed over empty space.

What the fuck?

I dug my knuckles into my forehead. It helped. It was as if I were pushing the headache back physically, commanding it, focusing it. This worked for about a minute and then the pain spread to my hand because the back was all torn up. My knuckles had been tenderized like meat.

A small shard stuck out of the raw flesh. I pinched the white fragment out, turning it this way and that in the moonlight. Odd. What was it? Bone? Porcelain?

I remembered the vanished nightstand. I swiveled around, regretting my haste when my neck started throbbing like a mother. I was in a bedroom.

A bedroom that did not belong to the London hotel. The mattress I was lying on was new, but cheap. The sheets were clean. I wasn't wearing anything beneath the sheet, though, and there were no clothes in sight.

I slid off the mattress and opened one of the doors. It was a closet. Mostly empty, though a few clothes of a feminine cut hung inside. That could mean nothing.

Frowning, I tried the other door. I was surprised when it gave without a catch. Unlocked.

Was this a trap, or mere oversight?

I stepped through the doorway, noting the carpeted floors. Probably not a bunker. To my left was a living room and a kitchenette. To the right, a bathroom. Could be a safe house — but where? The air here was dry, and sweltering. Not England.

A light was on in the living room. It came from the glow of an open laptop. I counted to three and braced myself for a fight I wasn't in any condition to provide.

I heard breathing, slow, even, and deep. I moved closer, then froze, unable to tear my eyes from the sleeping woman on the couch.

Christina.

They say you can't feel pain in dreams. I sure as

hell was doing that. Her hair was damp, curling around her face. I touched her cheek, letting my fingers trail to the swell of her lower lip.

She opened her eyes and let out a startled scream. I saw her right arm move, reaching for a — fuck, she had a knife. I knocked it out of her hand with a chop to her wrist and the blade went skittering across the kitchen floor.

Christina turned into a spitting, writhing hellcat. It was like trying to hold onto water — water that could also scratch, and kick, and bite.

"No!" she cried, balking when I knelt over her legs, keeping them pinned with my thighs so she couldn't kick me. "*Get off me.*"

I realized the dubiousness of our current position. "I'm not going to hurt you."

She wasn't listening.

"*Christina.* I'm not going to fucking hurt you, all right?" I leaned back a little for emphasis. I didn't let go of her wrists, though. Not yet. "But I'm going to need you to calm the fuck down before I let you go."

"Calm down?" she repeated.

"Yes. Calm. As in not screaming. That kind of calm." She was still gorgeous, but less girlish. Her high cheekbones stood out in relief in the dim light of her laptop. Her eyes narrowed up at me.

"Don't tell me to calm down. You destroyed my bathroom. You punched a hole in the floor — you could have done that to me. You could have *killed* me. Who do you think you are? Are you insane?"

Fuzzy images rose from the sea of drugs still soaking my thoughts. I felt the sweat on my chest grow chilled. *"Merde."* She watched me with a wary expression that bordered on fear. "Did I hurt you?"

My question seemed to surprise her. "You tried."

"I don't remember any of that very clearly." I recalled my earlier thoughts and looked away, not liking myself much. "What, exactly, did I do?"

"You threw up on me. Said some horrible, hurtful things. You also did about three hundred dollars' worth of damage to my bathroom."

"I don't give a shit about your bathroom. Hell, I'll pay for the damage. What I'm asking is whether I hurt *you.*"

"Do you really care?"

I gave her a flat look. "I'm asking, aren't I?"

Her body lost some of its tenseness but when she spoke, she was still angry. "What am I supposed to think? What happened to you? Why are you here?"

"It isn't something we can talk about now."

"Can't? Or wont?"

I felt my lips curl up in spite of myself. "Can't."

"Why *not*?"

"Your apartment's probably bugged."

Unsurprisingly, this statement did not make her happy. "I found one in the thermostat."

"That's the bug you were supposed to find. The decoy. Trust me, if they don't want you to find the bugs, you're not going to find a one." My voice broke. My throat was killing me. "Mind getting me something to drink?"

"I don't have any alcohol." Said sharply.

"Cute. I meant water. You do have water, right?"

She pushed away from me. I watched her pad over to the kitchen. There was something different in her walk, something that made it hard to look away.

"Did you know you were taking PCP?"

"I had an idea." I thought of Hawk's speech. He was like Richardson that way, fond of the sound of his own voice. The only difference was, it had gotten my old boss killed in the end. "If you're asking it was voluntary, no; it wasn't. How did you know?"

"I looked up the symptoms on PubMed." She

filled the water glass. "Who did it to you?"

"I'll tell you later." I rubbed my eyes and crusty gunk flaked into my lap. "Did you mace me?"

"Only after you attacked me."

"You said I didn't hurt you."

"I didn't say you didn't try." Her eyes were hot. "Everything's always so black and white with you, isn't it?"

"Me? Your life could be a chessboard — it's so black and white."

She sloshed the water in my face and set the glass down on an end table. I watched her storm out of the room with her laptop into the bedroom I'd just vacated. I walked over to the sink and refilled it, knocking back the water like a shot of whiskey. I drank three glasses before heading back for the bedroom I'd just vacated. I knocked first. No response. Quietly, I tried the handle. Locked.

"At least tell me where the fuck I am."

"Welcome to Arizona, you bastard."

I pinched the bridge of my nose. "All right. Where are my clothes?"

"I threw them away."

I let my hand fall to my side. "Why did you do

that?"

"If you want them back, you can fish them out of the dumpster."

The BN must have done a number on my head: her brusqueness was starting to turn me on. That was what had changed. She had lost that tentative, sheltered meekness. She'd learned how to harden her heart.

Just like me.

Fuck. What had I done?

"I'll be needing some new ones then," I said. "You have any plans on procuring some for me?"

The door opened. She leaned against the doorjamb, folding her arms over her chest. "Why did they bring you to *me*? Why not kill you?"

"I guess they want me alive."

"Why?"

"I have no idea."

"Well, why do you *think*?"

"Vengeance. Without going into too much detail, I was set up by a mutual friend of ours."

"Who?"

"Take a wild guess. First three don't even count."

Armed and Dangerous by Nenia Campbell

From the look on her face, she didn't even need one.

Armed and Dangerous by Nenia Campbell

Chapter Fourteen

Plan

There had been a time when Michael Boutilier had been the greatest evil my mind could comprehend — cold, cruel, and callous; the IMA had once considered him their best operative in the agency. Then I had been taken into custody by the IMA and realized that even among bad guys there still exists a continuum.

Staring up at him now, standing in my bedroom doorway, I was startled by how much he seemed to have shrunk. In my memories and nightmares, he was a giant. In a way, this was more imposing. Because all of that was fiction. This — this was real. This could be worse.

There were so many things I wanted to ask, I hardly knew where to begin.

In keeping with his perceptive nature, he said, "You and I need to talk." He looked down at his sheet. "Right after you get me some new clothes."

That snapped me out of my trance. Less than ten minutes conscious and he was already ordering me around. "No," I said. "I'm going back to sleep."

Michael studied me levelly, saying nothing.

"Night."

Armed and Dangerous by Nenia Campbell

He let me slam the door on him and lock it.

Let.

If he had truly wanted to, he could have stopped me. We both knew it. That took some of the satisfaction out of my resolve.

I wished I had my switchblade. But no, it was still on the kitchen floor, and I was too afraid to go back out there. Not after the way he'd looked at me.

I woke up the next morning to the smell of frying butter. I stumbled to my feet, momentarily startled when I found the door locked. *Why?* — *oh.*

Michael was standing in front of the stove. He had the sheet draped around him like a toga. I blinked. The image did not go away. He should have looked ridiculous, and most other men would have, but *he* looked like one of those marble statues frozen in the act of preparing for battle. *Mars,* my unhelpful brain supplied. *The Roman god of war.*

I decided to chalk that lapse in judgment up to a severe lack of sleep. "What the hell are you doing?"

He glanced over his shoulder. "What it looks like."

I peered around him. In the pan were the last of my eggs, some vegetables I'd forgotten about, and what looked like melted cheese. I didn't even know I *had* cheese. I pointed at the peppers. "I was going to throw those out. They're past the expiration date."

"You can cut out the bad parts, you know." He tilted his head. "Or do you always do everything by the book?"

I turned my back on him and grabbed the coffee pot. I filled it with water from the bathroom tap and sat down at the table while I waited for it to brew. It looked like I'd have to go out today after all. Shit. He had used up the last of my fresh food and I couldn't have him walking around like that.

He set down a plate in front of me, forcing me to lift my head. I cut off a small square with the side of my fork. It was surprisingly good. Really good. "I didn't know you could cook."

"I know how to do a lot of things."

The old Michael would have said that with a leer, and I half-flinched in anticipation, but he kept his eyes on his plate and his tone was as bland as if he were discussing the weather.

"How is it?"

"I—it's fine."

"Only fine?"

God, he was making me nervous. "I'm just going

to get changed. I'll pick up some clothes for you and we can, um, talk. Like you said."

"Don't you need my size?"

I froze. "What?"

"My clothing size," he repeated. The corner of his mouth lifted a little. "Or did you do more than look when you took my clothes off?"

"No," I said tightly. "I did *not*."

I yanked open a drawer and tossed a memo pad and a pen at him. I'd meant for them to hit him, but he snapped them out of the air.

"Unlike you," I said. "I respect people's privacy."

And then I turned and walked away before he could see that he had gotten to me.

Fifteen minutes later found me at the stupid drug store near my apartment with a stomach full of something too dark to be butterflies. His compelling presence made it hard to think. I didn't want to get sucked into this nightmare, though I suspected it was already too late.

I looked down at the crumpled post-it in my hand. The ink was smeared from my sweaty palm. *Shirt size, XL. Pants, 36. Shoe size, 15.*

Armed and Dangerous by Nenia Campbell

He was probably snooping through my things at this very moment. Anything not bolted to the floor would be considered fair game. I was trying not to worry about it. I had nothing to hide. Nothing except my pills, my pepper-spray, and the switchblade, and all three of those things were tucked safely away in my purse.

I bought three t-shirts, two pairs of shorts, jeans, track pants, socks, sneakers, and a pair of hideous leather sandals that looked like something my father might wear. It was my pathetic attempt at revenge, not that Michael would notice.

I could feel a stress headache forming. On impulse, I grabbed a six-pack of energy drinks and a bottle of aspirin from the racks of stuff near the register tempting you into a last-stand of impulse buying.

The Asian guy at the register gave me a strange look as he rang up my purchases. I winced when I saw the price glaring at me on the LED display. Michael's new wardrobe had cost more than my textbooks had, even with my student discount. Between this and the damage to my apartment's bathroom, he was going to ruin me.

I bet there are other ways you'd like him to 'ruin you.'

"Can you twist off one of those for me?" I asked

him, pointing at the energy drinks. "And the aspirin."

"Sure. Let me just finish bagging what you've got here." He trailed off. "Hey, wait, I know you."

He did? "You do?" I asked guardedly.

"You're the girl—" he snapped his fingers. "The girl whose dress was unzipped on picture day. Man, you really tore out of there fast."

Oh crap. He was right. "Yeah. Thanks. That was me."

He cut the tags and removed the sensors from the clothes. "Sorry. Didn't mean to remind you. I never forget a face or a place."

I was too mortified to speak.

"So," he said, nodding at the clothes. "These for your boyfriend?"

My head jerked up. "No," I said, too sharply.

His eyebrows zoomed up to his hairline. I felt like a fool. "Well, just so you know, our return policy is thirty days grace period with a receipt—oh, and a five-percent restocking fee on student merchandise. Would your—I mean, would you like a gift receipt for the clothes?"

"No. That's all right. Thanks, though."

He tore the receipt from the printer and handed it

to me with a flourish. "Have a nice day."

I was having anything but.

This is what normal feels like, my brain informed me as we left the store. *It looks like him.*

"Here are your stupid clothes."

Michael was reclining on my couch, flipping through my psychology textbook—proving my theory correct that he had done a casual search through my meager belongings. "Put that down," I snapped, batting it out of his hands. It hit the floor with a loud thud that made me jump and him smirk. "Put *these* on."

"Does bossing me around get you off or something?"

"No."

"Are you sure?" He bent down, his face was level with mine. "You seem to like it an awful lot."

I averted my eyes with a startled yelp when he let the sheet drop without pretense to step into the boxers. "For God's sake," I said. "Cover your shame!"

"I'm not ashamed," he said.

I struggled for words. "Those — those haven't even been washed yet."

"You want me commando?"

"I want you to put on some pants."

He laughed. "My God, you're acting like a virgin on her wedding night. Loosen up, darlin. I don't have anything you haven't seen before," he added, making me flinch. "Don't tell me you didn't sneak a look when you stripped me down, either."

The sting of my nails in my palms was a cutting reprimand. It hurt even more because he was right. "You're disgusting."

"Only if you're a prude."

I bit my lip and said nothing. The rustle of clothing filled the silence. I squeezed my eyes shut, trying to push away the series of images that came, unbidden, to my mind. "You can't talk to me that way," I said. "That is unacceptable."

When I felt his hand on my shoulder, I jumped. "Do I pass inspection?" His voice was low, and made my heart rate kick into overdrive, filling me with the urge to run —

Towards him, or away?

I steeled myself and turned around, putting a step between us as I did so. *Away.* He was wearing the jeans and one of the wife-beaters. The school logo warped across his muscular chest, which was all too visible beneath the snug white fabric.

I looked away. "Everything but good conduct."

"I think you like it when I'm bad."

"I really don't think so," I said, still not looking at him. I could see him in the corner of my eye, though. Walking around me. "The clothes fit then?" I asked loudly.

"More or less."

"What does that mean?" He had disappeared from sight again. "What doesn't fit?"

The sudden, tickling warmth at my ear was the only warning I got before his arms wrapped around me from behind. "My pants," he said. "They're too tight."

I whirled around. Standing this close, I would have had to tilt my head back to look him in the eyes. I didn't do that; it would have seemed like an invitation for him to kiss me. And he *would* have — I knew that instinctively.

"What are you doing?" I tried to ask. My lips moved, but my voice was silent. I cleared my throat and said, "You shouldn't joke about such things."

I was proud of myself; I sounded steadier than I felt. I felt like I was a step away from shaking to pieces.

There was a heavy pause. The set of his mouth

didn't change. I put my hands over his and lowered them from my hips. His hands flipped and closed over mine before I could completely pull away.

"I missed you."

My heart stopped. "What?"

"You heard me."

"Please," I said. "No. Don't do this."

"I dreamed about you." Pause. "Every night."

Oh God, I was weak. Weak.

He tilted my face up. I felt the burn of his words on my lips. "Want to know what you were wearing?"

The illusion shattered. I jerked out of his now-loose embrace and glared at him, furious at him for sneaking past my defenses so easily. Furious at myself for wanting him to. "I'm going back to bed."

"Is that an invitation?"

"No," I ground out. "It's a dismissal."

"Sounds more like a challenge to me."

I pointed a finger at him. "Stay *out* of my room."

"*Mais oui*, I'll do that. Let's just see if you can stay out of mine." He spread his arms, indicating the whole of the living room and kitchen. "Sweet dreams, Christina."

Armed and Dangerous by Nenia Campbell

Michael:

When she came out of her room two hours later she was wearing khaki shorts and a red tank top, her hair bound into an unruly braid. She shot me a defiant look. With a set-up like that it was tempting to say something, but I had always prided myself on my sense of restraint.

Or I had until Christina entered the equation.

As long as I didn't act on anything I was feeling, that wouldn't change. I just had to keep my distance.

I just had to stop having a cock.

While she brushed her teeth and glared at her reflection in a way that led me to suspect that it was really me she was glaring at, I said, "Where do students at your college normally go to have their chats?"

She spat in the sink. "Campus coffee shop."

"Good. We'll go there. Where is it?"

"On campus." She put the toothbrush in its stand. "It's pretty loud in there. Are you sure you wouldn't prefer to go someplace quieter?"

"I don't mix business and pleasure."

I liked seeing the color rise up her high

cheekbones like the tide coming in. "That's not what I meant."

"Well, you want loud, trust me. You never know who might be listening in." Her blush deepened. I hadn't meant it that way, but, well, looked like she had herself a dirty little mind. "How are we going to get there? You have a car?"

"No. But I live on the bus line."

"When's the next bus come?"

She glanced at her phone. "Twenty-five minutes."

"Good. Make sure we're on it."

"Do you ever say *please*?"

"You could have found that out last night."

Toothpaste spattered the rim of the sink when her mouth fell open. I saw a lot in her face. Desire. Fear. Anger. Pain. She was an open book. Always had been.

Not like me.

She saw me watching her and closed the bathroom door with a small cry. I left her to compose herself. Forcing my presence on her wouldn't do either of us any favors.

I picked up the psychology book and flipped through it some more. Some passages were highlighted in green. She had made notes in the margins. Cramped handwriting, slanted, with lots of flourishes. Distinctive, but not neat. That surprised me. I'd expected something more girlish.

Who the hell cares? What is this, Penmanship 101?

I closed the book.

About ten minutes later the bathroom door opened. She grabbed her purse without looking at me. "Come on. Let's go."

Heat slammed up against me the moment she opened up the front door. The night had been warm, yes, but it hadn't prepared me for this. *This* was like walking into a giant oven. Jesus Christ. It had to be in the triple-digits. What a fucking nightmare.

"Is the weather always like this in the summer?"

"This is a pretty bad heatwave." Her voice was tight. Still angry. Still defensive.

"Where's the stop?"

"Just around the corner from here."

I shoved my thumbs through my belt loops and settled in for the wait. Christina played with her phone. Sweat beaded on her skin, soaking into her top, making it cling. I was thinking of other ways to make her sweat when the bus arrived. From dreams about hot fucking to hot, fucking reality. At least the bus was air-conditioned.

She sat down beside me in silence, face grim. I wondered if she was remembering that ride to Seattle. I wanted to tell her to cut it out, that there was no need to worry or look around so suspiciously.

I also didn't want to lie.

"Don't look so tense," I said.

She glared at me. Definitely angry.

"Okay. You want to look like someone just shoved a taser up your ass and hit the juice, you go right ahead. Far be it from me to keep a woman from what she wants."

"Just leave me alone," she said. "Please. Please, just stop talking for a little while."

Her face was so raw. I nodded shortly.

When she'd mentioned her college to me I'd been expecting something pretentious. Redbrick buildings and grassy quads. Ivy League. I should have known better. It seemed like everything was crafted from white-hot metal and blinding glass.

Shame I didn't have the foresight to get sunglasses.

I paused, then chuckled to myself.

No pun intended.

"What's so funny?"

"Nothing," I said. "You lead."

She grabbed me by the hem of my shirt, dragging me towards a shaded alcove where students sat beneath sun-faded umbrellas, nursing iced coffees and talking. Bared breasts, midriffs, and legs abounded. So did my cock.

Christina gave me a cold look I had no trouble interpreting. Jealousy? I smiled at her as I opened the door. "Inside."

"You can't talk to me like I'm your hostage."

She said it quietly, but the fact that she'd said it in public at all made me mad. "Do you have no sense?"

For a moment, she looked chastened. Then angry. "More than you do, apparently."

"You want me to walk?" People stared at us curiously. I was still holding the door and she had yet to walk through. We were making a scene — that was the last thing I wanted.

"I don't care," she said.

I glanced at the students around us, checking none of them were within earshot, then back at her. "You know as well as I do that you need me to help keep you alive. Isn't that right?"

She shrugged.

"It's all on you, *bebe*. You tell me what I want."

Christina put her hands on her hips. "I want this all to go away."

"Tough shit. That isn't going to happen."

She continued to look at me levelly with those huge blue eyes. I fought back the approaching wave of irritation. "You going in, or you want to chat out here in the sun in front of everybody?"

She stepped inside.

"The way I see it," I continued, "I'm doing you a favor by keeping our interactions brief."

"Hostile," she said. "Abusive."

"You already hate me," I pointed out. "What have I got to lose?" *What have I got to gain?*

Her expression flickered. "I don't hate you. At least — " she hesitated " — not as much as I used to."

"You do a good enough impression. What happened to leaving me out with the trash to fuck flies?"

"Y-you heard that?" I let my silence speak for itself. She looked embarrassed, and that made her angry. "That was after you — after I found you passed out on my porch. After you tried to attack me. This is all such a shock. Excuse me if it takes some getting used to."

"Better get used to it soon," I said. The instant the words were out of my mouth, I knew it was the wrong thing to say.

Her eyes flashed. "Maybe it's easy for someone like you, but I can't just rewrite the past. I mean, you're here. At my school. I'm buying you coffee, for God's sake." For a moment I was afraid she was going to cry but she let out a shaky little laugh instead. "You, of all people. My — " she glanced at me and colored a little more " — well."

I grunted.

"Just last night you were out of your mind. Paranoid and psychotic. You treated me like I was your enemy. You made me relive my nightmares. Now you expect me to believe your claims that our lives our in danger. How is any of that my fault?"

"I didn't say it was."

"You were the one who walked away, Michael. You were the one who promised me that this was all going to end. You were the one who tried to hurt me. It's you. It's always been about you."

She drew in a deep breath.

"Do you understand now?"

"I'm beginning to."

"I don't know anything about you," she said. "Not really. I'm not so sure that I want to — I wouldn't even know where to start asking questions. I certainly didn't expect to have you in my life again. Right now all I want to do is scream at you, and I can't even do that. I certainly don't want to feel *sorry* for you."

Music floated up from hidden speakers. I couldn't place the song. She felt sorry for me? We stepped up in line and I said, "You could start by asking."

"To scream at you?" She looked surprised.

"No. If you want to know more about me — ask. I won't be able to answer all your questions. You always have been too nosy for your own good. But I'll answer what I can."

"Really."

"Quid pro quo."

"What's the quo?"

"Not feeling sorry for me, since I sure as shit don't want your pity." I let her hear the sharpness in my words, and was gratified when she flinched. "Maybe you can start by pretending I'm not so bad."

"All right," she said a little sarcastically. "I was going to assume you liked eating babies and sacrificing virgins, but I might as well ask, what do you do for fun?"

"I languish in sin," I replied in the same tone. "I take my babies rare, and my virgins over easy."

She made a sound of disgust.

"All right. You want to know what I really do for fun? I drink. I play cards. I read. I fucking watch TV. I work. When I'm not doing that I drink some more because drinking quiets the demons."

"And that's your definition of fun," she said slowly.

"The long evenings just fly by."

"No music?"

"Can't stand the shit. Gives me fucking migraines."

"Can you sing?"

"Not a note."

Christina folded her arms. "You must be a blast on long car rides."

"Oh, I am. You haven't experienced fun until you try to fuck in the front seat of a Civic."

She flinched again. This time, the pain in her face cut at me, too. Because I'd seen that face before more times than I cared to count. "Why do you always do that?"

"Do what?" I drawled. *Don't let her see you bleed.*

"Make it about sex. Is that all I represent to you? Is that what *all* women represent to you? Sex? Or are you doing this because you know it upsets me, because you're trying to push me away? It won't work." Her voice shook. Fuck. "It won't. You're disrespecting both of us by acting like such a misogynistic asshole."

"Don't ask questions you don't want the answers to."

"You just *told* me to ask," she snapped. "I'm trying the best I can, despite what you might think."

She was getting noisy again. People were beginning to look over in our direction. Glaring at me, like I was the bad one in all of this. Maybe I was. "Fine. You win, darlin. Conversation over."

"That isn't what I — "

"Over."

"You can't just — "

"*Over.*"

Soon after that it was our turn at the counter. We ordered our drinks. She looked pale under the fluorescent lights, the light brown of her skin bleached as if she wasn't getting outside much. A pretty impressive feat considering the force of the glaring sun overhead.

Callaghan had said something about her seeing a shrink. I'd figured he'd been laying it on a little thick but for once it seemed like he'd been telling the truth.

Her face was still tight with anger and frustration. I felt bad for winding her up now. "You all right over there?"

"Fine," she said shortly.

"You're looking a little ashy."

"I guess I'm a little dehydrated." Her full lips were cracked. She bit down on the lower as she thought. "I guess I haven't eaten much over the last couple days, either."

"Can we get some of that sushi?" I asked the barista.

"What are you doing?" Christina hissed. "I can't afford that."

She couldn't? When had that happened? Her parents were loaded — or had been. A lot could happen in a year. Guilt attempted another approach. I shoved it away. Slammed that mental door. "It's on me. Or will be as soon as I get some money wired over. You had a shock. You need to eat."

She really must have been feeling low; for once, she didn't try to argue with me.

Armed and Dangerous by Nenia Campbell

A group of Asians got up from one of the booths in the back corner. Perfect. We sat down and I watched her pick at her sushi with the chopsticks, working through the little rows one piece at a time. I waited, making sure she was eating it. Then I opened my own package.

"You realize we can't stay here much longer."

She looked around worriedly. "The cafeteria?"

"No. The school. The city. Here."

"What?"

"They know where you live, and they know that I'm with you." I popped a piece of eel in my mouth. "You've worn out your welcome in Bumfuck, Arizona."

All the color drained from her face. "But what about my classes?"

"Are they more important than your life?"

She didn't seem to hear me. "What about rent? What about my things? I already paid for tuition this semester. You can't do this to me. You told me this was over."

"This will never be over. Not until we're dead — or the people who're fucking with us are."

She whimpered.

"Now don't do that. Not here." I grabbed her hand, gratified that she didn't immediately shake me off. "Hold it in. Don't let them see you fall to pieces."

"I can't do this again."

I squeezed her fingers hard, as much in warning as in comfort. "You don't have a choice."

"What a change that is," she said bitterly. "What are we going to do? Am I going to have to spend the rest of my life running from the IMA? Is that what you're saying?"

And the BN. I released her. She didn't need to know about that yet. "First things first. We're going to have to stick around for at least a couple more days. Those assholes left me with nothing, so I need to figure out how I'm going to get my hands on money, ID—" I ticked the items off with the chopsticks "— transport. All that good shit."

"I just want to live my life."

"Yeah? Then stop assuming that you're going to die. That's step one."

She prodded at a limp piece of eel. "I can't fight them."

"You won't have to." I hoped to fuck that was true. "I'll do all the fighting for both of us. I can keep you safe. You won't come to any harm under my protection."

She didn't look like she believed me. "You and safe don't belong in the same sentence."

"Be that as it may, what have you got to lose?"

Christina folded her hands on the table. "My future. My life. My soul. My heart. Take your pick."

I crumpled up the plastic tray like paper and shot it into the nearest trashcan. I said nothing. I leaned back in the booth and waited, with my arms folded behind my head.

She crossed herself. "I can't believe I'm doing this. But okay. Fine. What's your plan?"

That's my girl.

Armed and Dangerous by Nenia Campbell

Chapter Fifteen
Escape

Christina:

Our talk ended after that.

I tried not to be aware of his denim-clad thigh, so close to my own in the cramped seats of the bus as we rode it back to my apartment. Or his muscular arms. Or how much fiercer he looked with a few days' worth of beard. He was the apple and the serpent all rolled into one. I knew that and yet I wanted anyway, despite knowing that acting on my desires would ultimately be my undoing.

His eyes slid my way. He slung his arm over the back of the seat and faced me. "Something wrong, darlin?"

"No." I looked away. "Nothing." *Everything.*

My hand shook a little when I turned the key, making it rattle in the lock. The dishes in the sink reeked. I'd forgotten all about them, but they asserted themselves now; I could smell sour eggs and milk from that morning's breakfast the moment I opened the door.

Michael shut the door behind us and leaned back against it, looking around my living room thoughtfully. "Do you have any money on you?"

"Why? Are you going to rob me?"

He stared at me. Then laughed. "Don't be ridiculous."

"I have some cash," I said hesitantly.

"Good." He tossed his empty coffee cup in my recycling bin. "If we're going to do this, we're going to have to a buy a few things. I'll wait here."

Now? I blinked. "We're going now?"

"No time like the present," he deadpanned.

I slipped into my bedroom and rolled out my last four twenties from a pair of mismatched socks. I shoved them into my purse and zipped up the pouch.

Michael was still where I had left him. "What's the nearest store to this place?"

I named the drug store where I bought his clothes.

"Do you have any food besides the cold stuff?"

"Um, ramen. Dried fruit. Cereal. Mac n' cheese."

"That'll be our first stop then."

We took the bus to the store even though it was starting to cool down outside. Michael muttered under his breath the whole time. It sounded like recitation, like prayer, though I knew firsthand that he wasn't a religious man. When I asked him what he was doing he growled at me to shut up, so I left him to his crazy act in peace.

The drug store had a small selection of grocery items. Most of them were the kind that students buy in bulk to munch on during final exams. Michael added pop-top cans of fruits and vegetables, sardines, soups, crackers, and a bottle of multivitamins. He was quick, efficient.

Why wouldn't he be? He's done this countless times.

I didn't appreciate being made to feel useless. Confiding my fear and desperation to him had been a mistake, I thought. Now it seemed as if he were trying to show me that I couldn't possibly function without him.

I marched over to the pharmacy section. I'd assembled a first-aid kit for a badge back in girl scouts. It was pretty simple — rubbing alcohol, band-aids, gauze, anti-itch, insect repellent, sunscreen, allergy pills, aspirin.

Michael came by with the cart. He glanced at what I had gathered but chose not to comment. I took that as a sign of approval. I waited until his back turned before adding Kleenexes, sanitary napkins, and Midol to the cart.

Flashlights, batteries, matches, bungee cords, and

a miscellany of other outdoorsy items completed the selection. I wondered if the eighty dollars I had was going to be enough. I'd seen him checking the prices.

At the register, the cashier said, "Going camping?" She said it the same way others might say, "Robbing a bank?"

"Not here," he told her. "Up north, where it's cooler—know any good spots?"

Did she ever. While the two of them bantered about the Sierras, I took the crumpled bills out of my purse and flattened them against the edge of the table. It was eerie, I thought, how quickly and convincingly Michael could lie.

How many times had I been on the receiving end?

On the way back, I was silent. How much of what we'd been through together had been real? The dynamic between us was disparate; he was specially trained to manipulate, and was skilled enough that I wouldn't be able to tell the difference between a truth and a lie from his lips.

If we were going to work together, I had to trust him.

His quickness to resort to sexual remarks was also worrisome. He knew it bothered me. Since he kept doing that, I could only assume that he didn't care.

I needed to sort out my feelings and I couldn't do that if he kept stirring them up by keeping me in a constant state of uncertainty and unease.

My apartment felt like a different place with the sea of plastic bags covering the floor. It was like a modern-day Ali Baba's cave. I guess that made sense, actually, since we were technically in the middle of the desert. Michael looked up from one of the bags he was sorting through. "Do you have an extra backpack?"

I nodded and went to retrieve it, grateful to be away from those piercing eyes that saw both far too much...and far too little.

I dumped my school bag out on the bed. Pens and pencils went rolling across the floor. I had a spare in the closet, an old Jansport. Neither of them were as nice as the Michael Kors leather satchel I'd used all of last year. It had disappeared after I'd been kidnapped, and I supposed that meant meant it was still back at the safe house—if the safe house hadn't been destroyed.

That was his agency's philosophy. Destroy all the evidence. Remove all witnesses. Leave no trace of the past so you can rewrite history as you would. Never mind who got hurt in the process, or how many.

Armed and Dangerous by Nenia Campbell

I handed Michael the trashed pack. He began dumping out the spoils, removing the items from the packaging with assembly-line efficiency, stuffing them into the packs. Without a word, I sat down and joined him. It felt oddly cozy, which was not only *wrong*, but also bizarre, and it took me a moment to realize that this whole setting reminded me of Christmas. Of wrapping presents with my family. The fact that we were sitting next to the AC helped.

"You'll want to leave some extra room at the top in case we need to stop somewhere and get more," Michael said. "Save the plastic bags. They might come in handy."

I could feel his eyes on me as I continued to assemble the first-aid kit, and so I nodded. I added fruit, ramen noodles, and small baggies of crackers to the bottom of my backpack. I muttered an excuse and went to grab an armful of clothes from my bedroom. Windbreaker. T-shirts. Tank tops. Underwear. I bundled these last up in the shirts so Michael wouldn't see them and offer comment. The fact that I cared made me doubly nervous. I tried to focus my thinking. What else did I need? Sleepwear? ID? Money?

"On the day we leave, go to an ATM and take out your max limit," Michael said, when I pulled my driver's license out of my wallet. "Then cut your card in half and throw it out. Leave your cellphone. They can trace us with it."

He was looking at me, but talking for himself, pacing around my living room like a caged tiger. Because he *was* wild. He was wild in a way most humans didn't have to be, and *hadn't* had to be for hundreds of years.

"We'll leave tomorrow, or the day after. No later."

In my writing class, we had been reading *Into the Wild*. Michael reminded me of Chris McCandless in some ways, except he had been heading into Alaskan wilderness. We were in the desert. He had also died, though I was trying not to think about that part of the book so much.

"Where are we going?" I asked him.

His eyes focused. "Anywhere but here."

"You have no idea, do you?"

"Trust me, darlin. I have plenty of experience when it comes to not being found. Now let's get some shut-eye. Tomorrow is going to be a busy day."

Michael:

Armed and Dangerous by Nenia Campbell

Arizona is one part sand, one part rock. Everything else is hot air. There are stretches of sand dunes that go on for miles. Sandstone labyrinths. Cacti and tumbleweeds running rampant. Some places are so hot and arid that nothing can grow at all. It was the perfect place to hide.

"Have you ever been through the desert before?"

"I'm a professional survivalist," I told her.

"So no."

I didn't respond.

"The IMA isn't going to have to kill us. We'll already be dead by the time they find us."

"Your faith in me is so encouraging."

She winced but she didn't apologize.

Before we went off the grid I made a last trip to the store and bought another backpack, which I filled with water bottles. I had Christina go through her apartment a final time. She called her utility providers and had them shift the payments to her mother's address. I then checked to make sure she had destroyed both her debit card and her phone. She had. We were off.

The sun beat down hard on the both of us and soon our clothes were plastered to our bodies like papier-mâché. I'd rubbed on sunscreen and still, my skin was blistering. It was too hot to feel anything but hot.

Sand crunched beneath the heels of her and my boots, punctuated by the occasional snap of dead branch or desiccated tumbleweed. The sky was the searing blue of a gas burner. Flecks of mica flashed pinpoints of blinding light from the sand every time I turned my head. It wasn't as bad as Louisiana in the summertime, with its hot wet heat that wrapped around your body like a serpent and squeezed, but it sure as hell wasn't a temperate Oregon September, either.

"So out of all fifty states to choose from, why Arizona?" I asked to take my mind off the heat and the weight of the two backpacks glued to my chest and spine with sweat. "I'm curious. Why this hell-hole?"

She turned around to glare at me. "It isn't a hell-hole."

"If this place isn't hell, then it's God's fucking ashtray."

A bead of sweat dripped down my forehead and into my drying eyes. I flicked my tongue out and tasted salt.

"All right," I said into the silence. "Why this not-a-hell-hole?"

"Because it's quiet and peaceful, I guess."

"You must have had some other reason in mind. The Olympic fucking Peninsula is quiet and peaceful, and *it* isn't one hundred degrees in the summertime."

She looked out at the desert. "I can't explain it. There's something about this place, like it absorbs sound as well as water. In the forest, everything is chattering and alive. The desert has this slow-paced stillness; it makes me feel calm."

Only because it was too goddamn hot to do anything else. I did understand what she meant. The Cascades were like that — standing pools of wilderness where you could let go of your inhibitions and focus on being alive.

That was the basis of my existence. Check your conscience at the door. Follow these rules. Do this, and you will survive.

A shadow skimmed over the sand. I shielded my eyes to search for aircraft. Just a large bird circling lazily overheard in the updrafts. I thought it was a vulture at first but the shape of the head and neck were all wrong. It was a red-tailed hawk.

I was a little glad it wasn't a buzzard. A buzzard would have seemed too much like a bad omen. Not that I'm a superstitious man, but it's hard to escape your heritage. Especially a heritage that comes from growing up in a fucking state whose population still predominantly believes in the *gris-gris* and all that other voodoo bullshit.

I wasn't about to look any gift optimism in the mouth, though. Lord knew, we needed it.

Christina continued talking. Apparently she had warmed to the subject of school. "I got accepted into Reed," she was saying now, and I remembered reading that in the file I'd done on her back when she had been my charge. "Stanford, Oregon State, Washington University." She looked at me—trying to impress me? I looked back, not impressed. I knew people who went to Brown, Harvard, Yale. "But all those schools seemed too high-profile."

"Too cool for school?"

She turned away. "No. It's not like that. None of that hipster 'don't label me' posturing. I really don't want to stick out. I've had enough drama in my life what with my mother, and being kidnapped, and never being able to just be *me*. I wanted to go somewhere I could just…quietly fade away."

"The desert."

She sighed. "The desert."

Armed and Dangerous by Nenia Campbell

"That's pretty fucking sad," I told her.

"Why is that sad?"

"You want to waste away in this million-degree sandbox. I don't know. Sounds pretty pathetic to me."

"Look at it this way: you can't understand, not until you experience it for yourself. The pictures don't tell you anything. Being here...it's existential."

I spread out my arms to indicate that we were standing in the middle of her so-called existential experience and I didn't feel shit.

"It's relaxing," she insisted, wiping sweat from her face. "The sandstone is beautiful at sunset, and I've never seen the stars as clearly as I do here at night."

"Too bad it didn't work," I stated.

"Yeah." Her voice was flat. "Too bad."

I eyed her. "You're starting to sound a little cranky. Why don't you drink some water?"

Christina caught the water I lobbed at her and took a long drink. The plastic crumpled. "You're a jerk."

"I'm the jerk who's keeping you alive," I reminded her. "I suggest you remember that."

She handed back the water with more force than

strictly necessary. "Is that all you think about? Survival?"

I shoved it into my pack. "It's all I can afford to think about."

"Now *that's* pretty fucking sad," she told me, quickening her pace so she didn't have to walk with me. I could have kept up, easily, but I didn't. Her statement cut a little too close to the truth.

We were both pretty fucking sad, getting our jollies where we could—except the Jollies Super Store was all sold out of "jollies." And right next door to that, the Give-A Store was all out of "fucks."

I leaned back. The red sandstone contrasted sharply against the blue of the sky. Christina was probably right about the view being something else at sunset, though I couldn't picture her coming all the way out here by herself just to watch the play of light on stone. That was ridiculous, even for her.

Such a strange woman, to see beauty in a deathtrap and goodness in a killer. I couldn't afford to indulge in such romantic dallying, and neither could she. Regardless of what she believed, this was survival, not a nature walk, and she was distracting me from my purpose.

On multiple levels.

Armed and Dangerous by Nenia Campbell

"Oh—look!"

"What? What is it?" I touched the hilt of the blade strapped to my hip. Looked around for scorpions or four-wheel-drives. *Or scorpions* on *four-wheel-drives.* I was disappointed on all counts. She was pointing at a sandstone cave yawning open before us, reddish mouth wide and heavily striated, like a bad case of strep throat.

Perfect shelter.

The way she pointed it out—not so much.

"Good eye." I ignored the hesitant smile that flickered across her face at the praise. I didn't appreciate her crying out what could have just as easily have been a warning as an exclamation of delight. "We'll camp here for the night."

She sucked in a breath. The small sound rippled through the caverns the way it did through my body. "It's beautiful." She spun around, and my throat ached in a way that had nothing to do with thirst. "My God — look at the walls. It's like someone made a frieze of a red ocean."

I watched her fingers trace the dusty red whorls trapped in the surface of the stone and found myself wondering what it would feel like to have her touching me with such reverence. It was a very appealing thought.

And a very dangerous one.

"Isn't it beautiful?" she whispered.

My cock bobbed in agreement. Yes, she was.

"Stop feeling up the walls," I snapped. "We're going farther back, around the bend. If I light a fire I don't want the flame being seen from the cave mouth outside."

"Fine." She lowered her hands and followed sullenly. I batted away the guilt that threatened to creep up on me like a rattlesnake. This wasn't a game. We didn't have time for her to exclaim over every rock and tree. Not if we were going to stay alive.

But this meant I was the goddamn bad guy again, setting parameters, curtailing her freedom. When we set down our gear for a quick dinner *a la* can, she sat with her back to me as if I'd had her sit in time-out.

Having her think of me as her captor, even now, was not conducive to our escaping. Knowing that I deserved it rankled me further. I didn't like being put in this position. "Look," I said to her spine. "We are on a deadline."

"I know." She didn't turn around.

"Emphasis on the dead if you don't start being a little more cooperative." I dug two tins of cocktail out of the backpack. After playing the part of pack mule in our little desert parade, my body felt buoyant without the supplies weighing me down. "Goddammit. I'm not your enemy."

No response.

"Are you going to eat, or are you going to pout? Either is fine by me, but only one of those options will put food in your belly. You need your strength."

"I'll eat." She slid closer, watching with suspicious eyes as I passed her the water bottle she'd been drinking out of earlier. As if I'd had time to drug it in the two milliseconds she'd let me out of her sight.

"You're welcome," I said coolly.

She ate without speaking, save for the occasional smacking sound that wore quickly on my nerves. It sounded like a sloppy blowjob. "For fuck's sake. Chew with your mouth fucking closed."

She jumped as if I'd slapped her, but after that her chewing was silent.

And I felt like a complete dick.

When we finished eating I gathered up the trash and tossed it into one of the empty plastic bags I'd saved. Christina made no move to help. My irritation crested again. I tamped it down and unraveled the thin, insulated blanket, flattening it out over the ground. I rolled out the stray pebbles, made myself remember my training.

However bad imprisonment had been for me, it had been twice that for her. Unlike me, she hadn't known what to expect. Unlike me, she hadn't been prepared for torture.

She hadn't asked for any of this.

It was hard to remember that.

I pinched the bridge of my nose. "We'll sleep here."

"W-we?"

"Did I stutter?" I stretched out my legs. "I'm sleeping here. You don't like that, feel free to lie on the ground in the corner with the scorpions."

"You're an asshole," she said.

"I sure am," I agreed, leaning back. My calves were burning. There was a heavy ache in my back from the double load. I was more than ready to sleep. If she thought I still had the energy to paw at her after all that, she was giving me too much credit.

I watched through half-shut eyes as she slung off her own pack and yanked a sweatshirt out. She wadded the sweatshirt into a ball to make a pillow and slammed it against her side of the blanket. As she leaned back, her dark hair fell across the fabric and I had to admit: few girls women her age would show such resilience in a situation like this. She was a trooper.

I sat up to strip off my shirt and folded it into a vague lump at one end of the blanket, following her example. She was still making a point of not looking at me, but her posture grew rigid. "My pants stay on," I said dryly.

"Please don't," she whispered. "Please."

The desperation and panic in her voice made my chest tighten like a vise. I sighed. "I won't. I didn't come out here all this way just to hurt you."

I curled an arm around her waist, reeling her in until her ass was pressing against my crotch of my jeans. She tensed at the contact of my fingers on her bare skin but didn't pull away. She was limp.

"I'm not going to hurt you," I repeated.

"You didn't have a choice. They made you come here. Don't pretend you're here for me."

"I chose to stay." I pulled down the hem of her tank top so it was covering her midriff. "With you. For you." I ran my hand back up her arm. "Here." She let out a shuddering breath. "It ever occur to you that maybe my intentions are benign?"

"People don't change," she said. "Not like that."

Armed and Dangerous by Nenia Campbell

"They can."

"No," she said firmly. "They can't."

Outside, I heard the roar of a helicopter. There was no telling how close it really was — not with the distortions caused by the many caves in canyons.

Christina heard it too. "Is that them?"

"Maybe." Possibly. Probably.

"Oh God."

"They won't find us."

"I hope not." She shivered, and I pulled her closer. "This wasn't supposed to happen."

"I know."

"I'm scared."

I know.

"You've changed, you know," she said suddenly, "but not as much as I'd hoped you would."

"I'm trying," I murmured.

"Not hard enough."

Hard being the operative word here.

I shifted uncomfortably so my dick wasn't jabbing her behind. "What do you want me to do? Apologize for the way I am?"

"It's not just about you, Michael."

Armed and Dangerous by Nenia Campbell

And there, I supposed she had a point.

Armed and Dangerous by Nenia Campbell

Chapter Sixteen

Regret

Christina:

When I opened my eyes I was dazzled by the sandstone. The rising sun turned the serene waves of mineral deposits into a mural of fire, bringing out rich amber, gold, and cinnabar that had previously lain dormant.

I rolled over, still half-asleep, and humbled by the cave walls. My face mashed against a man's naked chest. I looked up through the screen of my hair to see him watching me back with an unreadable expression.

For a moment I couldn't breathe. I didn't like it when he looked at me like that. It made me feel like I was taking a test I'd never know the answers to.

It made me wish that he would kiss me.

"W-why are you looking at me like that?"

"Because you look like shit," he said.

"You — " I'd forgotten that lazy, effacing grin. As if humor were something that could only be wielded with irony, because it made one too vulnerable. "You do, too," I said lamely.

"I know." He raked a hand through his own

mussed and greasy hair. "Ready for another day in hell?" His voice was husky from sleep, deeper than usual, with a gravelly edge.

This man was your kidnapper. Don't get attached.

I nodded. Yes, I was ready. Yes, I understood.

"Good girl." He rolled over, stretching his arms over his head. I didn't like myself much right now for being so weak and impressionable. I should not have been looking at him the way I was. But I didn't have the moral fiber to look away, either.

Breakfast was a bottle of water and another can of fruit. I drank the syrup down thirstily. I used to think it was gross but the sticky syrup soothed my sunburned lips.

Upon finishing, I packed up my things in silence and avoided Michael's eyes.

It was a few degrees cooler outside than it had been the day before. There was even a bit of a breeze to stir the heavy desert air, thick as whipped cream from the dust and the sand. A few clouds hung low on the horizon, though I had lived here long enough now to know that they would all evaporate before noon. By then, the temperature would be in the triple-digits.

The suffocating heat made it hard to think. I had

lost focus on what was really important here: I still didn't know *why* I was running away in the first place.

Seeing Michael again under such dire circumstances had been such a shock I hadn't had the presence of mind to ask him for more details. He had said the IMA was behind it, but to what end? There was more to the story.

I said as much to Michael once we resumed our trek. His eyebrows knit together. "I was wondering if you were going to ask me that."

"Are you going to answer?"

I had several arguments ready to use in case he said no. If my life was at risk again, I thought I had the right to know why. Plus, he owed me for not turning his drug-bloated corpse over to the cops.

Not that he'd believe you would.

I didn't believe I would.

"That all depends," he said, drawing my attention away from the Michael in my head to the Michael standing in front of me.

"On what?"

"Will you stop cringing every time I look at you?"

His request surprised me. The fact that a man

who could be so base could also be so complicated was frightening. "Maybe," I said. "I'll try."

"You'll try." His skepticism cut like a blade.

"It's the best I can do right now," I said. "Try."

"If that's all you've got to offer, I'll take it." He drank from his water bottle and began to tell me what he had been doing since the last time we had met.

The stories he told me made my own problems and concerns pale into insignificance. I listened with real horror as he told me that he had spent several months on the run from the IMA because he hadn't wanted to go back. They caught up to him at last because he had let them. Because out of some perverse sense of dignity he preferred to give in rather than be dragged in against his will.

He told me he had been taken to Scotland. He had been told he was going to head a mission against a rival group of mercenaries, only to find out that the whole thing had been a pretext for "retraining." He drew the air quotes himself, saying in the next breath that he had been tortured for his failures. Despite knowing he could escape, he was still virtually a prisoner because he was afraid of what they would do to me as a result if he left.

Michael cared about me beyond a simple matter

of quid pro quo. He cared enough to put his own life and well-being on the line. Something that had been hard to remember when his own life had been thrown into the mix right alongside mine.

Kent had been telling the truth that morning. In his own twisted way, Michael had loved me. He loved me enough to let me go — and it hadn't worked.

After completing his duties in Scotland, he returned to Oregon and found out immediately afterward that he was going to be deployed to England to deal with that same rival group, called the BN.

I interrupted. "Who are the BN?"

"Remember when you were being held in confinement at our base, and I was returning you to your cell right before they sent me to Lake Angelus?"

That had taken place just before Adrian had beaten me half to death. I'd nearly died. I nodded slowly.

I remembered.

"Remember that man you saw?"

"Who?"

"The other prisoner."

At first I had no idea what he was talking about. I was doing my utmost to forget what had happened to me, and little details like that were among the first to disappear because they were so inconsequential. But then I thought I might know who he was talking about. The handsome, dark-eyed man who had looked so thin and bruised. The one Michael had used as an example when he warned me about the IMA: *"As long as you're here, you still have a fighting chance. Just remember this: once they move you to one of our internment bases, it's over."*

"That's the man," he said. "He was a member of the BN. The *Bureau du Nuit*. His name was Pierre Dupont, and he was one of their leaders."

"Was? He's dead now?"

Michael nodded grimly.

That meant that man — Pierre — had been tortured to death in one of the camps; it meant that unlike us, he had not been lucky enough to get away. A terrible death.

"I bet the BN weren't too happy about that."

"No, they were not." Michael paused to wipe some sweat from his forehead with the back of his wrist. "In their own way, the BN are just as dangerous as us. They are willing to stoop to acts of massive violence to further their cause. They prefer to think of themselves as peacemakers, but any animal fights back viciously when cornered and the BN are no exception to this rule. They protect their own.

"Callaghan wants them eliminated because they pose a threat to the expansion of the IMA. They are encroaching upon territory that we have already claimed as our own, and killing our agents. I was chosen to head the expedition Callaghan formed to put them in their place. I never met the team I was allegedly leading. I just reported to that bastard, and he reported what I said back to them — filtered, of course. I figured he thought I might sabotage him, or decide to stage a rebellion of my own." He gave me a dry smile. "The thought did cross my mind."

"But that was the rumor *he* started about you in order to get Richardson to eliminate you," I protested. "It was never actually true."

"You've heard of self-fulfilling prophecy."

"Greek tragedies are all about self-fulfilling prophecy."

"There's a reason for that." He glanced over his shoulder. "They seem to get you in trouble, too."

He was right. This whole mess started when my dad hacked into the IMA's weapons database with the name of an old Greek god. "Maybe they're cursed," I said.

"Never talk about curses to a man from the bayou."

"You don't believe in that crap, do you?"

"This, coming from the Catholic schoolgirl?" His face didn't match the severe tone. It was a spot of lightness in his otherwise dark tale, and didn't last.

He told me how he planned to use the IMA's and BN's mutual distrust of one another to double-deal to both groups, feeding each faction a blend of half-truths meant to provoke them into direct conflict.

For a while, it worked — but then he had been found out, and the BN decided that getting back at him through me was too good of an opportunity to pass up. They risked his vengeance and his wrath by drugging him with the PCP that had caused him to nearly attack and kill me, and left him on my front porch for dead for me to find.

"Why not just kill you outright?" I wondered aloud.

He glared at me. "I don't know. I guess they were hoping I'd bump you off. Or that you'd kill me in self-defense, save them the trouble. Who the fuck knows how they think?"

"You used to," I pointed out.

"The deuces are wild as far as Callaghan is concerned."

"So what happened? How were you found out?"

"Someone caught on to me." Michael kicked a stone out of his path. I watched it go skittering away, making ripples in the sand. "Someone who knows my methods."

"Who?"

"Apart from Callaghan? I heard the BN mention someone named Villanueva. I think he's a rat."

"A rat?"

"That means the IMA have another double agent. One who isn't me, and whose loyalties seem torn between theirs and the BN."

"I know what a rat means," I said. "I watch *The Sopranos*. What I meant, was, does that happen a lot?"

"It's the danger of double agents. Sometimes they realize the grass really is greener on the other side."

"Is that what happened to you?"

"Me, I found out both sides were nothing but shit and decided to *passe* on the hell out of there."

I turned away so he wouldn't see my smile of relief and read something out of it that he shouldn't.

Armed and Dangerous by Nenia Campbell

It felt good to have Michael on *my* side once more. I felt more comfortable around him than I should have. On the other hand, he had shown himself to be the lesser evil. He said it best himself: he knew how to survive.

We took a water break every half hour. Around two in the afternoon we lunched on tinned sardines and a shared can of string-beans. He had me drink the vegetable-flavored water from the bottom. "You're not used to weathering it," he said. "You need the extra fluids."

That brief but welcome morning coolness disappeared much too quickly. The sand was too hot even to sit on. I found that out the hard way during one of our breaks when I tried to steady myself and burned my hand on the hot shards of rocks. We had to squat, leaning against the sandstone cliffs for support. Cast in their own shadow, they were cooler than the sand. My legs were killing me and my calves and hamstrings screamed at that new and unwelcome strain. "Why didn't we take a car?"

"Too easy to trace."

"What if we dumped it somewhere after?"

"You watch too much TV."

"At least a car would have air-conditioning."

Armed and Dangerous by Nenia Campbell

Michael snorted. "Yeah? What if some cop pulled us over to check our papers? I don't have any ID."

He was right — and I begrudged him for it.

The food was some consolation but it was a far cry from the milkshakes I'd started fantasizing about as my brain marinated in its own juices like steak tartare. A Neapolitan milkshake — strawberry, chocolate, and vanilla, so I wouldn't have to choose a single flavor.

Clearly my body was mad at me for putting it through this crap and was wreaking psychological warfare in revenge. Stupid body.

Michael was mostly silent, and didn't speak unless spoken to first. It was too hot to talk. All my energy went towards getting through the sheer exertion of walking and breathing through the shimmering heat. I was surprised he had said as much as he had. His face was creased in thought, so I suppose he was still mulling over what he'd recounted to me earlier, turning over each possibility in his mind like a man at a game of shells.

I was still reeling over it. How could one man face the world alone and still be sane, never mind *alive*? It made it harder to hate Michael for all the things he'd done, knowing he had suffered like that. I wanted to believe he had changed, that he was capable of change. But I also didn't want to get hurt, or set myself up for disappointment.

Michael looked back again, in that uncanny way of his, and it was as if he had read my thoughts. His expression was as hard and battered as the sandstone cliffs. I shifted the weight of my backpack on my shoulder, as if the sheer intensity of his gaze had added more weight to the load.

"Don't look at me like that," he said. "I didn't tell you all that because I wanted your goddamn pity."

Why had he told me then? "I wasn't. Pitying you, I mean. I was…just looking at the cliffs."

"Good." He nodded at a cave entrance. "We'll stop here for the night."

This cave was shallower than the one I'd found — it was a large embrasure denoting where massive erosion had occurred God only knew how many years before but not very deep. I was pleased that my cave was better than his.

Because he wanted to avoid being seen Michael refused to make a fire and allowed me to use the flashlight just long enough to procure the necessary provisions for the night.

"Looks like we'll be spending more time together than we bargained for." His voice came from the darkness without warning, perilously close to my ear as I snapped the flashlight back off and set it aside.

Swallowing, I agreed that this was so.

"In that case, I think we should clear the air about something I'm sure has been on both our minds."

My throat felt too dry. I wondered if I'd swallowed too much dust. "And what is that?"

"The sexual arrangements."

I nearly dropped the tin of fruit I was struggling to open.

He took the can from me, opening it easily. "Don't get me wrong. I got you into this mess, and I'm going to get you out. I owe you that much, and I'm not going to use sex as leverage. I'm not that kind of man."

He handed the tin back. *You were*, I thought, taking it. *You demanded that I sleep with you in exchange for helping my parents and A escape from that wretched island.* I drank the fruit, still warm from the sun. *Did you forget?*

"I'm not going to force you into anything you don't want. But I'm also not going to take a vow of chastity and pine away for you, or whatever the hell it is that men do in romance novels these days. I have needs. I'd rather satisfy them with you, but if you don't want me I suppose I'll just have to find someone else. Might take me a while, but I'll make do. I always have before."

My traitor heart faltered. "You said it was dangerous. To be together, I mean." I wet my cracked lips and my tongue made them burn. "You said that I'd be killed if I were around you. That's why you said you had to leave."

I sounded like I was whining, even to my own ears. Throwing out excuses as if they were weapons without looking first to see where they would land. Hoping one of them would hit.

He reached out, fingers brushing my face in a blind caress, before closing around the edge of my jaw. "Yeah, well, it's beginning to look like we're fucked no matter what we do. At least if I'm with you I'll know it wasn't because I didn't do enough to keep you safe."

I found myself leaning into his touch before I was quite aware of doing so, and his hand dropped as I began to understand the significance of what I'd done. "I — "

No, no, no. This is wrong. All wrong.

His posture shifted to watchful readiness in the dark. "Careful." I felt his hands come down on my shoulders. Keeping me from moving closer, but also keeping me from backing away. "I want you to think about this very, very carefully. What you're getting into. This won't be a one-time thing."

His words buzzed strangely in my ears. Was he...asking me to be his girlfriend? I couldn't make myself form the words. They caught in my throat like burrs. I wet my lips. "What if I decide to say no?"

"I won't touch you."

"That didn't stop you before."

Michael sucked in a breath. His fingers tightened on my shoulders. "No. And I made that choice. I let all that anger and pain get twisted up in my thoughts for you." He leaned in. "It fucking kills me. Every night. I relive what I did to you every night." His forehead rested against mine. "Until you," he said softly, "I never felt truly helpless."

My vision blurred. I swallowed back the sob working its way up my throat and looked away, even though he couldn't see it. He tilted my head up, though the feel of my tear-streaked face gave him pause.

"I am not a nice man," he said, even as he loosened his grip. "I don't do valentines or anniversaries or weddings or any of that shit, and I might very well break your heart, but I can promise you'll never be bored."

And then his lips sealed against mine, tongue slipping as expertly past my lips as he did through my common-sense, and I closed my eyes at the familiar taste of him as his thumbs dug lightly into the grooves of my collarbone.

No, I thought. *He is anything but boring.*

I thought that kiss would never end, but then it did. As if some taut string between us had been cut, he pulled away, and with him went some of the pressure weighing down on my chest.

"I am sorry." He caught my lower lip between his teeth, and dropped a kiss along the upper. "You deserved better. You still do. I'm giving you the choice now I should have given you then." My skin hummed when he pulled away as if an insect was fluttering its wings along the sensitive skin. "Until then, that's something for you to consider."

"Michael…"

"Don't talk. Go to sleep."

He didn't touch me again that night.

I realized for the first time just how hard and lumpy the ground was through that thin, cheap fabric. Since I couldn't sleep, I had the whole night to wonder how much self-control I possessed.

Michael:

I'd noticed her watching me. I'd be lying if I said I hadn't done everything in my power to keep it that way. I knew she liked my body, even if she was too shy to admit it, and I suspected she didn't hate me as much as she pretended. If she did, she would have delivered me to the cops when the BN dumped me on her doorsteps.

But she hadn't; she had taken me in, cleaned me up, bought me clothes. Grudgingly, but I couldn't blame her for that, even if I was still a little sore about the mace. The fact that she hadn't immediately gone for the knife said something. She still had that little switchblade. I'd gone through her pack when she went off to take a piss and found the knife wrapped up in a pair of panties right along with the pepper-spray. She could have used both on me as I slept, leaving me to die in the desert.

Oh, she didn't trust me, but I couldn't blame her for that, either. I didn't trust myself; I just distrusted everyone around me a whole lot more. I hadn't brought up the knife with her for that same exact reason — she *shouldn't* trust me. Asking for that was asking for a lot.

Armed and Dangerous by Nenia Campbell

But when I felt her yield and kiss me back, and I realized I had a fighting chance to make this all work out somehow, I had hope.

That was far deadlier than any knife or mace.

Armed and Dangerous by Nenia Campbell

Chapter Seventeen
Tension

Christina:

The next two nights followed the same pattern. We spent most of the day putting distance between Coswell and ourselves, wading through sweat and sand. The nights we spent sleeping in the rock walls like frightened animals.

He wouldn't touch me. Not unless it was by accident. He barely spoke. It was too hot and painful to speak with blistering lips. Harder still with a fevered mind. The minutes ticked away in sluggish silence, leaving me to the recess of my thoughts.

I relive what I did to you every night.

I wanted to believe him. He had spoken the words with such sincerity, such heart-wrenching sadness, that it was difficult not to — until I remembered his easy banter with the drugstore clerk, and the countless other lies that had paved the path down which he had happened upon me.

Was any of what we had real?

I decided not to dwell on it. Instead, I took a page out of Michael's handbook; I focused on surviving.

Armed and Dangerous by Nenia Campbell

Michael:

Our fifth day of playing Lawrence of Arabia brought us to one of those outposts that make Coswell look like a hustling, bustling city. I stared at the stunted pony looking at us from over the top of a wooden corral. It was grazing on yellow-green grass, watching us stumble into the town perimeter. A one-horse town in every sense of the word.

I hoped they had an inn. After five days in the desert I probably stank worse than the fucking pony.

We trudged along on the shoulder of the road. There was a general store, a gas station, a fire station, a police station. Empty shells, like the mining and lumber towns I'd passed through in the Cascades. Remainders of something greater, left to crumble to dust in the sweltering heat.

The road led to an old ranch house set back a ways on sandy soil, tufts of dead grass choked to death by the gravel. A sun-peeled sign read, "Bed and Breakfast."

I jerked my head towards the sign. "Here looks good."

Christina lit up, but the smile on her dirty face was chased by a more troubling expression I didn't care to think about. I walked purposefully towards the front door and a bell chimed overhead, signifying our arrival.

I noticed the foyer had been converted into a small lobby. It was a failed attempt. There wasn't even close to enough space and the plastic stand of brochures was partially blocking the door. Definitely violating fire code.

We squeezed past the rack, making our way further into the dim room. Most of the shades were drawn. To keep out the heat, I guessed. There wasn't any AC out here. I hoped the bedrooms were better accommodated.

"Hello?"

I blinked, my eyes only partially adjusted to the light. The speaker was a woman, mid-seventies, at least part Native if the cheekbones were any indication. She looked us over distastefully.

"Are you here to rent a room?"

"That all depends. How much a night?"

She named a price lower than I'd expected. It was obviously inflated. Considering the foot-traffic this place didn't get, I'd have figured that beggars couldn't be choosers. Her demeanor changed, however, when I paid in cash. It changed some more when I said we'd gotten lost while hiking, and hinted that we might stay an extra night or two if conditions were favorable.

"You poor dears," she said.

What a joke. Christina was staring at me in disbelief. I winked at her. She flushed and turned away as the woman came back from the back room with a key. Hand-tooled leather fob. How cute.

"The rooms are on the second floor."

Great. Stairs. My favorite.

There were several doors. The open door led to a bathroom, which I guessed we shared with the woman downstairs. It was the middle door, and the one to the left of it was labeled "guests."

I unlocked it, revealing brownish-red walls. It was an attempt to mimic the adobe houses scattered around nearby. A poor attempt. It looked like what it was: a botched paint job. The blankets, cushions, rug, and draperies were a particularly loud Navajo weave. Probably available for sale in some shitty gift shop nearby.

I wondered if Callaghan's goons had bothered to track us through the desert. The image of his henchmen sweating .45s in their own kevlar was enough to make me laugh out loud. Lead vests didn't do shit against those kinds of bullets. Then I remembered the helicopter I'd heard a few nights ago, distorted by the cave, and my amusement died.

Christina whipped around when she heard me shut the door. She looked cornered, and very dirty. I kept my face implacable. "You want to shower first?"

Her eyes darted between me and the door. I could see her weighing her options, trying to suss me out. "Okay," she decided. She grabbed her backpack and hurried inside. The door locked. A moment later, the shower started. I shook my head. She was acting as skittish as a kicked cat.

I sat on the edge of the bed and waited for her to finish. Trying not to imagine her standing naked under the cold spray. Head tilted back. Eyes closed in ecstasy as she ran her soapy fingers up her —

Fuck.

This was going to be more difficult than I thought. What if she said no? I'd have to honor her decision, and my cock might just explode from sheer frustration.

I tugged off the sweaty t-shirt and kicked it aside. I wanted to persuade her, but I didn't want to scare her, and I certainly didn't want to make her cry. I wanted her to be safe. I wanted her to be mine. I wanted to have my cake and eat it, too.

Armed and Dangerous by Nenia Campbell

The water shut off. I held my breath. The bathroom door unlocked. She stepped out in a red tank top and flannel boxers. It wasn't a corset but my mental Rolodex was already rotating around to accommodate for this new image. She flushed under my scrutiny. "It's all yours."

Are you?

Christina stumbled out of my way as I walked by her and I caught a whiff of floral soap. She was quite a bit taller than most of the women I'd been with. Petite women make me feel like a bull in a china shop and height differences require some creative rearrangement during sex.

Christina was the perfect height — I could kiss her without stooping down or picking her up. And if she let me, I could do a lot more. So much more.

Shit.

My cock tightened, pulsing with impatience. I shed my clothing quickly and jerked off in the shower, which was a bit like scratching an itch without using your nails; it did the trick, but it wasn't as satisfying. Then I washed all traces of that reddish sand from my body until I smelled like a fucking florist's from all that purple shampoo.

I shut off the water. Toweled myself off. The

mirror was still fogged up from Christina's hot shower, and through the blur of the steam I could make out a week's worth of beard. I ran my fingers along the bristles, then shrugged it off. I was too lazy to shave. Besides, it could make for a nice disguise; I went to work clean-shaven.

I pulled on some boxers and a loose pair of drawstring pants. Opened the door. Christina was in bed with the sheets wrapped around her. I pulled back on one end to get in beside her and she jumped. I saw her hands clutch around the sheet as she moved to cover her breasts, staring up at me with eyes that looked far too white.

I raised my hands, palms out. "Do you want me to sleep on the floor?"

Her eyes dropped to my chest. To my stomach. It wasn't a sexual look, there was too much pity in it — she was looking at my scars — but I stirred a little regardless. "No. That's okay."

"Thanks."

I felt a cool whoosh of air and saw that there was an old fashioned air conditioner mounted on the wall. Christina must have found it and turned it on while I was washing off. Goddamn, but it felt good to have a mattress at my back and cold air at my front.

Armed and Dangerous by Nenia Campbell

Christina:

I frowned at the unfamiliar ceiling. The cool, clean covers were an odd but welcome respite from the hot, hard sandstone I had spent the last couple nights sleeping on.

And then I remembered —

The door closed. I shot up, hugging the sheet to my chest. Michael glanced in my direction. "Did I wake you?"

That question made me blush. It wasn't sexual, but it made me feel as if we'd slept together. Which I supposed we had, but not in that way. "No. I was up."

"Good."

"Where did you go?"

"I was getting food."

Food?

He sat down on the bed, near my leg. I shifted it away and he noticed — of course he did — and tilted his head. He set the paper bag beside him and said, "You hungry?"

My stomach growled traitorously, but the way he was looking at me bespoke a different kind of hunger.

"Y-yes."

He reached into the bag and handed me a pastry. Then he got up to fill those chipping glazed mugs in the bathroom with lukewarm water from the faucet. I was going to wait, but he said, "Go on and eat while it's warm."

I hadn't realized how much I'd been craving something that didn't come from a can. The pastry had soft dough, crispy bacon, runny eggs. It reminded me of a breakfast burrito, except with flaky crust. We'd been so sparing with our supplies out of necessity but now I wanted a second pastry, then maybe a third. I couldn't choke it down fast enough.

"Don't eat so fast. You'll give yourself a stomachache."

I swallowed the mouthful I had, wincing. I remembered his snappish behavior from before, in the cave, when he had yelled at me for smacking too loudly. I'd been so embarrassed. Eating was a sore point with me, thanks to my mother, and one he had no right to make comments on.

I took a sip of water and uttered one of my fallback responses. "I don't care."

"You will if you throw it all back up."

He had a point there. I shrugged. "I'm fine."

"I think you'll want to save room for dessert." He produced a watermelon. My mouth watered. I loved watermelon. Maria used to make the best watermelon lemonade in the summertime.

That stopped me. I hadn't thought of Maria once until now. She had disappeared from the household when we moved. Had my mother even remembered to write her a recommendation or give her a reference? I pushed the guilty thoughts away. If — when — I got out of this, I'd take care of it myself.

"Where did you get that?"

"Do you want me to cut you some?"

"Yes. Please." I looked around. "What are you going to cut it with? You aren't going to use your weapon, are you?" I didn't like the idea of him using a killing blade to cut food. It seemed wrong.

"Don't you have a knife?"

"Yes, but I — " I froze. I hadn't told him about the knife *or* the pepper-spray. There was only one way he could have known that I'd brought them along. "You searched my bag."

I expected denial. He gave me honesty. "Yes."

Honesty didn't make me feel all that much better about what he'd done. "You went through my *things*."

He didn't blink. "Yes."

Armed and Dangerous by Nenia Campbell

"Did you take it away?"

"It's still in your bag."

It was? "Why didn't you take it?"

"If you feel unsafe, you should have a knife. Instincts save lives. I told you to bring what you needed. You listened." He shrugged. "You should trust your instincts."

He was wrong; I couldn't. "Okay. Well...good."

"I suppose I ought to thank you for not using it on me." I opened my mouth to protest. He stopped me. "Remember what happened on the sofa?"

Oh, yes. As if I could forget.

My heart hammered as I slipped out of bed to retrieve the knife. If he was angry, he was hiding it well. His mood had been so unpredictable these last few days, emotions oozing through the immobile stone facade like cracks in a weathering dam.

He had been like this before, back at the safe house, when I had been forced to watch him like a hawk to gauge his mood when he had began to lose his control. When he finally had, I had been the one to get caught in the deluge.

I handed Michael the switchblade. He flicked out the sharp edge in a practiced move, carving out two narrow slices. He handed the first to me. I tried not to think about what else he'd have use to cut like that.

The watermelon was perfectly ripe. The spongy red flesh seemed to almost melt in my mouth, making me aware of how thirsty I'd been all this time. I gulped down the rest of my water, not caring when drips of it ran down my throat to soak into my collar, and swiped the back of my hand across my mouth. "That was good."

He didn't answer, and I glanced over at him. He had the now-empty paper bag in his hand, and was in the act of putting his own depleted rind into it, but his eyes were on me. I felt the want in them burn as they flickered down to my chest, and my face flushed hot when I realized he could see my erect nipples quite clearly through the fabric.

"Oh God," I said, grabbing the sheet.

He caught my wrists. Loosely enough that I could pull away if I wanted to. "Don't do that, *cher*. They're beautiful." His voice grew lower. "May I see?"

"What do you mean?"

"I want to see you. More of you."

The creatures in my stomach fluttered awake, their wings fanning the flames that were building up slowly but surely from deep inside my body.

"Just a look. I won't touch."

"What's the point then?"

He whispered in my ear, something that made me turn red. "I told you I dreamed about you," he said huskily. "What did you think that meant?"

I thought it meant that we were on two completely different levels.

"You going to give me some food for thought?"

I nodded, and he let out a breath. He released one of my wrists, and ran the back of his hand down my cheek, down my throat, before gently taking the hem of my shirt in his fingers and dragging it down until one of my breasts was exposed.

I looked at his face, and then away when I saw the hunger in it. He pulled down the other strap and shook his head. "Why you'd want to look at the fucking sandstone when you could be looking at this in the mirror…"

I shook my head slowly and reached to pull my shirt back up. He held my wrists down.

"Not yet," he said. "You're beautiful, and it's killing me and I want to die a moment longer. Please."

He could turn on the charm, intensify his accent. He could lie as convincingly as any actor or con artist. I steeled myself and refused to fall victim to it.

Armed and Dangerous by Nenia Campbell

I was not successful.

"Oh Christina." He stroked the inside of my wrists. "You have no idea how much I want you." Michael turned my palm over, pressing an open-mouthed kiss to the back of my hand without taking his eyes off me. "Or maybe you do."

I froze, my breath coming shorter as he bit down lightly on the knuckles of my first and second fingers, before slipping his tongue into the space between them, licking the watermelon residue from the whorls of my skin.

"I could show you."

"What are you doing?" I said faintly.

He paused, nipping lightly at my fingertips. He set down my hand without letting going of my wrists, and leaned in. "Well." He let go of my left hand to pull my hair back from my ear. "That's what I want to do to your breasts, one after the other. Suck, and lick, and kiss, and bite—I'd do all those things until you squirmed down to that tight little pussy of yours. And everything above and below and in between. I want to fuck you with my mouth and I want to take my time at it, until all you can say is *yes* and *please*."

He paused.

"And then, when I felt like you'd asked me sweet

enough, I'd lay you back down nice and gentle. Fuck you face-to-face so I can see every single reaction on that beautiful face. So I can feel you say my name against my mouth while I'm kissing you. So you can see how much I want you when I bring you to the best orgasm of your life."

My stomach twisted violently, like a butterfly's tremors after losing its wings. "You don't just say things like that to people."

"You're right. You do them."

"I haven't said yes," I told him.

His eyes flicked to my naked breasts, then back to me. "You also haven't said no."

"You're not an easy person to say no to — that's enough." I tugged at my arms. He released me. Then he turned and walked away. I sat there unmoving for a full ten seconds staring at my limp, damp hand before realizing that I should probably get dressed.

He was gone for most of the day after that. "Making arrangements," he'd said, when he stopped back after the first errand to drop off more food and a few books for me. That was how I spent the time he was gone: reading paperback best-sellers and wondering what I was going to do about Michael.

The woman in the romance novel I was reading

suffered no similar problems. She was wearing a skimpy nightgown, getting ready to seduce the hero she'd been jerking around for the last 200 pages or so. I closed the book and let it fall to the floor. Her face leered up at me from the cover: a woman in a low-cut gown with a faceless, shirtless male embracing her from behind. Both of them looked badly photoshopped. I kicked it under the bed.

Michael returned at sundown. He was wearing a black shirt—different from the one he'd been in when he left. What had happened, to make him throw it away?

I recalled a time he had come back drenched in another man's blood and shivered.

Deep down, I knew he was still capable of that.

He nodded at me, dumping the pack on the table. With his back to me, he peeled off his damp shirt. There was a black strap cinched under his arm, crossing his back, where it ended in a low-slung pouch at his hip that contained a brand-new gun.

He definitely did not have that before.

And with no ID, it wasn't as if he could buy one.

I bit my lip. I had to ask. Had to know. "Where did you get the gun?"

Armed and Dangerous by Nenia Campbell

He pretended not to hear me.

He couldn't have bought it, anyway. He didn't bring the money; it's in my *bag.*

"Michael?"

Still no answer.

I hesitated. "Did you kill someone?"

"We'll stay here for another night or so. After that, I think we'll have worn out our welcome. We'll take a bus up north. I've got a contact in San Francisco who can help us."

I'd always wanted to see San Francisco — but never under these conditions. I pretended my features were made of stone, afraid of showing my heart to this powerful man. "Answer the question," I whispered.

He set the gun on the table beside the bags and unbuckled the holster, turning around to face me with his hands on his hips. "You sure you want the answer to that?"

I watched him pull on a fresh shirt with a sinking heart. "You did," I said. "Oh my God, you *did*."

He set a sandwich and a bottle of juice in front of me. They could have been alien artifacts and I wouldn't have known the difference.

"What did you do all day?" He leaned back in the chair, swinging his feet up on the edge of the bed. He knocked back an energy shot. "You have enough to do?"

"You killed someone," I said. "How can you act like nothing happened?"

He set down the drink. A little of it sloshed over the top, soaking into the Navajo weave. He didn't notice. "Because that's my job. It's what I've been trained for my whole life. Because it keeps me — and you — alive."

But I wasn't listening. He had kissed me, and then he had gone out and killed someone. One right after the other. What kind of a man did a thing like that?

"How?"

He studied me in that unsettling way of his. Then sighed and shook his head. "We'll talk about it tomorrow. Eat your dinner."

"I'm not hungry," I said flatly.

Michael looked at me for a moment longer. "Fine. Don't eat."

There had been a time when I had felt nothing for disgust for him. That had been easier, in a way. My raw hatred only served to reinforce my conviction that I should avoid contact with him at all costs. But now that hatred was tempered with something else; I found myself wanting to make excuses for him.

Excuses rooted in fantasy and wishful thinking.

He was a bad man, and I *knew* that, but a part of me was starting not to care. And the part of me that did care was quickly becoming a liar.

Armed and Dangerous by Nenia Campbell

Chapter Eighteen
Killer

Michael:

It didn't take me long to find the rat, camped up on the edge of town in a haphazardly erected tent. He was wearing desert fatigues, a beige undershirt. He didn't see me coming until it was almost too late, and then he tried to run.

I picked up speed and tackled him. He fell against the sand, and lost some skin as he went sliding across the sand. I hit him hard, and knocked him out. They make it look easy on TV. It isn't. It takes a particular amount of force to a particular location. Too hard, and you can kill a man. Too light, and they just get mean. This one was just right.

I sliced a few strips of canvas from his tent and bound his hands and feet. Then I helped myself to one of his beers while I waited for him to wake up. I was halfway through the can when he began to stir.

"Good," I said. "You're awake."

"Oh shit," the man said. "Shit. Listen, I didn't — "

"Shut up." I had the beginnings of a headache. I dug one of my knuckles into my forehead to cut off the pressure. "There are two ways that this can go down. You tell me what I want to know, and I'll kill you quick. You fuck around with me, and I'll kill you slow."

He swallowed. "I have a wife and three kids."

"You and every other fucking man in the world," I said. "I bet you also got a whore or two lined up on the side."

He didn't respond.

"That's what I thought." I folded my arms, knife in hand. "Who sent you?"

"I don't know his name."

"Describe him, then."

"Uh — tall. No, wait, medium height. Medium skin. Brown hair. I don't know, he was just ordinary, okay? Like someone you'd see on the street. Jesus, don't — "

I hit him. Once. Hard, on the temple. The description didn't sound like anyone I knew. Probably a grunt. They tended to get stuck with the dirty work. I'd know.

"You don't speak unless spoken to," I told him. "That's enough out of that question. They gave you orders?"

"Yes." He was sobbing now. I pretended not to notice.

"What were they?"

"To follow you."

"That's all?"

"And kill the girl, if I could."

"And if you couldn't?"

"Then to watch her, and record what I observed."

"What about me?"

"Same as the girl."

"But not killing?"

He looked away. "No."

I put my hands on either side of his head.

"What the fuck are you doing?" he yelped.

"Same thing as you," I said. "Only better."

It took a single twist. I felt the crack from his broken neck like the recoil from a gun. I let my hands fall to my sides and finished the beer. Put the empty can in my bag. I grabbed one of his socks and used it to swipe clean everything I'd touched.

He wore the same size shirt as me. I stripped off my sweat-stained one, now spattered with a few drops of blood, and slipped on one of his black shirts. I wondered if it was true what he'd said, about the wife and kids.

Armed and Dangerous by Nenia Campbell

It didn't really matter, either way.

Christina:

Michael was leaning back in the chair, wearing a t-shirt and the track pants. He had a half-empty bottle of cheap tequila with a Spanish label. He met my eyes over the neck of the bottle as he drank deeply.

"Morning," he said tonelessly.

"We need to talk," I informed him.

He laughed at me. It was a humorless, bitter laugh chased by another swallow of that vile tequila.

"You promised," I said. "You said we would talk about this today."

Michael waved the bottle at me. "What do you think this is for?"

He was daring me to react. I didn't give him what he was looking for. "You killed someone."

His eyes narrowed. I waited, watching the different emotions play over his face. He uncrossed his legs and ran his free hand along his temple. "Yeah, that sounds about right."

"How?"

"I made it so he wasn't alive anymore. Easy."

I threw down the sheets angrily, and got on my

knees. "How — did — you — *kill* — him?"

He was off that chair in an instant, and only a little unsteadily considering how much of the tequila he'd finished. I let out a startled yelp when he clapped a hand over my mouth.

"What are you thinking, shouting that? You want to get us both turned into the cops because you're sore at me for doing my job?"

I turned my head away, sliding out from beneath his palm. "How was it your job?"

Michael swore. "Because he was following us. Because he was going to *kill* you if he got you alone. So I snapped his neck." He was breathing hard. "There. Are you happy? I put both my hands around his throat and snapped his windpipe like a fucking wishbone. Is that what you wanted to hear?"

"Then you stole his gun," I said.

"I did it to *protect* you."

I paused.

"I need you alive. I need you breathing." He shook his head. "I need *you*."

"You're drunk."

"And you're fucking impossible," he growled. "You think I like this, coming back to you with news of a dead body like a fucking cat with a dead mouse? You think I expect you to be fucking proud of me? Fucker's kids are gonna grow up without a daddy. Hell, I'm not real proud of myself right now."

"So why did you do it?"

"To keep you safe," he repeated.

I sobbed in frustration. "*No.*"

"Yes. You're the only thing that matters right now." Michael, swaying a little over me, said, "You're trying to talk yourself into hating me when all I'm trying to do is keep you alive."

I wish it was that simple. I wish all I felt for you was hate. "That's not it. I feel something, and whatever it is, I feel too much of it, and it's driving me crazy. But I don't think it's hate — at least, not entirely. It'd be so much simpler if it was," I concluded miserably.

The silence stretched on for so long that I began to think he wasn't going to say anything else. "So, what, I'm supposed to take whatever crumbs you care to throw to me and be fucking grateful for it? Is that it? Grateful that not all you feel for me is fucking hate?"

"No!"

"Then what?"

"You can't just make me want you and then — " *refuse me.* That's what I had been about to say. I was about to tell him he didn't have a choice. " — expect me to let you threaten me, mock me, and treat me like crap. Just because you 'love' me. Because that's not love. That's something I want no part of."

"This doesn't come naturally to me, darlin. There's a reason we're having this conversation while I'm shit-faced."

"That's not healthy," I hissed.

He took another swig and tossed the bottle aside. I flinched, expecting a smash, but it must have landed on a pile of clothes because there was only silence.

"Okay," he said, planting his newly freed hand on the mattress. "I stopped. Now let me tell you what I think. I think *you* think that if you give in to what I want, and what I suspect *you* want, I'll make a killer and a whore out of you. You think I'll hurt you if you refuse."

I stopped flailing and fell back against the mattress. Was that it? It sounded accurate. "And?"

"Let me tell you something — killing one man doesn't necessarily make you a killer, just as fucking one man doesn't necessarily make you a whore. It's all about the choices you make down the road. Fate has the whip, but you're driving the pace as you pull the cart. *You* decide who you are and what you want.

Armed and Dangerous by Nenia Campbell

"But — once you decide, it's a helluva lot harder to go back. You get me?"

Yes, I got him.

"I'd like to know if I'm just wasting my time."

"No," I said, after a pause. "If you could prove that you respect me, and that you have respect for my limits, then yes. I...I think I could sleep with you."

"But do you want to fuck me?"

"What's the difference?"

"Not much sleeping going on in the latter." He gave one of his rare smiles; it made my heart hurt. The smile quickly disappeared. "You know I've killed before. What makes this time any different?"

"Because this time it was my fault," I whispered.

Michael tilted his head. "His boss sent him out here to kill you. Wouldn't that make him the killer?"

I blinked. "Maybe."

"Fuck yes, maybe. Listen. You spend your time worrying about who's at fault for what, you're going to drive yourself fucking crazy." He closed his eyes. "Just look at me. Drunk off my ass. Maybe it was my fault but it sure as fuck wasn't your fault. Don't ever blame yourself for the shit I do."

"Okay."

"Say it."

I swallowed hard. "I won't blame myself for the things you do."

"Close enough. Glad we had this talk." He stumbled out the door without looking back. Where on earth was he going? Quietly, I tiptoed after him, only to find the hallway empty. Downstairs, I heard a door close, and when I stepped outside into the chill night air of the desert I saw footsteps fading out into the sand, back to the sandstone caves.

He was sleeping in the desert darkness so that I could be alone.

I did not like this side of him. I did not like it at all. It made me want to care.

It made me want to love him.

Armed and Dangerous by Nenia Campbell

Chapter Nineteen

Disaster

Michael:

She asked herself why I thought feelings were so full of shit. This was precisely why. It seemed like they existed solely to keep you from getting what it was you wanted. An evolutionary clusterfuck.

I'd had it all planned out.

Out running errands — be back before noon.

I made a list of some of the things I like.

Check the ones you're interested in, underline

any maybes, and cross off your no's. I'm going

to do to of the things on that list to you when

I get back — your choice. Surprise me.

-M

That all seemed cheap now. She didn't deserve cheap.

Christina was still asleep when I got back. I tore my eyes away from her and stole into the bathroom to wash off the grit. The cold shower did nothing, they never do, but the time alone gave me a moment to recoup and clear my head.

She associated loss of control with sex. For her,

they were inextricably linked. Part of that — no, most of it — was my fault.

After last night, I could hardly look at her, let alone fuck her. Not knowing what I did.

I pulled on the sweatpants and shirt I'd brought in with me so she wouldn't have to see me change. Not while she was still so rattled. Beads of perspiration welled up along my spine.

What am I going to do with her?

The obvious answer was, nothing.

Armed and Dangerous by Nenia Campbell

Chapter Twenty
Travel

Christina:

We left early, before the desert had completely thawed out from the comparatively cold night air. It was a whirlwind of packing and chaos, checking and double-checking luggage. I scarcely remember what was said. We didn't say much, and both of us avoided looking at the unmade bed.

I felt...oh, terrible isn't even enough to describe how I felt. Not just ashamed, though that was part of it, too. This feeling went deeper than shame; it was powerlessness, paralysis, cause from an inner-battle so forceful that it sundered all control. Because that was what this came down to in the end.

Control.

Michael was sorry for what he had done. He wanted to repent. But he still acted as if he thought he owned me. I couldn't have that.

The bus stop was on the edge of the town proper. As luck would have it, the small town was on the route of *Las Jardineras Laboratory*, which had a sister lab in San Jose. We were able to snag last-minute seats on the commuter line.

It took an hour for the bus to arrive. We sat near

the front on scratchy seats that made the backs of my legs itch. Michael sat in silence in the seat beside me; he could have been chiseled out of some very disapproving stone.

I leaned back, keeping my legs swept to the side so our thighs wouldn't touch, and watched the desert scenery pass by on the other side of the glass. Periodically, I glanced over at Michael, hoping he would thaw.

He didn't. He stared straight ahead. His jaw was clenched, as if he didn't trust himself to speak.

I supposed I shouldn't blame him for being angry about me sending out the mixed signals I had. Only I hadn't meant to. I wasn't trying to be manipulative or anything like that.

And he had been sending out plenty of mixed signals of his own.

When I thought about it some more — and there was plenty of time to think, with Michael not talking and the estimated travel time hovering around twelve hours — I realized that maybe I wasn't entirely blameless.

I didn't want Michael as a gestalt, as a whole person. I wanted to be able to pick and choose. I wanted the side of him who liked to read, who could say such powerful things, who could kiss until I felt dizzy and who looked at me as if I were the only woman in the world.

That side was there, but it wasn't the only one. There were other sides to him. Terrifying, *dangerous* sides.

Sides that could kill.

With his body weighing down against mine and the musky, familiar scent of him invaded my nostrils, the situation became too overpowering.

It was one of those other sides that had slept with me, that one night on the boat. Those sides that frightened me, and had made me fear for my very life. Those sides had diminished, but they were still there. I could never be sure whether they wouldn't resurface when I least expected it.

On the same token, I didn't want him to follow through on what he said before, about not wanting to wait around forever for me to make a decision. I didn't want him to find another girl. Just the thought of him with another woman made me feel queasy.

I was stupid, so stupid. I deserved to be miserable if I was going to put myself through this.

As the bus traveled northeast the reddish-yellow of the Arizona sand yielded to reddish-brown earth peppered with tumbleweeds and tufts of crabgrass interspersed with ranks of hunchbacked Joshua trees standing sentry in the dusty sun. Tufts of chloris grew along the roadside, their seeds scattering like season when rustled by the wind.

The mountains were pretty too, when they finally appeared on the horizon. The bald, carved-out cliff faces looking out to the roadside, where huge hunks of volcanic rock had been scraped away by years of erosion, were shrouded demurely in veils of bluish haze.

I looked around the bus, and locked eyes with a creepy man in a suit. His smile was mangled, as if it had been put through a strainer first, and I turned away with a shudder. Adrian Callaghan had a smile like that. Superficial. Fake. A mask to conceal the horrors that swam beneath the surface.

I must have edged away because my elbow hit Michael in the side, and he swung around to look at me. "S-sorry," I said.

He shook his head and closed his eyes again.

I was sitting by the window, exposed to the sun, and the yellow beams covered me like a blanket woven from cobwebs and light. Warm, but intangible. Before long, Michael was shaking me awake.

Armed and Dangerous by Nenia Campbell

I yawned. "Are we there already?"

"No. Ten minute rest-stop." He was right. The bus was empty — I hadn't noticed. "Take a piss, buy some food, do whatever you need to do in ten minutes or less. They won't wait."

The bus had parked in a turnoff adjacent to the long stretch of freeway. We were in front of a slumping gray building calling itself "The Quick and Easy." It was just as tacky as the name suggested. Next to the convenience store were several Porta Potties that stank like a barnyard in the rain. The thought of the bus driving off with all my belongings made my decision faster than it might have been otherwise. I had to *go* and beggars couldn't be choosy.

I did, however, grab my purse which held my money, ID, knife, and pepper-spray.

The bathroom looked even more disgusting than it smelled on the inside. That was a first. I washed my hands for a third time before opening up the latch with a dubious piece of tissue.

It's still cleaner than Target Island.

I dropped the tissue. Memories of sewage-smelling beaches, of sweat and blood, and the bitter tang of death, all crashing down on me in a wave that threatened to drag me under and leave at the mercy of my tortuous incarceration.

What was my life becoming, that I had to resort to such comparisons to make myself feel good? It wasn't even working. I'd only reminded myself just how terrible the people pursuing us were.

I was so deep in thought, I thought I imagined the arm that ringed around my waist. And then I tasted the salty, meaty dampness of a man's spongy flesh as a hand clapped over my mouth.

Oh God — someone from the IMA?

"Hey there, *mamacita*."

I stiffened. No. It was that disgusting creep from the bus. The hand on my stomach snaked upward, towards my breasts, and I jerked forward with a yelp, causing my purse to smack against my side.

"I saw the way you were looking at me on the bus." His voice was as slimy and disgusting as the walls of the toilet. "Maybe your boyfriend ain't man enough to show you a good time, is that it?"

My purse. The pepper-spray. The knife.

His groping fingers left a snail-trail of dampness over my skin. I heard his breathing quicken. "You got yourself a pair of real nice titties. I'll give you a hundred bucks if you let me play with 'em while you suck me off."

Armed and Dangerous by Nenia Campbell

I grabbed the knife, and plunged it into his thigh. His grip on me tightened as he let loose a strangled scream, his dirty fingernails biting painfully into my skin. I twisted out of his grip and sprayed the pepper-spray into his eyes when he lowered his hand to the knife handle. He fell back into the Porta Potty. The door swung closed, muffling the resulting splash.

What did I just do?

I stared at my hand, speckled with a few drops of blood, and retched. Over and over, until I was coughing up green strands of bile. Then, shaking, I returned to the bus and waited for Michael, with an empty bladder, an empty stomach, and a heavy heart.

Michael:

Even after I'd bought $30 of crap from his piece-of-shit store, the owner still hemmed and hawed about letting me use his goddamn phone.

"It's a business call," I said. "It's important."

He folded his arms over his faded coveralls. "I'm afraid it's store policy."

I could tell he liked the sound of how official "policy" sounded, though I doubted a hick like him could give me a definition if he tried. "Please."

"It isn't an out-of-state number, is it?"

"No." Not that he'd know shit from Shinola.

"Well, all right," he said at last. "Though generally the phone is for paying customers only."

I eyed the paper bag he'd given me. *Just what the fuck does that make me then?* I said nothing. He was letting me use the phone. For that, I was willing to ignore him and his bullshit.

Kent picked up after several rings. "It's me." I eyed the owner, who gave no indication of budging an inch from his post.

"Can you talk?"

"No."

"Where are you, old boy?"

"So-Cal. Few miles north of Lancaster."

"So about eight hours away."

I snorted. "More like twelve. We're on a bus."

"You have her with you now?" he asked carefully.

Picking up on nuances was his specialty. I imagined they had entire seminars devoted to the subject at M16. "She can't go home, can't go back to school either. They left me at her house — they know where she lives."

"Poor girl."

A hint of accusation lay buried in those words. I could tell what he was thinking. This wasn't supposed to happen. She didn't belong in this world. But I'd dragged her back into it, kicking and screaming. I knew. I'd been thinking the same thing myself. All I said was, "Yeah."

"What are you going to do with her?"

"Well, I can't take her with me. Not if I'm going to have to deal with those assholes. Can't take her back to Oregon, either. Doesn't sound like things are very stable at the homestead."

I paused.

"Actually, I was thinking she might work for you. She has some valuable skill sets." Kent coughed delicately, pointedly. I pretended not to notice. "Bilingual, some basic knowledge of computer programming — we could use her as a translator or a coder. Either. Both."

"Have you discussed this with her?"

"No." I knew she wouldn't like it.

"Don't. She is too young, and far too impressionable. This line of work is not for her. She would hate it, and over time this would cause her to hate herself. Even if you don't put a gun in her hands, she will know that she is simply a means to that end."

"Fuck," I said softly. He was right. On both counts. "Well, what do you suggest?"

"I suggest you focus on arriving in San Francisco, safely and in one piece. I will ensure someone meets you at the location of your choosing. Let me know." He ended the call.

I handed the phone back to the store owner. It was good advice. Sound. Not what I wanted to hear. Good advice seldom is. "Thanks," I muttered.

"What are you, some kind of executive type?" He sounded hopeful now. *Trying to get out of your fucking rut?*

"No." I exited the store. Goddamn rednecks.

The bus driver was pacing outside the bus, stretching his legs while he made a phone call. Sounded like a wife. He gave me a short nod. I returned it with perfunctory courtesy, staying under the radar as I took a stretch myself.

Most of the passengers hadn't returned. The ten minutes were close to expiring so I assumed they were in the later stages of binging or purging in accordance with their needs. A greasy suit appeared from the Porta Potties. I'd noticed him glaring at me earlier on. Not one of ours. Far too conspicuous.

Smelled like shit, too.

Armed and Dangerous by Nenia Campbell

His eyes were red and he was clutching his leg. In his hand was a knife. That made me sit up and take notice. So did the bus driver. His face darkened. No civil nod for the suit. He said something, his other hand trailing to the walkie-talkie at his hip.

I watched the man say something else. The driver's forehead creased. He shook his head. The man tossed the knife into the grass and the driver picked up his walkie-talkie, speaking into it while the man presented him with some ID.

Well that wasn't good.

I looked closer. I recognized that tiny butter knife of a blade. Didn't Christina have a knife like that?

Oh, fuck. I ran onto the bus —

Thank you. Oh, thank fucking God.

She had her head leaned against the window. Her backpack was cradled in her arms, on her lap. There was a book beneath her folded hands, face-down. One of the ones I'd bought for her. Didn't look like she'd gotten very far. I watched her for a few seconds longer before rattling the plastic bag. "You all right?"

She peeled her face away from the window. Her cheek was red. I noticed her top was a little ripped, and there were similar marks on her breast.

I dropped into the seat beside her. "What the fuck

happened to you?"

"Nothing."

"Yeah? Then why does that guy look like he just got maced? That's your trick, isn't it?" At her pained expression I said, "Jesus, what did he do to you?" And then, "I'll fucking cut off his — "

"Don't."

"Don't?" I said. "He tried to assault you, and you expect me to just let him — "

"No. *I* took care of it. I stabbed him in the thigh with my knife. I think I nicked him in the, um, you know. In the balls."

My own junk shriveled in sympathy. I crossed my legs. "Yeah?" She nodded. I felt a little impressed, in spite of myself. "And what did you do after you went knife-happy on his nutsack?"

"I sprayed him in the face with the pepper-spray. He lost his balance and there was a splash — I think he fell into the toilet."

I couldn't help it. I laughed.

She jumped, startled.

"Shit attracts shit," I said, earning a shaky smile. "Good to know you can take care of yourself."

"Y-you're not mad?"

"At you? Fuck me. No. Him, yes, I'd like to carve him up like a Thanksgiving turkey for what he did to you. But you? No." I softened my tone. "You were amazing, darlin. You hungry?"

"Let me have the first-aid stuff first," she said. I watched her scrub her hands methodically with the rubbing alcohol. She dropped the used cotton-balls on the floor of the bus, and shoved everything back in the bag. "I can still feel his hands on me."

Fucker. I repressed the urge to look at him, and pulled up her shirt. She flinched a little. *Can she still feel my hands?* "I'm sure he can still feel your knife in him, *bebe*."

Christina looked up, and then away. For a moment, I could almost taste her lips. She was so close. I patted her cheek, letting my fingers linger where I longed to put my mouth. It felt like there was a spring in me coiled up, and ready to burst.

Goddammit.

This was just like what I went through every night. What she went through every time she met my eyes. What I'd done to her. What I might continue to do if I couldn't keep my distance. She didn't fucking deserve that. She didn't fucking deserve *me*.

I was a monster — we both were.

Armed and Dangerous by Nenia Campbell

I pulled away before I could do something stupid and gave her a bottle of soda and a bag of chips from the $30 phone call. She turned them over in her hands. "Fried onion puffs and pineapple soda? These don't look very healthy." She bit down on that sexy lower lip. "I don't suppose you have any fruit juice?"

I rifled through the bag and tossed her a greenish package that had a cartoon apple with a bucktoothed smile on the front. "Apple Rings," I said. "I'm sure there's some real apple buried somewhere real deep beneath all that sugar and ascorbic acid."

"Contains no fruit," she read from the label.

I laughed again as I tore open the bag of onion puffs and her expression softened just a shade as she gave me a shy smile that pulled all my internal strings taut. I wanted her to look at me like that all the time. "We should be in San Francisco in ten or twelve hours."

"Then what?"

My mouth was full. I chewed and swallowed before saying, "Guess we'll find out when we get there."

There was a long silence, and then I heard her say, hesitantly, "Michael?"

"What?"

"Thank you for being so...kind." I felt those gorgeous lips of hers brush against my stubbled cheek. "It means a lot."

"Don't thank me for giving you what you deserve." I could still remember how bright her eyes had looked filled with tears. How young it made her look. How that childish pettishness and pampered softness had made me want to tear her to pieces. How the power trip had gotten me halfway off.

Could that happen again?

"Don't," I said, sharply, shrugging off her arm, and her kiss. I saw that hurt again, the widening of those eyes, and felt like I might fucking fly apart.

Christina:

The bus coursed down the oak-spattered Tejon Pass. I ended up eating a few of the Apple Rings after all because I was starving, and they alleviated the popping in my ears.

Most of the passengers on the bus were older, in their late sixties and seventies if I had to guess. There was a middle-aged woman with a baby that kept crying and two little boys who kept kicking the seats in front of them; two teenagers I suspected were boyfriend and girlfriend and who looked far too young to be traveling alone; a black man wearing headphones who spent most of the trip asleep (and since he was the one stuck in front of the monster twins, I didn't blame him).

The creepy man was gone. He'd gotten off at the last stop. Nobody seemed sad to see him gone. The girl teenager even clapped, though her boyfriend stopped her with a scowl. *Pig*, I thought.

I shoved the book in my backpack and adjusted the neck of my shirt. Michael had been asleep for the last hour or so. His breathing was slow and even. The rise and fall of his chest was as constant as a metronome.

Looking at his slack face made me want to sleep, too, but at least one of us had better stay awake and I'd slept more than my fair share.

God, I was so tired. I reached over and snatched an energy drink from his pack, wincing at the fizz that sputtered out when I popped the can. Liquid foamed out and I held it away from me, over the floor, so my clothes wouldn't get all sticky.

At the sound, Michael jolted awake. The sleep cleared from his eyes as he assumed a ready stance.

"Sorry," I said, holding up the can in what looked like an awkward toast, "It's just me."

"Don't do that."

"Do what?"

Michael muttered something incomprehensible and leaned back against the seat, stretching his legs out as far as the seat would allow.

Seconds later, he was asleep again.

Armed and Dangerous by Nenia Campbell

Chapter Twenty-One
Fatality

Michael:

The bus dropped us off in San Jose. About goddamn time, too. I've never been a big fan of public transport. Too much hassle. Too much time spent in enclosed spaces. Too easy to find yourself trapped.

After a quick and inexpensive lunch at a Korean deli we made our way to the crowded BART terminal. It wasn't peak rush hour, but in a city this big there was bound to be some foot traffic at all hours. Luckily, the tickets weren't as expensive as I'd feared, though between the BART tickets, the bus tickets, the *kimbap*, and the shit I'd bought at the rest-stop, we had depleted most of our cash.

One-way SJ—SF ticket in hand, I slid the blue card into the machine and stepped through the turnstile. The card appeared through a slot on the other side of the partition. I yanked it out, only to see Christina having some trouble.

I sighed. Dammit. "Don't pull it out," I instructed. "It's not a scanner. Feed the card into the thing, *then* walk through. It's not fucking rocket science."

"Oh," she said, flushing unhappily.

I took her by the wrist. "It's fine. Come on. Help

me find where we board. We're looking for the westbound train."

The trains came far more quickly, and in greater numbers, than the bus had. We only had to wait about five minutes before one of the bullet-shaped trains glided up on the rails. Then we stepped over the yellow safety line and into the car. I tried not to read any symbolism in that.

There were two empty seats towards the rear. That pleased me. Nobody would look back there. Most people were too focused on the automatic doors, and getting off at the right stops. I caught Christina's eye and nodded at the seats, making sure she got in first. Old habits die hard.

When I got stressed, I relied on instinct. It was as automatic as breathing, or taking a shit. All this sitting around in one place was putting me on edge. When Christina had popped the lid on that can of soda, it was as if she had pulled a gun at my head.

The BART ride took about forty minutes and the terminal was right in the heart of the city. A gush of cold air breezed down the steps and Christina tugged her sweatshirt on, staring dubiously at the darkened sky. "Is it going to rain?"

"Nah. It's just fog coming inland from the bay."

Armed and Dangerous by Nenia Campbell

Navigating through the crush of people gave me something to focus on. I let my thoughts narrow to one goal. Find Kent. Find a phone to call Kent.

"Are you hungry?"

"*Yes*."

Our best bet was a takeout place that made deliveries. Somewhere with a company phone with an answering machine, that got a lot of customers.

I spotted a frozen yogurt place. A sign in the window said they did catering. Bingo. "How do you feel about ice cream?"

Her face fell. "Um, okay, I guess."

"Good. Buy yourself something. I'll only be a minute."

While Christina disappeared into the restroom, I located the manager. I dredged up the important business call excuse, but this time I embellished it a little with a stolen cellphone. She was quite sympathetic. Must have had to deal with that crap from all the idiot tourists.

I punched the extension number to dial out and then Kent's number. "I'm in the foggy city," I said.

"You're only arriving just now?"

He might as well have told me outright that I was

losing my edge. My smile faded. "We took the BART. I figured it'd be safer."

Harder to trace, in any case. Certainly better than taking a cab or renting a car. I resented having to explain myself. Kent knew my methods.

"I won't bother asking if you paid in cash."

"What do you take me for?"

"Where are you now?"

I told him.

"I'm familiar with them. Quaint little place. Good ice cream."

"Frozen yogurt."

"They have both." I could hear the shrug. "I'll send over a friend of mine who owes me a favor. Do you have a location in mind for the pick-up?"

We ended up agreeing on a Starbucks near the shopping mall. Close enough that we could get there quickly. Far enough away that the frozen yogurt store owners wouldn't be able to give a description of the giveaway car, assuming we were even traced that far.

I collected Christina from the table she was sitting at. She had a small bottle of juice. She offered me a sip. I declined; I didn't want the taste of her in my mouth. Not now. I couldn't.

Armed and Dangerous by Nenia Campbell

It was a cold, cloudy day. Quite a contrast from the hundred-and-ten-degree heat of the Arizona desert. The bay-chilled weather felt a lot like a freezer in comparison.

I used the last of our money to buy a drink of my own while we waited for Kent's contact. The coffee didn't do much. I've had so much shit in my system at one time or another that nothing does, not anymore.

Not unless it's the hard stuff.

While I drank the triple-shot espresso, it occurred to me that this was one of the riskiest gambles I'd ever taken, going into fucking No-Man's-Land without money or backup. It went against all my training. Most of what I found myself doing these days did.

I glanced at Christina. Did a double-take. "What the fuck are you drinking?"

"Aloe juice."

Like the skin lotion?

"It's healthy."

"I'll bet..." Where the hell was Kent's contact? We'd been sitting here for at least fifteen minutes. Had something gone wrong? Kent was nothing if not timely. "You see anyone looks like they're waiting?"

"That woman is staring at us."

Armed and Dangerous by Nenia Campbell

"What? Where?"

"Over there, in the gray."

I glanced over in the direction she indicated. There was a black woman sitting alone in one of the corner tables. Her skin was that dark black that looks blue in some lights, as it did now in the silver reflection of the window. The formal pantsuit was at odds with her shaved head and hoop earrings. Christina was right; she was staring. And now, thanks to her lack of subtlety, she was coming over.

I'd never seen her before. Shit. She could have been Kent's, but she could just as well have been an agent. I reached for the backpack that held my gun.

"Michael?"

She had a soft accent. African. Probably central. I wasn't sure. I relaxed my grip on the backpack's handle a little. "Who the hell are you?"

"Kent sent me."

"Who?"

She extended a slim hand to me. Her nails were unpainted, manicured. "Angelica Connors. He said you would say that. He also said to ask if you remember this: You once chased after an assignment after getting shot and sustaining a potentially fatal bullet wound. *After* nearly drowning. *After* being tied up and locked in the trunk of — "

"Okay, okay." I raised my hand to shut her up. She was Kent's, all right. Now that I knew that, I wasn't sure whether to laugh or pop an aspirin. "Still spreading that bullshit about me around like toast at teatime?"

When she smiled she revealed very white teeth. "He never stopped — unlike his smoking habit."

"Quit again, has he?"

"Yes."

"What's he on now? Nicotine patches?"

"Junk food." She looked at the both of us. "I suggest bringing an offering of Corn Nuts, so he does not toss you out on your asses."

She laughed, though whether at the phrase or the idea I wasn't sure. It was a nice laugh. She probably wasn't on contract. Looked younger than I'd guessed, too.

I was also surprised that she claimed to own the car: a surprising luxury for the city, and further proof that she probably wasn't a criminal. You had to register vehicles and getting fake IDs were a bitch if you were strapped for cash and didn't know the right people. I said as much, probing for more information, and she answered evasively, "I commute."

Armed and Dangerous by Nenia Campbell

The parking meter for her space was just about to run out. That meant she had been waiting here for a while. At least fifteen minutes from the look of it. Well before I'd called Kent. I kicked myself for failing to scan the parked cars. What a shit impression I was leaving.

"I like your accent," said Christina, while I was busy mulling that over. "Where are you from?"

Angelica laughed. "Michael, you have not told her such questions simply are not asked in your line of work?"

"Oh, I've tried. But Christina here has a hearing problem when it comes to following orders — 'specially when they come from me."

To Christina she said, "I am Sudanese."

"When did you come to the States?"

She just couldn't take a hint.

"I came here along with several others from my village in Sudan to receive a full scholarship to Stanford for my achievements. In school, I majored in Chemical Engineering. I am very lucky to be where I am now."

It was a nice elevator speech. I bet it was a pretty close approximation of the one she'd given Kent when he'd asked her why she wanted to work for him.

"Chemical Engineering? Does that mean you design weapons?"

Oh, for fuck's sake. "*Christina.*"

"Not precisely." Angelica let the subject drop, swerving to avoid a Mercedes that immediately began laying on the horn.

Well played. She could have been in Information. They could be pleasant people. Had to be, to get anything out of the people whom they were being paid to exploit.

On the other hand, that would be a waste of a perfectly good Engineering degree. Those were hard to come by, and they generally reverted to the soft sciences for their psychobabble bullshit, though I supposed it was possible she was also doing all that on the side....

Better not to know.

Angelica parked in front of a cluster of tall office buildings. Their one-way mirrored surfaces reflected the sky, while revealing nothing of their interiors.

Because all the parking spaces were taken, Angelica stopped in the middle of the road. Angry honking blared at us from behind. The fucking Mercedes again, with friends. I'd have given them the finger, but Angelica just raised her voice a little to make herself heard over the noise.

"Take the elevator up to the eleventh floor. Number eleven-forty-five is the room. He will be expecting you."

"Hopefully he'll be the only one."

"Pardon?"

"I've had my fill of surprises for the day." I shot Christina a look. She glanced away. Angelica got back into her car and drove. The line of blocked cars followed, still honking.

"Don't ask him any questions," I said to Christina. "Leave all the talking to me. If you ask people what they do in my line of work, they're liable to take it as a threat — or an interrogation. Same result, either way. Fortunately for you, Angelina works for a friend. She knows you're a civ."

"I'm sorry."

"You should be."

"But I didn't *know*."

"That's not good enough."

But it wasn't her nosiness I was thinking about. It was that night in bed when she had all but begged me to fuck her, and then turned around and started crying. These fucking mixed messages. Emotional blackmail. That's what this was.

Christina was silent all the way up to the elevator. Room 1145 was set up like a delivery office, replete with waiting room front and plenty of magazines. All of them were current and up to date.

The receptionist pulled back the sliding glass door. "Can I help you?" She was wearing an 80s-print dress. Wire-rim glasses. Curly, nondescript hair. Very convincing.

"Michael. I'm expected."

"Come right in — sorry, I'm afraid you'll have to wait." This latter was directed to Christina. She looked at me. I appreciated that, but shook my head.

"Do what she says. I won't be long."

Christina:

I looked at the receptionist. She hadn't closed the window yet. I thought her face looked a little smug. Maybe that was my own bitterness manifesting itself in the face of somebody else.

"Will you keep an eye on this?" I nodded at my pack.

"This office assumes no responsibility for lost or

unsupervised items left on the premises. If you — "

"Never mind." I packed my ID, the last of my change. Part of me hoped that the snotty receptionist would take offense at the implication that I thought she might steal something.

There was a vending machine down the hall but it was out of order. I thought I *had* smelled something food-like on the way up, though. Surely they wouldn't keep all these business people locked up in a building with no food. Not with parking being what it was. Not if they didn't want a mutiny on their hands. Too bad I hadn't asked about a cafe.

Michael had said to stay in the waiting room. He would be angry if he came out and found me missing.

On the other hand, he did have a lot to sort out. He needed a new ID, money, and weapons. I had at least fifteen or twenty minutes. This beat waiting around in the lobby for him like a dog under the eye of the hateful receptionist.

He had been *so* hurtfully, cruelly dismissive, to the point where I wondered if all that talk about letting me have my choice had just been another attempt to sleep with me. He was a good liar. A good person? Not so much.

I didn't want him to think that I was just going to

roll over and do everything he told me to do — no more than I did already. I didn't want to be that kind of girl. But I was beginning to understand that not every girl has a choice in the matter, not entirely. It was a revelation.

It was depressing.

The elevator doors opened with a beep. I walked with my head down, trying to look as if I belonged. With my shorts, boots, and baggy sweatshirt, I felt like a desert explorer. Hardly appropriate.

The upside to being in the city was that there were people outside wearing far stranger ensembles. I guess the city folk were used to weirdos. I didn't even have to put the theory to the test; the corridor was empty. I could hear voices coming from the depths of the various closed doors, though, which reinforced my suspicion that this was really the skyscraper equivalent of an office park.

Two voices separated from the buzz, sharpening in focus. I found myself listening without meaning to. Habit, I suppose. One I hadn't acquired until meeting Michael.

Maybe one of the men would bring up the cafe and I could follow them. If they sounded nice, I might even ask them for directions.

" — have to be around here somewhere."

"This building has thirty-two stories." The second voice was impatient, frustrated. "Can you imagine how many rooms this place has?"

I silently agreed. This place was a nightmare. Not as bad as the mind-bogglingly claustrophobic underground base that the IMA had in Oregon. At least here there were windows, and the doors were wood — not steel.

Maybe they're looking for the cafe.

I started to move out of my hiding place, to ask if they had any idea where it could be — because I could *smell* that coffee and it was reminding me that I hadn't slept well for several days now — when I heard the other man say, "Move upstairs, then. They couldn't have gotten far."

They?

As in, Michael and I?

No, it couldn't be. We just got here.

"According to this, they haven't moved. Find out which of the offices are open in that section of the building. I'll search upstairs. Call me as soon as you figure it out."

Shit. *Shit.* That did not sound good at all.

Armed and Dangerous by Nenia Campbell

I dove back into the elevator and slammed the button for the eleventh floor. The voices grew louder as they rounded the corner. "You take the stairs, I'll take the — *hey*, could you hold the door, please?"

Oh, yeah, sure. How about no?

I pressed "door close." I heard a curse as the door slammed shut seconds before he reached it. "The fuck—"

He would have done worse if he knew who you are.

I hoped he hadn't seen me, then.

Does he have a gun?

It occurred to me that the man might be watching the elevator to see where I got off. He'd sounded pissed for the door bit, regardless of what suspicions he may have entertained. Just in case, I stuck my foot in the door to keep the sensors from closing it, and palmed the buttons for all thirty-two floors. The elevator would stop at each one.

The receptionist looked up briefly when she heard the door open. Then back down again when she realized it was only me. I rapped on the frosted window until she opened up and said, shortly, "what?"

"Let me in." I was short of breath.

"You don't have clearance."

Armed and Dangerous by Nenia Campbell

"It's an emergency," I said.

"Please. I need to speak to Michael."

"I can't let you in. If it is truly an emergency, I can page him. What's the message?"

"Tell him *they're* here. They him that they've followed us. He'll know what that means." She stared at me, still holding the phone. "What are you waiting for? Tell him! Now! Right now!"

She gave me a startled look. Hung up the phone. I thought she was going to let me in, too, but then I heard a door open and close further on down the hall. Muffled, urgent conversation. The reception door swung open.

"Are you sure?" Michael had both backpacks and a tight expression. The receptionist was at his heels.

"Yes."

His eyes narrowed. "What were you doing downstairs? I told you to wait here. In the *waiting* room."

"If I had waited, you wouldn't know we were being followed in the first place."

He stepped out of the door frame. "I don't understand it. I made damn sure not to leave a paper trail. Cash only, everything strictly low-tech. There was no way they could have — "

A series of changes passed over his face, each in quick succession to the other, and he looked at me in a way I didn't like. "You had an encounter with the Sniper, didn't you? Before?"

"Encounter? He attacked me at school — but I didn't tell him anything. And that was weeks ago."

"Did you bring anything with you that you had on when you saw him last?"

I stared at him blankly.

"Jewelry. Clothing. Anything like that. Anything he could have come into contact with if he touched you."

If he touched *me?* "He didn't — "

Wait, why was I defending myself to Michael? After the way he had treated me? I shook my head emphatically. "No. He didn't do anything like that. Touch me, I mean. Just my — "

We both looked at my backpack at the same time.

"Is that the one you use for school?" he asked in a dangerous voice. At my silence, he let out a frustrated growl. "You fucking idiot. *Fuck* me."

"How was I supposed to know? You didn't say anything. I figured you would have said something if it wasn't okay."

Armed and Dangerous by Nenia Campbell

I watched him unzip the pouches with a sinking heart. He went through the smaller side pockets. Pockets I hadn't gone through personally because they couldn't hold enough for me to consider them useful.

Michael sucked in a breath and let out another curse. He stormed away to one of the windows as the receptionist and I looked on. I saw him cock back his arm and hurl something small and metal outside. It winked briefly in the sun before plunging down eleven stories below.

"We need to get out of here."

One look at his face kept me from saying anything in response. I had screwed up. Big time.

Just when I thought things couldn't get any worse the floor beneath us rumbled, sending us both to our knees. With a series of "fucks" Michael yanked me out of the door and down the hall.

"Earthquake?" I whimpered.

"Bomb," he snapped back.

I was sorry I had asked.

There was another explosion. The elevator doors dinged. I started towards them and Michael yanked me back as a fireball burst out of the open doors, blasting into the office across from them and setting that whole wall ablaze. The smoke alarms went off with a scream, dousing us in cold, foul-smelling water.

"Stairs." He shouted to be heard over the shrill alarm as we raced for the emergency stairwell.

Other people were coming out of their offices, too, some of them screaming and shouting, others crying or speaking desperately into their cell phones.

The alarm was shrill and loud in the echoey corridor. "What about your contact?" I asked. "Kent." The blue-white lights rendered my peripheral vision fuzzy and blurred. I felt faint. "Is he okay?"

"Keep running."

"Michael — "

The door slammed open. People raced through, disregarding years' worth of fire drills as they shoved past us to run for their lives. Over the sound of panicked breathing, sobbing, and desperate calls for help, I heard one of the men from before.

"Michael!" I yelped.

"Goddamn it. Not *now*."

"They're shooting at us!"

"Of course they are." He yanked me down. "Jesus *fucking* Christ."

Armed and Dangerous by Nenia Campbell

A bullet ricocheted off the stone with a loud crack, slamming into the body of a man nearby. He went down clutching at his neck, spurting blood on the floor and wall.

"Oh my God, someone's got a gun!" a woman's voice screamed, which set off a whole chain reaction of panic.

The gunmen had followed us here because of me. The two men were shooting at us because of me — because I hadn't been smart enough to check my own bag. All these lives were endangered because of *me*.

I felt bad, terrible. I felt worse for not feeling what I considered to be bad enough. Mostly, I just felt numb. That was the shock. I was sure the pain would come later.

Angelica's car was across the street. Out of the way of the emergency vehicles zooming towards us, with their sirens like a high-pitched death knell. She rolled down the window. "Get in. Get in — *hurry.*"

Armed and Dangerous by Nenia Campbell

Chapter Twenty-Two

Exposure

Michael:

Angelica dropped us off at a hotel. Nice one, view of the city and the piers. Looked expensive as hell.

She saw my look. "You have a reservation. Kent wired you some money before he — " She cleared her throat. "He wired you some money from your Swiss accounts."

"Great."

She ushered Christina ahead. Then she took one of my hands in both of hers. "I am so sorry. You were like a son to him." How would that even compare? I'd never had a father, and he'd never had a son. "Do not blame yourself."

"At least it wasn't the cigarettes that killed him."

"Yes," she said softly. "There is that."

"He'd have wanted to go out with a bang."

"I'm sorry," she said. I pulled away. She let her hands fall to her sides. "Be careful."

"Yeah. You, too."

I walked up the concrete ramp and into the opulent lobby, clutching the room key. Her face was blackened with soot from the explosion. I imagined I looked far worse.

"What floor?"

"First."

Well, that was something.

Christina:

Michael went straight for the drinks cabinet.

I protested. "You shouldn't be drinking right now."

"I can't think of a better time," he snapped. "Move."

I stepped out of the way, watching helplessly as he downed two shots of scotch in a row as if they were water. Then he reached for a third. I thought of alcohol poisoning and knocked it out his hand. "Don't do that!"

The glass smashed. So did the expression on his face; it rendered his expression as jagged and deadly as a broken bottle. I backed away from him but he walked right past me to the bed and let his body collapse.

"Michael, please. Don't do this."

"Fuck off," was his muffled response.

"I'm sorry," I whispered. "I'm so, so sorry."

Armed and Dangerous by Nenia Campbell

Michael threw his arm over his eyes and didn't respond. I saw his other hand clench into a fist, making the veins in his wrist pop out like steel cables beneath the skin. He blamed me for Kent's death — and maybe himself, too. You didn't act this self-destructive if you didn't also hate yourself.

I hesitated, torn between approaching him and leaving him alone. People were blowing up entire buildings trying to kill us, so it wasn't as if I had anywhere else to go.

He was human, even if he didn't act like it at times. Those fleeting glimpses of humanity just made his condition all the more pitiable. He was like one of those children psychologists found, abandoned and left in the woods, who had somehow managed to survive against all odds without language, without comfort, without love.

I put my hand on his arm. He shrugged me off. I got on the bed and put both hands on both his shoulders, leaning over him in such a way that it was impossible to ignore me.

"Get off me." He sounded genuinely angry. "I told you to fucking go away."

"I am not leaving you alone like this."

"I could make you." His voice sent a chill through

me, daggers of emotion lancing through every word. "Do you want me to do that? Do you want me to make you? We both know I could."

I lowered my hands, regarding him for a moment. He was scaring me. I was shaking. I knew he could feel it; I couldn't even keep my hands steady.

"You wouldn't hurt me."

"Go," he said, in those same even tones. "Now."

No. I sucked in a breath and wrapped my arms around him, pressing my face against his chest. As much to protect myself as to comfort him. He stiffened.

Had I made a terrible mistake?

His heart was pounding against my cheekbone. He squeezed me to him, startling me, his grip so tight that it hurt. I felt the weight of his chin on my head.

I ran my fingers beneath his chin and down his neck the way one might pet a cat. His unshaved beard scraped and pricked at my fingers, the skin beneath waxy and rough. Not at all like my own skin. Michael seemed to find my touch relaxing, and, like a cat, he tipped his head back.

When my hand was over his heart I stopped and looked up at him. His cheeks were wet. It took me a moment to process that. He was crying. *Michael* was *crying.*

"It's okay," I said hesitantly. I felt like I was walking along the edge of a cliff. I wasn't prepared for situations like these. "I-it's going to be okay." I kissed him softly on the cheek. He closed his eyes and turned away, making a noise of impatience. But he didn't move and neither did I.

We lay there for a while. The only sound was our commingled breathing, and the incessant baseline of his heart against my ear. The tightness of his arm and the quickness of his pulse were the only signs he hadn't drifted off to sleep; he was very still. He smelled like salt and fire and that strange, musky scent that was inherently his.

"That's the first rule." I jolted, not expecting him to say anything. Hearing it come so calmly from his broken face was like being pierced with a lancet. "Don't fucking get attached."

It took me a moment to respond. "That's no way to live, Michael."

"It's a worse way to die."

"No — "

"I've told you before. Emotions get people killed. Feelings make people stupid. Forming attachments means more fuel to add to the fire when somebody wants to see you burn. I knew that and still, I made exceptions."

"You can't help caring about those who care about you," I said uncertainly.

Michael shook his head. "If I hadn't fucking asked him for help, if he hadn't met up with us, he might still — "

He went quiet for several minutes.

"It was wrong to blame you. For the building. And the GPS. I knew what to look for. You didn't. I keep forgetting that." I felt his breath stir the hair on my neck. "I'm not used to caring. I'd seen it so often on the other end, but I'd never realized. I never knew…how much it hurt."

I was awed. He had revealed fleeting glimpses of himself before, but never anything like this. I also knew instinctively that if I showed the slightest hint of satisfaction or smugness in his pain, I'd lose him. Forever.

"Feeling things is human nature," I said carefully. "What's *stupid* is to bottle up all that stuff inside of you until you crack from the pressure."

"Did you just call me stupid?"

I ignored him. "You're like a savant, in a way. An emotional savant. You can do all these amazing things, but you're missing something. Something vital you had to give up in exchange for who you are now."

"Does something like that even exist?" He snorted. "All right, I'll bite. What did I give up? What am I missing?"

I tapped his chest. "Your heart."

"No." He lapsed into another silence. He also didn't push me away, and his other hand covered mine, keeping me against his heartbeat. "That might have been true once," he said, startling me. "For the longest time, I couldn't feel a thing. I was living numb. But not now."

"Really?"

"I feel you." He slid his hands beneath the hem of my shirt, locking them over my stomach. "Soft, warm, alive. Beautiful. Brave." His head shifted, tilting so he could look at me. "When I think about it I'd do almost anything to keep you breathing. So I try not to. *You are my beating heart, Christina Parker. I wasn't truly living until I met you, and if you were to slit my throat right now I wouldn't lift a finger to stop you, and I'd die a better man because of it.*"

"Oh, Michael."

"What?"

Armed and Dangerous by Nenia Campbell

"You're making me feel depressed."

"I won't talk then," he said. "I'll just hold you."

So we stayed like that, until his chest stopped its painful hitching and the exhaustion outweighed the pain.

There, in the warm darkness, I drifted half-conscious. Just before I fell asleep, I thought I heard a voice — his voice — saying, *Don't take her away from me. Don't make me watch her fucking die.*

Please.

Armed and Dangerous by Nenia Campbell

Chapter Twenty-Three
Revelation

Michael:

There's a reason people find "mob rule" so terrifying, and it isn't because they've watched *The Godfather* too many fucking times. It's because justice is absent. When nobody is looking out for you, you're the one who's gotta do all the looking. Most people aren't equipped for that.

Me, I get by.

I downed a shot of scotch and picked up the hotel phone. *It comes to this.* Liquid courage, my ass. The only thing that comes out in liquid form is cowardice — and fear. He picked up on the first ring. "You fucking prick."

"Hello, Michael." He sounded distracted. "Back from the grave again, I see."

"You would know." I kept my voice low, so I wouldn't wake Christina. "You tried to put me there."

"I'm as surprised as you are."

"Bullshit."

"Aye, well, perhaps not so surprised. They do say vermin are hard to kill. That's what I thought when I heard you were killed in action in London. I found it odd nobody stepped forward to claim the bounty on your head."

"You didn't know."

"I figured you could have lost your touch. You're getting old, boy. Slow. Stupid."

"Are you saying you didn't betray me to the BN?"

"Right in the thick of things?"

"Somebody did," I snapped. "Why not you?"

"You were doing good work for me — and for starters, you're still alive. If I were well and truly after you, you wouldn't be." He spoke with quiet confidence.

I didn't want to believe him, but it made sense. A lot of what had happened so far *had* mostly been left to chance. The phencyclidine wouldn't kill me. There was no guarantee either that I'd kill Christina while I was on it.

Callaghan was a professional. He didn't have to leave things to chance. That was the move of a rank amateur.

The explosion in the office building hadn't been his style, either. He knew how to rig up a bomb and wouldn't blink about taking out a handful of civilian casualties, but now that the IMA was going global he had vested interests in keeping things quiet. Massive explosions in the middle of a major city didn't fit in with that.

Christ, I was starting to believe the bastard.

"If you didn't do it," I said to myself, "who did?"

"That's the million dollar question, isn't it?"

I remembered the notebook Kent had presented me with, all my enemies color-coded according to means and threat. A lump formed in my throat. "Do you know anyone who goes by the handle of Villanueva?"

My voice was louder than I intended. Christina stirred and sat up. She looked at me, then at the phone.

"Someone who works at the IMA," I clarified.

Callaghan laughed at that. Laughed long and hard.

"The fuck is so funny?"

"I think I know who our ratty little friend is, Michael Boutilier. Yes. It all makes sense now."

"Tell me who it is."

"I think I'd rather you puzzle it out yourself."

I felt something punch into my chest. Christina screamed. I looked to the hotel door—it was open. Silently, which meant they'd had a key, or picked the lock. A man with a portable tranq gun was standing there, loading for a second shot.

Christina:

It was like a nightmare. Huge, empty room. Cold, gray floors. The smell of cardboard and chemicals gave the air an acrid, stale tang.

Something was pressed up against my back, firm but yielding. It moved and I let out a yelp. The something hard groaned. "Christina?"

"Michael?"

"Yeah."

"Where are we?"

"I don't know."

I stared at the dull concrete walls. It reminded me of the warehouse in the video that Adrian had shown me — the one of Michael torturing and killing that man. I swallowed. "They're going to kill us, aren't they?"

"Probably. Eventually."

A door opened. Footsteps echoed on the floors — loud echoes, like the kind you get from fancy, hard-soled shoes. "We meet again, Mr. Boutilier." The words were spoken in a British accent. I twisted around but couldn't see him.

"Hawk," he said tightly.

"I see you've brought a friend this time." He moved, stepping into my periphery. Some old guy. He was studying me. "The hostage, I presume," he said, folding his arms. "Not quite as pretty as I'd imagined. Certainly not worth throwing one's life away for."

"Don't talk about her like she's a fucking object."

The door creaked open. A second set of footsteps entered the room. "I would like to speak to the prisoners alone, if you would be so kind."

"Of course, Mr. Villanueva. You have been most forthcoming. It would be our pleasure."

Michael twitched.

"I can assure you, the pleasure was all mine."

I'd have known that voice anywhere.

The moment I met that dark gaze, I felt my heart stop in my chest.

The Sniper was the Villanueva Michael had been so concerned about?

All this time, it had been the Sniper following us and leaving threats. Not Adrian. Not the BN. "*Michael*. It's the Sniper."

Armed and Dangerous by Nenia Campbell

"Yes, it is me."

"You're Spanish?"

"For the moment, it would seem."

I felt Michael strain against the rope. "Traitor. You're the one who's been following us all this time?"

"Took you long enough to figure out."

"And the helicopter?"

"Yes, the BN are surprisingly generous with their limited funds. To a fault, it would seem. But in this case, their weakness was to be my strength."

"You turned me into the BN. You convinced them to fucking shoot me up."

"I had hoped you would kill the girl. Or that you would force her to kill you — all in self-defense, of course. That plan was not fail-safe in any sense of the word, but the damage sustained would have been adequate payback for the bullet — " he walked over to me " — and for the mace."

"You set off the bomb, too?"

"Ah, yes, I heard about your friend, Michael. The esteemed ex-agent from M16. I suppose it is true what they say, that smoking kills."

"Why the *fuck* did you do that? He didn't do shit to you. None of the people in that building did."

"All in a day's work, Michael. You understood that once. But not anymore it would seem. You truly have gone soft. You never used to mind a little collateral damage — it was a necessary damage."

"You're not getting paid for this. I *know*. Callaghan told me about your attempt to get extra credit. So I'll ask you again — *why*?"

The Sniper snorted. "Because I do not like you."

"I've got news for you. Adrian Callaghan doesn't like other people fucking calling the shots."

"I believe that in your case Mr. Callaghan would be willing to make an exception. It is my firm belief that the world would be a better place without you in it."

"Fucking bullshit. You don't give a shit about any of that; you'd see the world burn if they paid you enough."

"Spoken like a true mercenary."

"Just like they paid you to fuck with me."

"Well, yes," the Sniper said. "I suppose it was too tempting an opportunity to pass up." He circled around the chair again, until he was standing in front of me again. "I do not care for you, either, my dear. At least your death will be quick. You can consider that my favor to you."

I spat at him. The gob of spit hit him right in the eye and made him wince.

My fleeting sense of satisfaction didn't last long. He hit me — hard. The slap echoed off the floors of the empty warehouse. It felt like hundreds of needles were pricking at my cheek.

"Don't you fucking touch her, you son of a bitch. Don't take this out on her. It's me you want."

"Indeed." The Sniper touched a knife at his belt. "I haven't forgotten about you, Michael."

"No," I said. "What are you doing? Don't hurt him!"

I felt his body tense; a spasm went through him, betraying his pain. "Suits you, actually. Now everyone will know you for what you are. Better suited to the gutters and the streets."

"Fuck," Michael said hoarsely. "*Fuck.*"

"What did he do? Are you okay?"

"Goddammit. I'll kill him — "

"So nice to see you again. Hopefully it will be the last."

The British man must have been waiting somewhere nearby, watching, because I heard the door open again as the Sniper approached the exit.

"Have you said all that needed to be said?" he asked.

"Yes."

"What are you doing?" Michael snarled. "Are you fucking blind? You can't let him go. This man works for the IMA. He's Adrian Callaghan's right-hand man — he was sent here to betray you."

"I was under the impression that was your position."

"I wasn't a traitor until I was cast into the role, and that wasn't by choice. I was framed then, and I was framed now. This asshole is one of their riflemen. He—"

"Mr. Villanueva has already informed us that you would tell us this. It is easy to lie, isn't it, when you are superimposing your life onto that of someone else? Rifleman, photographer, contract killer — "

"*What?*"

"He's lying!" I raised my voice to be heard over Michael's profuse swearing. "*He's* the one who does all that. Search him. He's probably got several cameras on him now."

"We have already searched him. He was clean."

"Fuck," Michael snarled. "I don't fucking believe this. You've got your man right in front of you and you're too fucking stupid to see it."

Armed and Dangerous by Nenia Campbell

"Permission to leave?"

Hawk barely glanced at him. "Granted."

I watched the Sniper walk out, briskly but steadily. Why was he in such a hurry to leave? He hated us. He'd said so himself. Surely he'd want to watch us die.

Something was wrong.

Hawk picked up a metal implement. "Let's get down to business. You are going to start by telling me everything you know. If I feel you are lying, or withholding information, I'll start removing pieces from your friend. Starting from the bottom-up, I think. We'll save her face for last."

I choked back bile. "Wait — please, you can't do this."

"Christina," Michael said, "shut the fuck up. Please."

"I know why he left. I know why the Sniper left. He's got another bomb. This time he's not leaving things up to chance." The British guy looked at me. "Don't you see?" I fought to contain my rising panic. "He's going to kill us by blowing up the warehouse."

Michael:

Armed and Dangerous by Nenia Campbell

It all made sense.

The reason the BN job had reeked of such amateurism was because it had been. The Sniper didn't know shit about subtlety. Not unless it was on the other side of a magnifying lens on a rifle or a camera. His shoddy attempt at kidnapping Christina had been proof enough of that.

But making a bomb didn't require subtlety; it was the fucking *opposite* of subtlety.

"Christina?" I pitched my voice low. "I have a plan, but I need you to work with me. Can you do that?"

I felt her give a full-body nod.

"Good. When I give the say-so, I need you to push with your legs and jump to your feet."

"What are you — "

"Just say yes," I growled, "and follow my lead."

Hawk came closer, still twirling that metal implement in his hand.

"Now," I shouted.

It almost didn't work. Without the use of my hands, I couldn't get much lift. If we had been bound to the back of the chair we would have been goners. Luckily, we had the element of surprise on our side.

Armed and Dangerous by Nenia Campbell

The metal chair clattered underfoot with a screeching sound on the stone floors. I swung around, using Christina's body for momentum, and kicked from the hip. Hawk was older, and didn't have the training to dodge the attack completely. Just to make sure he wouldn't be able to get back up, I kicked him a few more times, not stopping until I saw the blood dribble out of his mouth.

"Are you insane?" Christina screamed.

"You bet your sweet ass I am, darlin," I said. I turned around, figuring I'd have a better chance at running backwards given her slow pace. "Now run for your fucking life."

Hawk might have been down for the count, but he had called for reinforcements. Doors on the second story of the warehouse were sliding open. I heard their shouted commands to each other growing closer.

"Hurry — faster goddammit!" She headed for the door the Sniper had taken and cursed. "What's wrong?"

"It's locked."

Hawk had to have the key. I eyed his fallen body in the center of the room, beside the upended chair, which was now surrounded by guards. *Beaucoup de* fuck.

"Michael — look out!"

I swung around, narrowly avoiding a clip to the head. Motherfucker. I dropped to my knees, yanking Christina down with me, and hoped to God I'd be able to get back up again.

"Slide," I shouted. "Anyone comes within kicking distance, aim high, and aim hard."

Hawk was wearing a lightweight coat, business casual, pockets on the bottom. I bent down and grabbed the hem of it between my teeth and shook — hard. Goddamn it. How humiliating. Change fell out, a wallet, a cell phone.

"What are you doing?" Christina yelped.

"Trying to give him a fucking hard-on," I snapped. "What the hell do you think?"

I leaned over him, to get at the other side of his coat, and saw a weak movement in the corner of my eye. Fingers curled into hawk-like talons — aimed for my face. That son of a bitch just wouldn't stay down. Now he was trying to blind me. I whipped my head back, and felt him sink his nails into the wound the Sniper had slashed with his blade and twist hard. *"Goddamn it motherfucking fils de putain bastard son of a bitch I'm fucking going to end you."*

Armed and Dangerous by Nenia Campbell

I slammed my knee into his crotch, grinding his balls against the stone floor. He released my face with a high-pitched scream. I bent for the other pocket again, purposely putting more weight on that knee as I did so, and shook an electronic key loose. "Come on," I said to her. "Move closer. Ignore Mr. Falsetto here and bend to the side. I need you to grab that card."

I heard her grunt and felt the strain in the ropes around my wrist as she groped for the card. "Got it," she gasped.

"Drop it." One of the guards pointed a gun at my chest. "Drop whatever it is you've got in your hand *now*."

"Michael, we're surrounded," Christina whimpered.

"Don't you think I know that?" I sucked in air, looking at each of the guards in turn. At their rifles, cocked and ready. Too bad I hadn't been trained as a negotiator.

"Okay," I said. "You got me. But listen to me. If you don't get out of here right now, this place is going to blow."

I could tell the rookies straight-off; they were the ones who nudged each other and laughed. *Yeah, right.*

The veterans among them remained expressionless.

"That man who left, the man that *this* dipshit — " I nudged Hawk with my boot " — knows as Villanueva, is an IMA operative — better known as the Sniper."

That elicited a reaction from some of them.

"Call someone." Drops of sweat rolled down my spine. "I'm sure you've got some patsy keeping watch outside. Call them and see if he turns up anything. What have you got to lose? Apart from your lives, that is."

Without lowering his rifle, the man across from me slipped a hand into his uniform and pulled out a cellphone. "Hello — yes, this is Berkeley. Yes…they say there's a bomb…I know, just check…real quick…"

Christina's hands were trembling. I stroked her palm with my thumb. "Don't worry," I muttered. "We've lived this long. No reason to stop now."

"Shut up." The gun dug into my neck. "No talking."

I waited, counting my breaths as they filled the silence.

"Well, that settles it. He says there's…what?" The guard glanced at the phone, and his fingers tightened around the receiver minutely. A slight contraction of the metatarsals like piano wire beneath the skin. "Fuck."

"Is there a bomb?" one of the guards asked.

"Fuck," the first guard repeated. "Yes. *Fuck*."

An ominous rumble shook the walls. On the other side of the cellphone, I could make out screaming.

"Run," I said, to Christina. "Run."

"But — "

"Not that way," I shouted. "Not the one he took! Other door! Back, back, back!"

We shuffled to the door. Christina slid the keycard through the door. Clean air flooded through my nostrils, tinged by smoke and plastic explosives. And then, as the blast burst through the door the guards had been foolish enough to open, the smell of cooking skin and burning hair.

Christina gagged. I heard her sobbing, and then praying, under her breath.

"There's no time for that," I said. "Run."

Flames burst through the doorway, singing our backs, sending us rolling across the concrete in a tumble.

Using one of the parked vans for leverage, we

struggled to our feet. "Keep running," I said hoarsely. The smoke poured out heavy and thick now. If the flames reached the parked vehicles and their gas tanks, the explosions would only increase in strength.

We stumbled through the open metal gate ringed with curls of barbed wire. And then we walked through the endless zones of industry, with the warehouses, the parking lots, the abandoned train track with the parked cars covered with urban graffiti.

When we came to an open field, marked "land for rent," we collapsed, and let the darkness take us.

Armed and Dangerous by Nenia Campbell

Chapter Twenty-Four
Incentive

Christina:

A crow squawked overhead. I itched. And where I didn't itch, I ached.

When I opened my eyes, they were pierced by the blinding blue of the California sky. Then it came back to me — the warehouse — the explosion — the burning bodies. We had collapsed in the middle of a field. I could hear the distant roar of traffic, the calls of birds in the oaks nearby. No sirens.

How long had we been here?

I was still lashed to Michael, but I couldn't see him. I could feel him, though, the tension on the cord around my wrists marking his presence.

"Michael?"

I received a grunt.

"You there?"

"What do you think?" his voice was hoarse from the smoke. "Come on. Let's see if we can get up. The barbed wire on that fence ought to be able to slice right through this shit."

After Michael cut the ropes on the fence we trudged back into town. It felt like a death march. I would know — I'd been on one before.

After what felt like, and probably was, hours, Michael found a place that was willing to let him use the phone despite how dirty we both looked. He called Angelica, who gave us a ride back to the hotel. I was so tired, I fell asleep on the ride over, and then lost consciousness again the moment I made contact with the bed.

When I awoke, I felt refreshed but no less conflicted.

I had been thinking about what Michael had said about the Night Bureau. He had said that they were not much different from the IMA. Hawk seemed like solid proof of that — in some ways he was as bad as Adrian Callaghan. But since he had come alone, and appeared to be doing his dirty dealings with the Sniper on the sly, maybe he was the exception to the rule.

They prefer to think of themselves as peacemakers, Michael had said. *They protect their own.*

Maybe that was vigilantism. I didn't care. I had slipped through the cracks so many times, I liked the idea of someone waiting down below to catch me if I fell.

I glanced over at Michael. The slash on his face

was healing slowly. The Sniper had gouged a slanting line down his left cheekbone, an obvious knife-wound. One that would mark him as a criminal for the rest of his life.

He stirred and I watched his fingers trace along the healing skin of his face, as though seeking out an itch that needed scratching. His arm fell back to his side. "What time is it?"

"Eleven, I think."

"Jesus. My *head*. It's like fucking Armageddon in there." He closed his eyes, massaging the lids. "Close the blinds. Now. Please," he added, as an afterthought.

"Sure." I closed the curtains, catching a fleeting glimpse of the foggy city skyline, half-shrouded in the low-hanging clouds, before the room plunged into darkness.

He muttered something rebellious. I heard the crack of a can opening and hoped it was an energy drink and not more alcohol. "Michael?"

A loud swallow. "What?"

"Was that man — Hawk — was he your boss at the BN?"

I heard a metallic clank as he set the can down on the nightstand. "No, thank God. No. That was Perry."

"Like Perry the Platypus?" I wondered aloud.

"No, like Perry the Peregrine. They're all a bunch of bird-brains, named after a bunch of fucking birds." He picked up the can and took another swig. "Why do you ask?"

"I was thinking about what you said about the BN in the desert. I was wondering if they were all like Hawk."

"No."

I paused.

"Do you still have the number to contact him?"

Michael groaned a little. "Number for who?"

"Perry. His phone number. Do you still have it?"

He definitely sounded more awake now. "Why the fuck would you need that?"

"Because I have an idea that could get us out of this mess." If the BN were a social party, even a militant one, I was sure that they would be interested in what I had to say. "Do you trust me?"

His skeptical silence made me shift uncomfortably. I felt like Aladdin, holding his hand out to Jasmine on the magic carpet. A ridiculous comparison under the given circumstances, and yet oddly apt.

Armed and Dangerous by Nenia Campbell

"I shouldn't," he said. His hand moved up to his face, testing the ragged edges of the knife-wound. "But you were right about the bomb."

"I guess watching TV can be helpful," I said.

"Yeah, yeah. Don't let it go to your head or anything. Shit." He reeled off the number.

His head tilted like a cat's at the beeping noises coming from the hotel phone as I dialed. "I hope you're half as confident as you're pretending to be," he remarked, leaning back against the pillow to watch me make the call.

"Shh."

There was a small click on the other end. Hardly noticeable at all, really, unless you knew what to look for. Just a few months before, I hadn't. But I'd heard the sound several times since then, enough times to know it was the sound of another line tapping in to record.

"Who is this?" The voice was British, suspicious, very posh-sounding. He reminded me of the Alfred character from the Batman films I'd watched with my dad as a kid.

"I'd like to speak to Perry, please."

"I think you have the wrong number."

"I don't think so," I said.

Michael growled and reached for the phone. I pushed him away. The man on the other line had gone silent, but he hadn't hung up yet, either. I had to fight my own battle.

"I know you're probably asking yourself how I got this number. I'm a friend of Michael Boutilier. I want to work for you."

"We are not hiring at present."

I pushed on. "I think your boss will be very interested in my proposition."

"And why might that be?"

"Because I'm the daughter of the famous computer hacker, Rubens Parker. The man who broke into the unbreakable. He broke into the IMA's database — I want to be the one to help you do the same thing again."

"You have my attention."

I gave Michael a thumbs up. He rolled his eyes and shook his head. I didn't care. I'd passed the first test, and I'd received a time and a place for my efforts.

Michael:

I thought she was being a perfect fool. Telling her this would have been even more foolish; when it came to my orders, she tended to disregard them — just for spite, I suspected at times.

Or as I phrased it: "If you're so insistent on marching in for the slaughter, then at least let me make it so you don't look like such a lost little lamb."

I took her to one of those ridiculously overpriced boutiques. She protested. The idea of me buying clothes for her made her feel uncomfortable, I could tell. She prided herself on her independence.

"Make her look intimidating," I told the hovering assistant. "Find something that plays down the sweet face. I'm going to find a suit," I said to Christina. "Stay here."

I found what I was looking for easily. The stylish shit was always placed up near the front. Black suit, simple cut. White shirt. No tie. No cufflinks. I paid for the clothes and walked back over to the women's section.

I found the shopping assistant outside the fitting rooms. "Has she got a selection going?"

She darted a look at me, and then away. "Well."

"No?" I turned towards the doors. "Christina — where are you? I want to see what you have on."

"I look ridiculous," came her muffled response.

I headed towards that first door. The shopping

assistant made as if to stop me. I threw her a look, freezing her in her tracks, and rapped on the door.

"Open up."

The door swung open.

She was wearing a white blouse tucked into a navy skirt. A navy coat fastened just beneath her breasts, cinching in her waist, cutting an imposing figure. She needed to unfasten the collar — she looked like a librarian. A little cleavage would give her some edge; most men are frightened by a sexually confident woman. But apart from that, yes, this was the look she needed.

I snorted when I saw her sneakers, though. "You need new shoes, darlin."

"Stilettos?" she offered.

"Yeah. Those." I lolled my head towards the saleswoman. "You got any in her size?"

She scampered off to get them.

"I think she's afraid of you," said Christina.

"You think so too, hmm?" I pulled her closer and loosened her collar. "Wear your blouse open," I said, running my fingers down the smooth skin of her neck. "It makes you look more confident. Just make sure you don't stutter."

Armed and Dangerous by Nenia Campbell

Christina:

The man sitting across from us in the airport cafe matched my stereotype of the British man. He was medium height, nondescript features except for a very full white mustache. He was wearing a brown suit that looked like tweed.

So this was Perry the not-a-platypus.

A cup of black tea sat in front of him, several cubes of sugar waiting on the side. Michael sat at the table while I ordered. His posture was stiff as the two of them spoke in hushed undertones. I carried my coffee back to the table

"Well," said Perry, straightening as I sat down. "I believe we have much to discuss."

Michael was a pillar of intensity beside me. I glanced at him, warily, and read the warning in his face.

I swallowed. "Yes. That's right."

"I will be honest; we did consider simply eliminating the two of you. Michael has already proved somewhat of a disappointment." His disapproving gaze fell on Michael, who returned it with a much more convincing glare of his own.

"The feeling was mutual."

"Quite." Perry cleared his throat. "I tell you this not as a threat, Ms. Parker, but as a token of our good faith and...honesty."

The fact that it is a threat probably doesn't hurt, though.

"That said, I do implore you to be honest, Ms. Parker. There is much that we know; it is not wise to lie."

"You already know who I am, then."

Rather than responding directly he said, "Our records show that your abilities with computers are only slightly above average. I'm not sure you can live up to your claims."

"I'm still in contact with my father. I planned on asking him to teach me what he knew."

Dad wouldn't like that but he owed me that much. I could no longer stay out of the fray, and I didn't want to spend the rest of my life looking over my shoulder. It seemed only fair to ask him for the means to defend myself against redundancy. He owed me that much.

As if following my line of thought, Perry said, "Why shouldn't we hire him, then? Skip the middleman."

"Because my dad is a coward."

Michael snorted.

I gave him a dark look. It was a truth that had taken me a year to come to terms with, but there it was. I turned back to the British man.

"Hacking is like a puzzle to him. A game. I don't think he really understands the consequences of what he does. When he realized what he'd gotten into with the IMA, he tried to run away — to hide from the situation. Instead, he ended up putting the fall on the people he loved … or claimed to, anyway."

I hadn't planned on saying that. The truth of it stung like an open wound. I took a hasty swallow of scalding coffee, stalling for a few precious seconds.

Stick to the script.

"The IMA destroyed any chances I had at living a normal life, forcing me to start over from scratch at nineteen. I can't go home. I can't go back to school. I've decided I'm going to stop living the way other people tell me to, and start living it the way I *ought* to — on my own terms. I want to work for you.

"I'm a good candidate because nobody would ever suspect me. Because I'm a girl, people assume that I am weak. Because I am young, they assume that I'm foolish, as well. Because I'm Latina, they figure I must not be able to speak English well, let alone code."

Perry leaned back in his seat. "A very moving speech."

Was he being sarcastic, or just British? "I have knowledge of the system level, the user interface, the network, and utility. I'm comfortable with Macs and PCs. I'm also well versed in Java *and* C-plus-plus, and recently I have been reading up on D, as well."

"I believe you."

I drank my coffee.

Perry sipped his tea.

Michael said, "Are you going to answer her?"

"This is unprecedented, to say the least. Many will question your motives — both of you. The very nature of your relationship is circumspect, you understand."

"That isn't relevant."

"But it is, Mr. Boutilier." Perry set down his tea. "You have betrayed two organizations for one another. Who is to say that you will not do it again? I would be interested in knowing your long-term plans, to get a sense of where your loyalties lie."

"I want Adrian Callaghan dead," said Michael. "I hate that son of a bitch, and I intend to see him in his grave. If you hire her, I'll leak you any information I'm able without also incriminating myself."

"Yes, we did find it odd that the information you provided us with was so...accurate. Double agents are not usually so forthcoming."

"Honor has a price, like anything else." Michael laced his hands behind his head. "I have no set loyalty."

"I don't quite believe that, but I see your point. Alliances fall and crumble. Even the most powerful."

Michael nodded. "Just look at those poor bastards in Rome."

"Yes, quite." Perry inclined his head towards me. "What about you, Ms. Parker? What are your thoughts?"

"I used to think killing was wrong. That judgment was something one should leave entirely up to God." I hesitated; I was on shaky ground here. "After I was kidnapped, I thought differently. I can't believe that God actually wants people like Adrian to continue to exist. It doesn't make sense. Maybe we should wait for divine judgment, ideally, but in the meantime how many more lives will be lost? How many more people will suffer? Either we're wrong, God is, or something got lost in my translation — and

I'm betting on the latter."

"Even if it goes against the law?"

I bit my lip. "From what I've heard, the law can be bent like the people who serve it."

"I like you, Ms. Parker," Perry said, after another long pause. I let out the breath I'd been holding. "You have a good head on your shoulders, and it's in remarkable condition. I admire your pragmatism."

"Does that mean you're going to hire me?"

He smiled. "It means that there's a chance. No more, no less."

Epilogue

"Well," Michael said, closing the door behind us. "That went better than I thought it would."

"How did you think it would go?"

He looked at me over his shoulder before flicking on the light. "I thought I might have to use this, for a start." He held up his gun before setting it down on the table. "We're getting a reputation, you and I."

He looked good in the suit, very James Bond. Exactly how one might expect a secret agent or an assassin to look. The black brought out the golds in his skin and hair, and the green of his eyes.

I was still coming down from the adrenaline high of meeting the leader of such a deadly organization. Dizzily, I said, "A bad one?"

"The worst." Michael leaned against the wall beside the table. "Congratulations on the job."

"He hasn't hired me. He said there was a chance."

He laughed. "In this line of work, sweetheart, maybe means yes, and yes means without a doubt. I'm pretty sure you've got the job — if you want it."

That gave me pause. I was working for the BN. An organization that, in its own way, was just as dangerous and secretive as the IMA.

Armed and Dangerous by Nenia Campbell

"Oh my God."

"*Do* you want it?"

"I...I don't know." Yes, I did. If only because I knew that if I turned it down, I would wonder about it for the rest of my life. Computer coding. Computer hacking. They'd have me working with the best.

This must be why Dad did what he did. This rush. This challenge. This thrill.

I would be more careful; I would carve out limits. I wouldn't let myself lose control, as he had.

"How do you feel?" he asked.

"I — I don't know. Different?" I folded my arms. "I feel exactly the same...only shocked."

"The shock wears off." Michael shrugged off his coat. "So does the thrill."

His words jarred against my conscious mind; it was as if he had read my thoughts.

What was it about him that made me captive? He was beautiful in his way, but looks can only go so far. Was it that I wanted to be the one to save him? Or was it that we had an understanding of one another in a way that nobody else in our lives had of us?

Maybe it was both. Maybe it was something that couldn't be put into words. Emotions are so complicated. We take our ability to explain them for granted, failing to take into account the fact that words frequently fail us when we need them most.

"You looked great — very in control. He seemed impressed."

"In control?" Me?

"You're a brave woman, Christina Parker. It shows. Whether you think so or not. It shows."

I took a step back. "I'm not brave."

"You think just anyone could go through everything you went through and live?"

Well...

"You have."

"I'm not just anyone."

What made me walk up to him? What made me say, "No, you aren't," and kiss him? That moment of fragile vulnerability, something all the more precious because of how easily it could be crushed. I began to understand.

There was a beat of surprised stillness and then he kissed me back, pulling me towards him as his hands untucked my blouse from my skirt and slid up my back. He tasted like the black coffee he'd been sipping, sour and dark and not at all sweet.

Armed and Dangerous by Nenia Campbell

The arm around my back pulled away a little. I felt his fingers stroke down my spine the way one might pet a cat. With each pass, he altered the pressure of his callused fingers, and the rasp of his skin on mine was like the swish of silk — a sibilant, sexual sound.

He moved back, catching his breath. Then I felt his mouth right beneath my ear. "Don't front with me." His fingers slid through my hair, making my scalp tingle. "You want to fool around, that's fine. But tell me where the limits are."

I unfastened his collar. He watched me silently as I loosed each button from its hole. Each rise and fall of his chest was an epoch. I let my hands fall to my sides and he caught them in his, bending to kiss me.

But he froze a hairsbreadth away. "No," he said, quietly but firmly. "Not until you tell me what you want."

"You," I said. "No limits. Just you. Only…I don't want to be hurt."

"I'll try to be gentle." His lips brushed against mine as he spoke. "But only for you." I was aware of being propelled backwards. The bed hit the back of my knees. He grabbed my butt, forcing me to grab onto his neck as he scooped me up and then levered me back. The air hissed out of my lungs like a balloon deflating.

The pad of his thumb caressed the knot of nerves at the base of my skull. When I arched against him, he unsnapped the row of buttons on my blouse with a dextrous slide of his fingers that seemed practiced.

"I have a favor to ask."

I clapped my hand over my chest, over my heart, to keep the fabric from gaping open. "What?"

"Don't let them turn you into a killer."

His breath tickled my dampened skin. He pulled away from me, sliding his shirt off his shoulders. The gold crust of hair on his chest was matted with sweat, and I realized, suddenly, just how hot the room was.

"A killer?" I repeated.

"Once you let them do that, they own your soul. They own it for the rest of your life."

I hooked a finger through the strap of the holster running across his chest. I could feel his beating heart. "That's a bit hypocritical."

"I don't want that goodness inside of you destroyed." He began to unbutton his pants, but I pushed his hands away and unbuckled the leather strap keeping the empty holster at his hip. He tossed the whole mess on the floor. "That would break you."

Armed and Dangerous by Nenia Campbell

"Okay," I said.

"They'll want to teach you how to use a gun, take you to a firing range. Say no."

"Okay."

He pulled my blouse out from beneath my fingers, letting it gape open. "Don't mention me, either. We're enemies now. They won't just say you have Stockholm syndrome. They'll think I'm pumping you for information."

I felt my face heat up. "I wouldn't do that."

"I know." He kissed me quickly on the mouth, leaning his forehead against mine as he kneaded my breasts through the top, working it down to pool around my elbows. "You're good."

He circled a nipple through my bra with his tongue while reaching around to unfasten the clasp. I gasped when his mouth found skin and felt him smile. "Very, very good."

His hands were on my thighs, rough and warm. But gentle, as he'd promised. I'd been afraid that it was going to be the way it had been before — but this time, I wasn't scared. I had control. And I knew, that if I wanted, that this time he would stop if I asked.

"You've changed," I said.

"You said that last time, too."

His voice was husky. I was surprised he remembered. "Well, I guess you've changed more."

"Is that good?" he asked distractedly, bunching my skirt around my hips. He hooked a finger through my underwear and pulled hard. I winced when the elastic snapped against my thigh, and he kissed my shoulder. "Fuck. Gentle. I forgot."

"It's okay. And yes, I think so."

Michael lifted his eyes. "What?"

"I think you've changed for the better."

"I'm glad, darlin. Real glad." He pulled his wallet out of his pants pocket before shoving them down his hips. "I'll be gladder still when I've got this fucking condom…out of the fucking wrapper. Dammit. Where the hell did it — *there*."

I felt a twinge of dizziness as he pushed into me, the first stirrings of déjà vu that I'd been dreading. He could try to be gentle, but he couldn't reduce his size or change his appearance. He was still the same man.

"Oh," he panted. "Right. I think you might like this." He rolled over so that I was on top, and the momentum of it pushed him in deeper, and for a moment, I was falling, with nobody to catch me —

Nobody but him.

I inhaled sharply, looking down at him in shock.

"I fucking love you, you know," he said. "You made my life complicated as fuck, and I could care less."

"Thank you," I said.

He laughed. "*Thank* you?"

I flushed. "I…care about you too, I think."

"You care too much."

It felt different, being the one on top, like I was the one in control. His body was no less powerful, but now I could feel the pliant softness of his skin sheathing his imposing musculature. I was more aware of his many vulnerabilities.

His eyes narrowed, and he tightened his grip a little, moving me up and down until I matched the pace he set. "What does that look mean?"

"N-nothing. It's just…my father got a hit put on him for hacking into the IMA on accident. What will happen to me? I don't have any training. What if they send someone to kill me?"

He pulled my face down by my hair. "I wouldn't worry too much about that, *bebe*. Those lips of yours could kill a man."

"I'm serious," I said.

"So am I."

Armed and Dangerous by Nenia Campbell

He was intentionally side-stepping the issue. I knew that. And he knew that I knew that.

And that scared me, more than anything.

Seeing the fear on my face, he pulled back and said, "Don't worry. They'll train you — they'll train you well. You'll be locked and loaded and ready to go by the time they're through with you."

"Really?" I whispered.

"A real *femme fatale*." He slid his hand up my thigh and squeezed. "Nobody will be able to touch you."

Except you, I thought, but didn't say, caught as I was in the crossfire of my own raging emotions. *Except you*. He had his fingers on the trigger of my heart.

I was starting to fall in love with Michael Boutilier. Quickly, violently. It was a love that was both armed and dangerous, a ticking time-bomb of destruction that threatened to send my whole world up in flames — and it felt good.

The end.

Armed and Dangerous by Nenia Campbell

(Ack!)nowledgements

- Thanks to McQuinn for her help in the *Revelation* chapter. She made me hate it much less. She is also responsible for Michael's "hard-on" zinger.
- Squishy hugs to Louisa, for her beautiful covers and her willingness to listen to all my whining.
- All my other whore-cruxes from PH.
- Venus Smurf, president of my fan club.
- All my friends and fans within the Goodreads community, for taking a chance on and supporting a little indie author like me.

Printed in Great Britain
by Amazon